Praise for *Swine Branch* and *Skunk Creek*

"With his melding of magic realism in the front-porch-sittin' talltale tradition of the Ozarks, Todd Parnell weaves a story about the bigger-than-life citizens of Edenesque Hardleyville that is a Scheherazade tapestry involving political intrigue, corporate hog farmers, and, of course, murder."

– Dr. Fred Pfister, founder, *The Ozarks Mountaineer* magazine

"It's a good ol' boy tellin' a long tall tale around a pristine creek campfire. It's a comedy of horrors. I really liked it!"

– Ken LeSure, author of *Cold Feat*

"*Skunk Creek* is interesting, it is fun, it is serious, it has a boffo early piece of excitement and then the excitement just keeps coming. It contains a lot of "learning" information . . . all in all a total delight! Absolutely, positively, just terrific . . . I didn't want to put it down!"

– Jane Brite, former executive vice-president and managing partner at Young & Rubicam, Inc., New York, NY

"*Swine Branch* is a colorful Ozarkian tale of murder, mystery, politics, history, and adventure. Chapters weave a series of incredible stories with colorful characters who keep you reading for more. It is a shadier side of the Ozarks with fantastic twists and turns from Hardlyville to Washington, DC to my own native Lebanon that makes any other roller coaster child's play."

– Rita Baron, architect and Drury University trustee

"Hardlyville. Where 'Dogpatch' meets 'Valley of the Dolls.'"

– Craig Endicott, retired editor, *Advertising Age*

Swine Branch

Swine Branch
Copyright © 2016 by Todd Parnell

All rights reserved. No part of this book may be used or reproduced in any manner, including electronic storage and retrieval systems, except by explicit written permission from the publisher.

Brief passages excerpted for review purposes are excepted.
All characters appearing in this work are fictitious. Any resemblance to real persons, living or dead, is purely coincidental.

First Edition
Printed and bound in USA

ISBN: 978-1-68313-045-1

Cover design by Kelsey Rice
Formatting by Kelsey Rice

Swine Branch

The Legend of Lettie Jones

The Ozarkian Folk Tales Trilogy
— Book Two —

by Todd Parnell

P
Pen-L Publishing
Fayetteville, Arkansas
Pen-L.com

Also by Todd Parnell:

Skunk Creek: The Ozarkian Folk Tales Trilogy, Book One

The Buffalo, Ben, and Me

Mom at War

Postcards from Branson

CONTENTS

DEDICATION

The Ozarkian Folk Tales Trilogy is dedicated to my wife, Betty, who challenged me in retirement to write fiction. When I complained that I had been raised to tell the truth and wouldn't know where to begin, she advised, "Start with something you know—the Ozarks, small towns, creeks, and rivers—then make it a mystery. Add a little violence, sex, humor, politics, exaggeration, even a hint of the supernatural. And have fun!"

I am grateful for her recipe. The first words I wrote were Skunk Creek, and the rest has just followed. I can only hope that this celebration of life amidst chaos and confusion entertains, as well as frames an often misunderstood culture as brave, resilient, and deeply rooted, with ultimately Village as hero. It has been fun to try.

Thank you, Betty, for pushing me and my personal envelope!

AUTHOR'S NOTE

A branch is a dance 'neath heaven's sky.

This is another novel about the Ozarks—that vague notion of geography and culture tucked into Southwest Missouri and Northwest Arkansas. I was privileged to grow up there, and I treasure the history, the beauty, the humor, the toughness, the kindness, the independence, the gentleness, the lore and the legend, the bonds that bind us.

Swine Branch is an Ozarkian folk tale* featuring the village of Hardlyville as hero, beautiful Skunk Creek as backdrop, and a large supporting cast of colorful Hardlyvillains facing grave natural, unnatural, and environmental threats to their way of life. It is a mystery grounded in Ozarks waters, culture, and history, and set in the tragedy, love, lust, and resilience of a fictional Ozarks village. Crafted in the long tradition of Ozarks storytelling, *Swine Branch* is bawdy, irascible, and irreverent. Its reach extends far beyond the city limits to centers of government and distant foreign cultures. It is a sequel to *Skunk Creek* and the second volume in a trilogy.

The Hillbilly caricature of bibs, corncobs, white lightning, ignorance, and bliss is often a self-inflicted and profitable iteration of the hardscrabble life many of our forefathers lived in forging an existence in a beautiful but unforgiving landscape.

Dark tales of violence, drugs, and abuse are but one side of the Ozarks. Herein, I have sought to meld the tragic with the exaggerated to honor the mythical Arcadia of ancient lore and the dogged resilience of a people and place beset with a myriad of contemporary challenges. Humor underlies it all, as it has served as an antidote for tough times and rough lives throughout Ozarkian history. And yes, the threats to tradition and precious natural and water resources are real and ongoing.

I was raised in a giving and extended family and community, short of perfection, but long on love. Characters and locales featured within are fictional but grounded in the imagination and tall tales of my youth. At the same time, jabs at prevailing political and moral hypocrisies play out every bit as well alongside a beautiful Ozark stream as in a teeming metropolis. Earthy and ribald moments are meant to soften body blows and bring an occasional chuckle, not to offend. Beyond all, I smile at my homeland—its rugged elegance, its many special characters, real and imagined, fond memories, and huge hopes.

Todd Parnell

* *Folk tale: A tale or legend originating and traditional among a people or folk having to do with everyday life, and frequently featuring wily peasants getting the better of their superiors.*

Cast of Locations

Hardlyville – Fictional Town
Hardlyvillains – Residents of Hardlyville
Skunk Creek – Fictional Creek
Swine Branch – Fictional tributary to fictional creek

List of Characters: (current)

Pierce Arrow—Editor, *Hardlyville Daily Hellbender*, Congressman
Lettie Jones—Genuine Hero, partner of Pierce Arrow, wife of deceased Lucas Jones
Lucas Jr., Vixen, Mona—Young children of Lettie
Lucas Jones—Genuine Hero, Deceased
Jimmy Jones—Entrepreneur
Sally Boswell Jones—Wife of Jimmy Jones
Sheriff Sephus Adonis—The Law
Airreal Flambeau—Sheriff's wife
Pastor Pat—Minister
Dylan "Ol' Dill" Thomas—Deaf owner of family still
Muffle—Ol' Dill's Dog
Donald "Dinky" Doodle—Village Jester, aka The Donald
Sisters Sledge—Old-maid sisters
Doc Karst—Town Physician
James Bond (PB)—Postmaster, Civic Leader
Bob Klunkerkokatus—Undertaker, Civic Leader
Matilda Peaches Klunkerkokatus—Undertaker's wife

Josephus Dudley—Mayor, Civic Leader
Florence Hormel—French porn star, sort of
Larry Larrsnist—Congressman
She—Demon Lady, Devil Woman
Flotilla Hendricks—Bakery Owner
Chuck Hendricks—Flotilla's son, Hot Shot CPA
Billious Bloom—Exec. Director of Rosebeam Foundation, School Teacher, Librarian
Rifleman—Small Businessman
Steele—Rifleman's wife
Lil' Shooter Abdul—Rifleman and Steele's daughter
Booray Abdul—Lil' Shooter's husband
Abdul Abdul, Kiri, Obi, Uvi—Booray Abdul's family
Tiny Taylor—Owner, Greasy Spoon Grill and Bar
Jamin Bennell—Banker
Mabel Bennell—Banker's wife
Captain Happy—Banker's best friend
President—The President of the United States
Principal Aide—Advisor to the president
Crazy Mary—Demonstrator in Washington, D.C.
Paul Michael Peters (Pomp)—Hardlyville high schooler
Aimless Bevel—Really Bad Guy
Cletus Bumrum—Occasional Deputy
Dan the Man Rutan—Occasional Deputy
Kay and Ed—Anorchia Anonymous members
Delegation Leader—Investment Banker
Big Man—Investment Banker
Doin and Goin Voit—Property Managers
Quarter Bogus—Jimmy Jones' best friend
CiCi Cobb—Jimmy Jones' worst friend

Characters: (Historical)

Thomas Hardly—Founder, Hardlyville
Petunia Perfidy Hardly—Thomas Hardly's 2nd wife
Hardlita Hardly Rosebeam—Thomas and Petunia's daughter, Ms. Octavia Rosebeam's mother
Octavia Rosebeam—Bequeather of Rosebeam Foundation

Institutions, Groups and Organizations:

Hardlyville Daily Hellbender (Newspaper)
Bank of Hardlyville
Skunk Creek Church of Christ
Skunk Creek Ranch (Hog Farm)
Big Pork (Pork Lobby)
Anorchia Anonymous
Redneck Army: Pierce Arrow's Hardlyville supporters
Agenda 21ers
Lolly, Gag, and Maggot, LLC, PC: Investment Bankers

Spring Rains

Spring rains came early to Skunk Creek valley, earlier than any old-timers could remember.

The skies opened wide in late February, and with higher than normal temperatures, not a drop of precipitation froze. Hardlyvillains were used to freezing rain and sleet, accustomed to losing power now and again, and adept at utilizing time lost to outages for sex.

Pierce Arrow, editor of the *Hardlyville Daily Hellbender*—so named in honor of a rare Skunk Creek inhabitant on the verge, if not there, of extinction—once conducted an informal study of birth month frequency over Hardlyville's recorded history. He had concluded that the highest birth rates occurred nine months from the season's first killer ice storm, within normal standard deviations.

Of course, no Hardlyvillain would acknowledge such aberrant behavior, except the venerable Dylan Thomas, now approaching eighty-five years of age and anxious to claim credit for bedding anything or body. Always the first to claim paternity for any out of wedlock event, Ol' Dill lived a life of offering child support payments to anyone desperate enough to accept them, funded from the proceeds of his family still. There had been few takers over the years, but Ol' Dill proudly kept "manning up," as he called it.

These rains were a different matter. Ol' Dill was one who claimed he had never seen anything like it. He could recall scorching summers and brutal cold, tornadoes and ice storms, floods and droughts, but never spring rains of this magnitude in February.

Postmaster and civic leader James Bond, who carried the monicker PB, had even cancelled one mail delivery this spring, the first in his storied tenure as mailman. Nothing—not wild beasts, snake bites, wicked winds, or wanton women—had ever occasioned him to not deliver the goods. But this spring, and it wasn't even spring yet, was different, he confessed.

Beautiful Skunk Creek ran gnarly and brown, carrying ancient trees torn from her protective riparian corridor and an occasional car parked along her banks all the way to the big waters along the state lines below. She was out of her banks more often than not for days at a time, even lapping at Skunk Creek Bridge and threatening its time-tested moorings. Basements flooded from seeping ground water, and wells overflowed.

Even town founder Thomas Hardly's original house, placed on a knoll to overlook the creek circa 1872 and empty since he was brutally murdered there, had rushing waters seeping into its remains. Decades of Hardlyvillains had left it standing as a tribute to the founding father as it slowly crumbled to dust. Some questioned the tribute part, as many had used it as a romantic getaway during their teen years and were wont to give up the memory of their first or second or even third precious introduction to the "deed." Those memories were now at serious risk.

Jimmy Jones, who had lost his virginity on its back porch just a few years back, organized a sandbagging brigade to provide temporary relief. That was until his recently betrothed and impregnated wife, Sally, figured out she hadn't been the one and disbanded Jimmy's brigade. No. Jimmy, cousin to Hardlyville's most recent deceased hero, Lucas Jones, would not get away with memorializing his first conquest in the name of founding history.

Speaking of which, Lucas Jones' gravesite had become a regional shrine. Lucas had given his life to protect Hardlyville's youngest from a coven of evil. A wicked priestess had blessed a covert reign of murder and sex, all in the name of religion, before Lucas, Editor Pierce Arrow, and Sheriff Sephus Adonis had ferreted out their hiding place and led authorities to disband it. Lucas Jones lost his life in the ensuing raid. The legend lives on but is too broad and brave to recount in these pages. A Pulitzer Prize awarded to Pierce Arrow's coverage of the tragic series of events speaks to its importance in Hardlyville history.

Pastor Pat, minister of the Skunk Creek Church of Christ, prayed incessantly for relief from the rains. He generally had good luck with his supplications, but not now. It set him to wondering whether his sidebar affair with town librarian, Billious Bloom, had displeased the Good Lord. It was not like they were cheating on anyone.

Their relationship had begun innocently enough, as most do. Ms. Bloom had come to Pastor Pat, who had long ago given up his last name for fear of legal reprisal, to confess. He had listened in his church office with patience and a sympathetic ear. He had also become quite turned-on during the process.

Seemed Ms. Bloom was a virgin. And at her advanced middle age, she was not going to give up her red badge of courage recklessly. Truth be known, no one had ever requested the honor of initiation. She shared with Pastor Pat that this often left her feeling a bit like the last pork chop at the barbecue. She was not unattractive, to which Pastor Pat had nodded vigorously, and was occasionally flirtatious—coyly unbuttoning then relatching the top button on her blouse with a quick wink. Pastor Pat had blushed uncontrollably.

Beyond these complications, she was wracked with guilt over lustful urges to offer her prize to the town sheriff, one Sephus Adonis.

Sheriff Sephus presented as an overweight, overwrought, oversized specimen of humanity, blessed with a big heart, a large appetite, and good humor. In addition, Sheriff Sephus was a local legend as a lover. From otherworldly tenderness of touch and technique to size and staying power, word of his unique skill set had registered and remained on Ms. Bloom's radar.

She had admired him from afar, occasionally casting a stray wink or smile his way, but could not bring herself to beg. Sheriff Sephus, never lacking for attention, was not the type to reach out beyond a generous response to a genuine request. Their delicate dance was acknowledged by neither and remained just beyond embrace.

As Ms. Bloom had shared her muddled tale with the good pastor, she noticed him staring at her breasts. This both flattered and confused her. She smiled back a quiet *do you like what you see?* Pastor Pat blushed again and excused himself to the men's room.

While he was gone, Ms. Bloom had removed her bra and stuck it in her purse, leaving little doubt as to what dwelled beneath. No one had ever looked at her that way before, and for it to be a man of God was beyond serendipitous.

Pastor Pat had returned, staring skyward. He had willed himself, in the name of the Holy Ghost, to look at the ceiling during what remained of Ms. Bloom's confession so as to avoid getting caught in a lustful gaze again. He awkwardly navigated the path to his desk and plopped on the edge of his chair, only to feel it slip away, dropping him to the floor. Still fixated on a rain-stained ceiling tile, Pastor Pat remounted his chair and spun it to face his confessor. Ms. Bloom asked what on earth he was doing. Pastor Pat had assured her that he was seeking heavenly guidance as to how to address her virginity, as well as that nuisance of an obsession with Sheriff Sephus.

This had presented Ms. Bloom with yet another challenge. How could she ever regain his gaze long enough to assess the purity of his intentions? This was a new frustration, but she had gone too far to back off. So it being confession and all, she simply confessed it. Her plaintiff plea for advice as to how to get him, Pastor Pat, to look at her breasts again, broke his steely gaze, and he yielded to temptation right there in the church office—where he had done so, on occasion, with other congregants.

Pastor Pat's bug-eyed focus on Ms. Bloom's erect display had caused him to break into his own confession. He had never seen such a lovely sight, he moaned, and he wondered if he might engage with them. Ms. Bloom wasn't sure what that meant, having never shared them with another, but she assured him with a nod that she was game. Shared confession was surely good for the soul.

It was only in the afterglow that Pastor Pat had provided the biblical reasons for his advances. Noting that it was better to give than receive, he had given her freedom from virginity so that she would not have to lust over Sheriff Sephus anymore. She could, of course, choose to do so, but he was hopeful she might find his divinely inspired ministrations worthy of her continued indulgence to the exclusion of a mere commodity—in total secrecy, of course. Ms. Bloom's satisfied smile spoke to the beginning of what would become frequent and passionate engagements for both confessors.

Both were slow to reclothe, basking in the righteousness of their coupling, as Pastor Pat had put it. Thankfully, Ms. Bloom had restored her bra to its proper place just as a loud banging at Pastor Pat's locked office door demanded entry. Speak of the devil, it was Sheriff Sephus himself standing outside, seeking Pastor Pat's help with an urgent spiritual matter.

A nude male body had just been discovered floating down flooded Skunk Creek, buoyed by large helium balloons tied to every, and Sheriff reemphasized the every, extremity. Jimmy Jones had dragged it ashore with his sucker-grabbing rig, but no one knew what to do next.

Sheriff would begin an investigation immediately, but something had to be done with the body in the meantime, and Sheriff Sephus wondered if Pastor Pat could handle the spiritual side of things. Undertaker Bob Klunkerkokatus was processing the cadaver, and if Pastor Pat would provide a brief blessing, ritual would be served. Even an unidentified, naked dead man deserved the benefit of a proper benediction, observed the sheriff, especially in Hardlyville.

Sheriff had nodded to Ms. Bloom, then turned quickly and strode to his police car, waving for Pastor Pat to follow. Pastor Pat blew a secret but heartfelt kiss to Ms. Bloom and went along, only to return soon thereafter for his pants, which he had forgotten to restore to their proper place. Fortunately, his communion robe, which he had donned to defrock Ms. Bloom, had covered his own nakedness. But it hiked up when he crawled in next to the sheriff, revealing nothing but skin from the knees down. Sheriff Sephus Adonis had simply smiled and urged him to move quickly, nodding his approval of the obvious.

As Pastor Pat reflected on the events of that bizarre day, he reasoned that surely God Himself could find glory in such a happy ending for a forlorn damsel and would not reject Pastor Pat's increasingly urgent entreaties for dry weather because of mitigating circumstances. He prayed for forgiveness, nonetheless. And dry weather.

Then again, maybe the dead body had something to do with it.

No, this spring would be different than any Hardlyville had ever known. Spring rains would see to that.

Death By...

Sheriff Sephus Adonis sat hunched over his fried squirrel with gravy at Tiny Taylor's Greasy Spoon Grill and Bar, so named to emphasize food over booze. He complimented Tiny on the freshness of her squirrel offering, and she confirmed she had shot the little bugger just yesterday evening, one of three on that day's menu.

Sheriff thought a lot of Tiny. Though relatively new to town and seemingly without a past, she minded her own business and did what she did best. Tiny, at four foot ten and ninety pounds on a good day, could simply fry the shit out of anything. From chicken to peanut butter cups to wild game to canned pineapple to chocolate ice cream, Tiny would lather on the batter and dip into thrice used grease to crisp up the most mundane offering. She refused to throw away good grease, believing prior use assured proper seasoning, but stopped at three days for fear of disease. She had never sickened a customer that she was aware of, and she took great pleasure in warming the hearts and bellies of even the most despondent visitor to her table.

Sheriff also admired her seemingly one-track mind. Her sole goal in life appeared to be customer satisfaction—nothing more, nothing less. She showed no interest in gossip, local politics, or sex, and had never once cast a glance at Sheriff Sephus' bulge. Rumor had her particularly fond of Dylan Thomas, despite their age difference. Ol' Dill had fed and probably planted the whole suspicion that they had a thing going on. Sheriff Sephus just couldn't see it.

That day, Sheriff had come in early. Discussion turned quickly to the naked dead body discovered twenty-four hours earlier. Tiny probably knew more about what was going on in Hardlyville than any other citizen because she was a good listener. As such, she walked a thin line between gossiping and reporting and was pretty adept at the latter.

She reported to Sheriff Sephus all that she had heard in hopes of providing a clue. Most of it was consistent with what the sheriff knew to be true.

The victim was a man, buck naked, with large helium balloons tied to every appendage to keep him afloat in raging Skunk Creek. She had heard that every appendage included his arms, legs, and penis, which was of average size. One report included his ears, which were deemed unusually large, but Sheriff debunked that one. The carcass was a fresh one, and cause of death was not obvious.

Sheriff Sephus confirmed that this was what baffled him most. Undertaker Bob could identify no wounds beyond Jimmy Jones' sucker-grabbing treble hook, no bruising or marks of violence, no bullet holes or knife cuts, no nothing. Except, and here Sheriff would take Tiny into his confidence, the man had no gonads—no balls, just an empty scrotum beneath his limp dick with the embedded balloon string ring. And furthermore, there were no signs of extraction, no cuts or scars, no entry marks—again, no nothing.

"What the hell?" was all Tiny could mutter, followed by the observation that he could have been born that way. She confirmed that she had never seen a man with no balls but quickly corrected herself to exclude her first and third husbands, who were cowards and chickenshits through and through. That was the first personal information Tiny had ever shared with Sheriff Sephus, and he filed it away without comment, beyond wondering how many there had been in all.

Ol' Dill showed up for breakfast and garnered the second squirrel, fried with gravy, of course. Tiny did pat his hand lightly as she took his order. Maybe there was something going on there, mused the sheriff, then revoked the thought before it had time to settle in. Just good customer service, he concluded, before paying Tiny and moving on.

Sheriff Sephus Adonis sought out his most trusted and admired friend, Pierce Arrow, at his *Daily Hellbender* office. They traded pleasantries about Pierce's live-in partner and lover, Lettie Jones, and the new baby they were expecting. Try as he might, Sheriff could not understand why little Lettie insisted on keeping her deceased husband and town hero Lucas Jones' name and had turned down Pierce's proposal of marriage, despite their obvious infatuation and cohabitation. Pierce had explained her rationale to Sheriff several times and seemed at peace with little Lettie's decision. Sheriff just didn't get it, but who was he to understand matters of love?

Sheriff asked how Pierce's campaign for Congress was coming, and Pierce nodded in the affirmative. This was Pierce Arrow's second effort to unseat the incumbent, Larry Larrsnist, an unsavory shill of politicos and lobbyists, whose principle claim to fame was voting NO. Larrsnist was even known to vote against his own bills from time to time, simply to pad his numbers.

Pierce Arrow had never contemplated politics and, in fact, despised the whole arena and those who played in it. But when a large-scale industrial pig farm popped up in the Skunk Creek watershed just miles upstream from Hardlyville, without due process or public input, threatening the beautiful waters of Skunk Creek with environmental mayhem and disaster, he took notice. Representative Larrsnist's allies were involved in back-door payments and political shenanigans that circumvented both rule of law and common standards of decency and landed several in jail.

Pierce was moved to action. And he almost won. Only a last-minute vicious and blatantly false personal attack on his morals and character, orchestrated by supporters of his opponent, derailed his campaign. They had planted abhorrent photos of young children engaged in lewd sexual acts in his office at the *Daily Hellbender*, accused him of trafficking in child pornography, and demanded his withdrawal from the race, which he granted them in stunned and shocked silence. He had known that politics was a dirty game, but even his cynical nature could not absorb that one.

As details of their devious and illegal maneuvers began to surface post election, pressure for him to run again began to percolate. And as his passion for new partner Lettie had stirred his passion for life and pushed every right and wrong button in his soul, he rescinded his pledge to never again seek public office and redeclared his candidacy. An army of passionate volunteers embraced his unconventional campaign, and with just eight months left until election eve, most informal polls showed him in a dead heat with the incumbent, despite Pierce Arrow's refusal to accept campaign contributions. Could an honest guy with no campaign coffer compete in the sleazy world of national politics? Sheriff, Pierce, Lettie, and most of Hardlyville believed he could.

Sheriff then got down to business. He explained to Pierce the mystery of the missing gonads, seeking his opinion on what significance it or they might have to the investigation. He reported that Undertaker Bob and Doc Karst—the village medicine man who specialized in live births, human and other—had never seen anything like it.

Pierce confirmed that he had heard of eunuchs, or something like that, in journalism school and even read about them in the Bible, as he recalled. He noted that his Lettie was pretty good on the internet, and if she could hold a connection for any amount of time, would gladly do a little research. Sheriff Sephus was grateful for any assistance and asked Pierce to keep this part of the mystery to just himself and Lettie.

Sheriff reported that he had shared the story with regional law enforcement officials, seeking any reports of missing naked dead persons, but could find no leads. Maybe if he added the missing gonads piece it would strike a chord with someone, but he would wait a bit to go there. Pierce felt obligated to report something to the community in the *Hellbender* but could hold off, for now.

Dinky Doodle ran in to announce that he had just heard that the naked dead man had no nuts and had been horribly tortured during their removal. Citizens were frightened and upset that a sexual pervert was on the loose and, in fact, might be one of their own. Rifleman, who owned the community's only manufacturing operation, a customized wood gunstock production, was lending firearms to any in the community seeking to arm themselves against this ominous threat. Sheriff could only shake his head and ask Pierce to go to press immediately with a more accurate story.

Sheriff surmised that Jimmy Jones had noticed the naked dead man's empty pouch as he was removing his sucker treble hook and thought a little sensationalism might move the needle on his dope business, which had flattened with the torrential rains. Jimmy's own marketing analysis had revealed an interesting theory: no sleet, no sex, no weed. Jimmy was smart, in his own way. Jimmy had a day job with Rifleman, so communication of Jimmy's discovery would have been swift and sure, if inaccurate.

Sheriff's immediate task was to disarm the community without violating their Second Amendment rights and before someone got shot.

All of this in the midst of yet another torrential downpour. Inches of rain fell in hours, and Skunk Creek and her tributaries were again bursting at the banks.

Swine Branch

The owners of Skunk Creek Ranch cast a wary eye to the heavens as well.

So named to draw a curtain around a ten thousand pig industrial swine farm perched on a spring branch that fed directly into Skunk Creek fewer than ten miles away, this confined animal feeding operation had been approved by the State Oversight Board for Water as a boon for local economic development.

Ironically, the only economic development that occurred involved the owners of the property, the owners of the production facility, the international conglomerate that lent out the piglets to the ranch for fattening, the Hardlyville banker, now deceased, who made the development loan, reaped generous fees, and happened be one of the land owners on the sly, and the chairman of the State Oversight Board for Water, who received a large bribe for shepherding the permit through commission approval.

The owners had claimed state-of-the-art technology and zero threat to Skunk Creek and Hardlyville. They spoke of entrepreneurial risk and expansion into the Skunk Creek watershed to create jobs, but all six of those went to members of a local religious sect who wreaked havoc on innocents with holy furor. The owners' true prize was cheap land, favorable permitting rules for which exceptions could be bought, and essentially a guaranteed return on investment.

Hardlyville's Pierce Arrow had simply asked: Why an industrial piggery in the Skunk Creek watershed? He had nothing against pigs or pork and could revel in a slab of baby back ribs with the best. But why not Iowa or a locale without karst topography, essentially a Swiss cheese underbelly, that didn't have much to lose in their quality of water? Why so many pigs crammed in together within shitting range of nearly pristine Skunk Creek? Why four million annual gallons of manure and sordid waste water, three hundred thirty-three thousand per month, give or take a turd or two, eleven thousand per day, four hundred sixty-three gallons of toxic waste per hour, all upstream with nowhere to leak but down? Why there? Why now?

The answer was Big Pork, pure and simple, and his campaign against the shadows they dwelled in resonated with all in the region who valued God's special creation over dollars. His loss had left an open wound on a community that was subject to the worst of infections.

The two local owners sat with their ranch general manager, contemplating the next steps. The early spring rains had already swept hog waste applied to fields the previous months down the spring branch and deep into Skunk Creek. No worries there because it would all flush through the flooded waters, perhaps depositing a little rotten residue along the way, but probably indiscernible from Hardlyville's own neglected septic systems.

Clearly of more concern was the large sewage lagoon. Rain had not stopped ten thousand pigs from defecating and had only added water to their waste. Built to withstand a twenty-five year flood, the lagoon was close to breach and actually showed cracks in the concrete lining from the pressure build up. There was no way more than three hundred thousand gallons of hog shit and waste that month alone would go unnoticed. It was potentially a very large problem.

The ranch general manager threw out a novel idea that would cost little and likely escape detection. What if they were to pump the sludge into a large sinkhole upstream of the ranch and spring branch rock formation to relieve pressure on the sewage lagoon and buy time for a return to normal weather patterns? Sure, the sinkhole would disperse into the water table, and maybe sour their own drinking water for a while, but natural karst filtering would dilute the really toxic mess before it took on a life of its own and poisoned those idiots' special Skunk Creek. Besides, the crazy religious cult that had resided in the shadow of the natural rock formation fortress for several years was now scattered and beyond risk, at least of a natural bent.

They had to take action before stinking liberal Pierce Arrow got something to use against them in his current campaign to unseat Dr. No, he reasoned. Larrsnist needed all the help he could get, and this might provide protection beyond laundered funds.

The owners liked the idea but wanted assurances that no one would ever find out. The ranch general manager said he would go online to see if anything like that had been tried in other corners of hogdom but that they had little time to waste on study. He was concerned the lagoon could split apart within the next forty-eight hours if rains did not abate, and there was nothing in the forecast that lent much hope to that. A full-fledged avalanche of hog shit cascading down the branch into Skunk Creek would be hard to miss in Hardlyville. Hardlyvillains would see it, they would smell it, and Arrow would latch on to it like a silky breast. All laughed at his metaphor but knew it was true of that liberal Pierce Arrow. Go for it, the owners decreed. Just camouflage the damn pump, and don't get caught. We'll worry about residue once the damn rain stops, was their general sense of urgency.

Piping was easy and quick to put in place, camo tape included. Installers wondered why the secrecy and time push but performed as demanded. They were paid well for their silence and assured of additional business.

As pumps whirred their putrid mess uphill before dumping it into the bowels of the earth, pressure on the lagoon eased, waste levels dropped, and a massive case of subterranean diarrhea began to gurgle in the guts of the watershed's karst belly. The owners breathed a sigh of relief and cut the ranch general manager a check for ten thousand dollars right on the spot for his quick and entrepreneurial thinking.

And the rain kept cascading down.

That very morning "Girl" Jones, first daughter of Sally and Jimmy Jones, entered the world at six twenty-three a.m. Little did "Girl" know what she was getting into. Her first clue should have been her name, or lack thereof.

Jimmy and Sally were beside themselves with joy. Jimmy initially wanted a boy so he could name it after his deceased hero, cousin, and best friend, Lucas Jones. After all, the baby had been conceived in an Ozarkian Garden of Eden buried deep beneath the spot where Cousin Lucas had sacrificed his life for his hometown, Hardlyville. Jimmy had even felt Lucas' presence that day, and he had confessed to Sally, who had blushed at the thought of anyone seeing their crazy naked frolic and fruitful consummation.

The only sad part about their discovery of paradise was that they couldn't tell a soul about it. Pierce Arrow had convinced them that to expose so precious a place would be to jeopardize its future existence, from both well and foul intentioned corners of humanity. It was so beautiful only because no one knew of it or could study the pristine spring and rare creatures, including the Ozark hellbenders who called it home. It thrived because it had been spared human intrusion and its related by-products.

In fact, the only sign of humanity they had encountered that day was a single silver dollar, marked vintage 1803, that was probably dropped by the last person to set foot therein. Pierce Arrow considered it a rare coin that would set others to seeking more of the same, so they had to sit on that as well.

He had also asked them never to go back for fear of someone seeing them and following later. They refused to take that oath, but promised to be CIA careful when they did. Sally loved the romance of the place, Jimmy wanted to check for deceased Lucas from time to time and watch hellbenders frolic in their natural habitat, and both believed it would serve as a special and holy baptismal site for their first born. So they committed to all of Pierce's suggestions, except to never go back.

Jimmy didn't really much worry that a baby girl popped first because it would be one of many. Sally and Jimmy probably differed on their definition of "many" but were too elated to discuss it just then.

Jimmy's job with Rifleman, manufacturing handcrafted wood stocks for shotguns, paid him okay and provided a stable, if limited, income. On the other hand, Jimmy's weed business was booming, if sometimes cyclical. Dope dealing was a boom and bust kind of enterprise, though Jimmy didn't really like to use the second "b" word beyond bragging to buddies about wife Sally's. As long as the good sheriff, Sephus Adonis, focused on local meth heads and looked the other way for Jimmy, as a loving surrogate father would, Jimmy would be able to feed a lot of mouths far into the future.

Jimmy was so excited about his new daughter that he pulled out a mason jar of Ol' Dill's finest and snuck back in the small clinic where Sally was recuperating that night to share it. He inquired about sex. Sally whacked him upside the head for such a stupid suggestion.

She did, however, love the thought of sharing a sip or two as baby lay quietly in a small crib next to her. And she loved Jimmy for his thoughtfulness.

She and Jimmy got bombed, really bombed, through the wee hours of the morning. When Doc Karst made his bedside rounds about seven a.m., both were in la-la land, convulsed in alternating giggles. Doc smiled, stuck the newborn on Sally's ample breast, and checked out her privates. All was well, and they had saved him some Percocet so Doc wasn't much concerned about their celebration. He told Jimmy to go home and get some sleep. Which he did. Forty-eight hours' worth.

Jimmy awoke to Sally snuggled in next to him, nursing his precious baby girl. He learned that Doc had finally brought them home from the clinic when Jimmy didn't show for checkout time and made a mental note to thank the good doctor for his kindness.

Jimmy asked if Doc Karst had any parting words of advice. When Sally shared the no sex for six weeks part, Jimmy paled visibly. Maybe he didn't want quite so many babies after all. He joked with Sally about visiting her single friend Mable Orb while Sally was out of business. Sally didn't laugh, so Jimmy took that for a "no."

"What's the use of getting stoned if you can't go for a roll afterwards?" he wondered aloud.

"No more of that for me either, at least for a while," Sally confirmed.

It was going to be a long spring, but the baby would get them through it. They smiled together, grateful for the shared blessing.

A couple of days later, Jimmy was looking through the clinic bills and found his daughter's birth certificate.

“Why did you name her Girl Jones?” he asked Sally.

“Think we forgot that part,” laughed Sally. “Guess Doc Karst needed a filler for the record, but why not?”

Simple, honest, straightforward, just like their daughter would be. Both agreed that neither would forget the grand celebration in Girl’s honor the night of her birth and would look forward to sharing the memory with her.

The second clue to little Miss Girl that she didn’t know what she was getting into would have been the vague rumbling noise building to the east. Even if Girl had sensed it, she probably would have placed it as gas in her mother’s womb. Her metaphor would not have been far off.

And she may have wished to crawl back in.

Absinthe and the Hellbender

The slimy, ugly creature slid slowly upstream with bursts of brilliance. Slipping between rocks and slate bottom with ease, she nursed the native habitat for all the survival it could offer as she had for half of her thirty-year life cycle. She propelled through the swift current with her rudder tail, occasionally grasping a rock bottom corner with tiny finger-like appendages. Her mottled brown-green slime bled seamlessly into the creek bottom, invisible to even the trained eye.

She felt danger today through her slimy skin—skin that she needed to suck in oxygen from the water. She sought shelter for herself and those who remained of her offspring deep in Skunk Creek—not sure what she feared through her ten million-year pedigree, only that it was real.

The Ozarks hellbender, at only a fraction of its recent population, was an endangered species. Found only in springs and streams of the highest quality, the mother and her lineage were at risk in ways she could never imagine.

Pierce Arrow sat at his desk at the *Daily Hellbender,* musing over what this unprecedented deluge of spring rain might mean to Skunk Creek and Hardlyville herself. There was high drama at play. As a newspaper man, he could feel it.

He bridged a decade of memories, back to when he had arrived in this quaint community after a lifetime of soul searching and depressing existence in the gutters of big city journalism. He had distant roots there, tracing back to Thomas Hardly's founding days, and had little trouble reconnecting physically and emotionally with his history. He was different in terms of education and experience than most of his new neighbors, but he sensed that the hypocrisies and foibles of urban life played out as well along the banks of a beautiful creek named Skunk as in a rancid, drug infested, urine scented back alley in Philadelphia, Pennsylvania. He preferred this version of Arcadian naiveté to base his reporting and analysis on. And it was the creek that drew them all together in the end. He would report it all fairly, honestly, and with compassion and humor.

That day, he was worried. He was worried about what was playing out east and upstream of Hardlyville, probably pouring into the Skunk. He knew the hog manure sprayed on fields adjoining what he called at every opportunity these days in the *Daily Hellbender* "Swine Branch" had already made it to the village edge, depositing in abundance along the way nitrogen, phosphorus, and whatever else spewed from a hog's butt. Who knew what that would look like when spring rains gave way to summer solstice? Creek critters would feel the wrath of the grossest deposits money can buy first, then perhaps Hardlyvillains themselves.

Pierce Arrow worried also about what remained at Skunk Creek Ranch: the ten thousand swine, the barns of their residence, and the lagoon of their waste. What was happening in that toxic wasteland tucked into the heart of paradise not yet lost? Would the rains flush down more gunk and destruction?

In a spontaneous sidebar, Pierce couldn't help but wonder about his daily's namesake, the hellbender. Pierce had seen only photos of this grotesque but lovable survivor of ten million years of civilization.

He had chosen the hellbender for his masthead because of its one-of-a-kind appearance and demeanor, its longevity and survivability, and the escalating threats to its very existence, all parallels to his brand of journalism. The hellbender fit Pierce Arrow's sense of purity, durability, and nobility, beyond superficial beauty and popularity.

In his research, Pierce had also learned that a respected fishing lure of the 1950s and '60s was named after the hellbender. Though more a lake than a stream lure, it was described as a three-inch-deep diver, manufactured by a company named appropriately "Whopper-Stopper." Consistent with its namesake, it was a bottom scraper, and also the ugliest fishing lure he had ever seen.

Pierce was worried about the real little buggers. They actually breathed through their slimy skins. No gills, no nose hairs, just osmosis of a sort. As such, they would always be the consummate barometer of water quality, more sensitive with measurement than any scientist could every record. So—Pierce concluded in his near obituary editorial explaining his name selection in honor of the ugliest amphibian in the world, one so gooey and slimy that only a mother's love could abide—we must do all within our power to shelter and protect the beloved icon.

That very day, the few remaining hellbenders in the Skunk Creek watershed were more at risk than any time in their long existence. Pierce's political campaign against the powers behind the Skunk Creek Ranch Confined Animal Feeding Operation, aka CAFO, was gaining purpose and traction. Big Pork be damned forever if it destroyed what had taken forever to evolve into a Skunk Creek water quality gauge.

~

As a toxic subterranean witches' brew began to simmer upstream of Skunk Creek, Dylan Thomas and Donald "Dinky" Doodle huddled around a large copper cooker at the third generation Thomas family still, hidden in a shallow cavern just outside Hardlyville. Hidden was all in Ol' Dill's imagination as everyone, including the law, had known where it was for generations. Still, he clung to the fantasy. Bootlegging was fun, legal or not, and no one ever turned down a mason jar of Ol' Dill's finest, even Sheriff Sephus Adonis himself. Ol' Dill had met bail with the heavenly elixir on some occasions of incarceration.

Ol' Dill and Dinky were the best of friends and the worst of enemies—competitors on the stage of Hardlyville life for any attention they could draw to their frantic antics. Separated by age but little else, Ol' Dill was the town braggart and Dinky the village jester. Ol' Dill was a stone-deaf, mid-eighties, self-proclaimed sex machine, who could not have heard a proposition from a naked cherub, let alone answered it. Dinky, whose nickname sprung from the rumored lack of pack in his privates—kind of the yin to Sheriff Sephus Adonis' yang—generally displayed insecurity through his wardrobe, which bridged both taste and gender.

With a guffaw, Ol' Dill would ask Dinky when his penis was going to grow up, generally in a crowd of no fewer than ten citizens. Dinky, knowing that Ol' Dill couldn't hear a hoot owl pluck a fedora off his head, would whisper a comparable insult from between smiling lips, leading Ol' Dill to think he got away with another one. Then Dinky would rip off his blouse and chest bump Ol' Dill in a double-D bra stuffed with dirty socks.

"Get them smelly things out of my face!" Ol' Dill would scream.

"Too much for you to handle?" Dinky would taunt.

"Touch my candle?" Ol' Dill would ask in disbelief.

"Handle, you idiot," Dinky would correct.

"You touch my candle and I'll have you arrested for sex abuse," Ol' Dill would threaten, noting he was saving it for his next date.

And on and on they would go, back and forth, keeping Hardlyvillains doubled over with laughter.

That day, Ol' Dill was actually trying to help his buddy. Dinky did not qualify as a legitimate virgin, as he had supped from the cup on several occasions. He had just never really enjoyed sex because it meant someone would actually see or handle his least proud part and might laugh. His encounters were always in a very dark room and generally with a stranger he would not have to meet on the street in broad daylight. He often wore silly masks, consistent with his village jester persona, most thought to entertain. In truth, they were to preserve anonymity if he was feeling lucky and often cost him consummation if his partner insisted on mask removal. He reveled in getting laughed at, just not for that.

One of the milestones of recent Hardlyville history was the visit of French porn star, sort of, Florence Hormel, brought to town by Pierce Arrow's college roommate and her boyfriend de jour, Dr. Felix Feelgoode. It was a long and passionate stay borne of Flo's desire to get to know more about Hillbilly culture after reading the book *Winter's Bone*. She literally and figuratively fell in love with at least a quarter of Hardlyville's male population during her two week stay and shared her generous bounty as a gesture of international good will.

Ol' Dill was her proudest customer and crowed his success to the heavens. As an equal opportunity purveyor, she served love to all comers from Sheriff Sephus to Pastor Pat and points in-between. She even tried to help Dinky Doodle but found it difficult to rouse him to his full, if somewhat limited, potential.

She worried about Dinky's self-esteem and as a parting gift left with him a plastic bag containing several clusters of seeds she called "le wormwood." She crushed one between her fingers and held it to Dinky's nose so he could smell the pungent, powerful herb scent. Then she simulated the consumption of a drink. What Flo lacked in English, she made up for in personal communication skills, and she unzipped his pants to pull out his tiny appendage. As it began to grow, she spread her hands to twice its length with a sly smile and pointed to his new bag of seeds. She kissed him on the lips, leaving him dangling in the wind, and waved him a sultry goodbye, mouthing the words "Absinthe Verte."

Dinky thought long and hard on her message and finally went to Ol' Dill for advice. Ol' Dill had heard of Absinthe but thought it was illegal due to its hallucinogenic powers. His father had called it the "Green Fairy" as he recalled and said he had been given a bootleg bottle of it by a grateful Frenchman during World War I. He had fallen prey to its dreamlike spell and tried unsuccessfully to replicate its color, bouquet, and texture in his still until his death.

Ol' Dill was all for helping Dinky grow his penis, as he was still young enough to get plenty of use from it if he could just overcome his insecurities. So Ol' Dill set out to distill an experimental liquor, utilizing Flo's wormwood seeds and the old family mash recipe. He labored for days but could only produce a foul-smelling, greenish-brown liquid that he wouldn't even feed his old dog, Muffle. Warm memories of Flo helped mute the putrid bouquet.

Desperate to help his buddy Dink, he finally poured a dollop into Muffle's dog food one night and tucked the smiling mutt into his kennel to sleep. Not long after, old Muffle was howling like a banshee and scratching to get out. Upon release, Muffle bolted through the front door screen and disappeared for several days. He returned exhausted and bearing nip marks on his flanks, but in as peaceful a state as Ol' Dill had ever seen the mutt. He could have sworn that Muffle looked satisfied, and subsequent complaints from neighbors about Muffle's sexual escapades of the past several days with their pets and farm animals confirmed Ol' Dill expectations.

He had seen enough to know that he had a product that Dinky needed to try. It probably wasn't the Absinthe of his father's time, but the source material was legitimate and the impact on Muffle undeniable. The problem was that no one in their right mind would ever take a sip if they smelled it. He would have Dinky to dinner and disguise the stink beneath a haze of hot sauce and rancid turnip greens.

His plot unfolded the next evening. Dinky wanted to know why the stew tasted so bad and was making him sweat so much. And what was the greenish-brown goo at the bottom? Ol' Dill pretended not to hear even the small parts he caught, and Dinky ultimately cleaned his bowl, sopping up the final drops with a crust of white bread. He thanked Ol' Dill for the shitty dinner and headed home.

Dinky's old-maid sister neighbors were sitting on the front porch as he walked down the lane past them. They were neither attractive or not, pleasant or not, neighborly or not, sexy or not. Very neutral. They were generally all business, although one had a crush on Dinky that she did little to hide. She had once flashed a large, saggy breast at Dinky through an open window, which he took for a plucked chicken with its head still on and simply hollered "fry 'em up" to her dismay. Dinky could never remember which one was named what, but he always smiled and was never rude.

He knew the old maids had spurned suitors in the past. Generally, one or the other would attract attention, leading to courtship and rumors of liaison, just never both at the same time or place. They came as a package deal, no more and no less, and the community honored their vows of interdependence.

Dinky was feeling a little lightheaded that particular evening, and he wondered if he should have had a second sip of Ol' Dill's finest. He reasoned that he needed something to kill the taste of the stew or he could never have finished it.

He waved at the ladies, which he rarely did, and was surprised to see both wave back. In fact, they both actually seemed to be staring at him with shy smiles on their faces. *What the heck*, he thought, *might as well be polite and wish them a good evening* as he slowly sauntered up. He couldn't remember which one usually flirted a little with him and certainly couldn't tell tonight as they both appeared flushed. As he stood looking up to the porch, one invited him in for a drink and the other asked what he might prefer. He said he would just have a sip of what they were drinking and was surprised to find it strangely reminiscent of Ol' Dill's finest in texture and taste. He hadn't realized they tipped every now and again and enjoyed their shower of attention.

As they stood staring out into the gathering dusk, the sisters kept glancing straight at Dinky's mid-section and whispering back and forth. As he looked down at the object of their attention, he was shocked by the bulge beneath his belt. One could actually see the outline of what lurked therein. Dinky's broad smile was met with each sister gently taking one of his hands and leading him through their front door.

When Donald Doodle walked back through that door and down the porch stairs ten hours later, he left "Dinky" in the old maids' flushed toilet. He was spent but a new man in every sense of both words. He would never answer to Dinky again, never wear a mask to bed with another, and never doubt his abilities as a first-class lover. Both sisters, scantily clad in gauzy if dated nightwear, waved goodbye to him with promises to anxiously await his return. A modified package deal had been sealed, keyed to the value of sisterly sharing and conditioned only by Donald Doodle's stamina. Hybrid Absinthe obviously did not breed abstinence. Whether it altered physical attributes was unlikely, but its effect on self-confidence was undeniable.

Soon most of the town was aware of what was going on down Doodle Lane and began smiling at Donald Doodle for new and different reasons. His gait was proud and steady, and though he looked worn slick on occasion, a satisfied smile never left his face. This did not keep him from the antics required by his job description as Village Jester, but he wore pride and confidence on the sleeve of his outlandish cross-dressed outfits.

Ol' Dill was happy for his buddy, if kicking himself for missing out on some of the Sisters Sledge good stuff. He still taunted The Donald and called him Dinky, but he soon tired of his refusal to respond. The Donald was his friend, and he had helped him find what lay within. His batch of homemade "Absinthe Verde" had changed a life for the better. He tried a little himself but found it lacking in anything beyond its foul odor. Ol' Dill guessed he had enough confidence and bravado without it.

Pierce Arrow laughed out loud when he heard about The Donald and the Sisters Sledge. He would miss typing the word "Dinky" in his occasional byline but celebrated the man's boost in confidence courtesy of another needy corner of their amazing community.

Pierce also marveled at lovable Flo, who was the gift that kept on giving. With her gift of Absinthe, she had etched her passion and memory into the Hardlyville psyche in yet one more way. Though he had not partaken of her pleasures personally, despite her determined efforts to entice him, she had aroused him in more ways than any physical touch could have managed. His proposal of marriage to Lettie, his decision to run for Congress again, his inflamed attacks on Big Pork, and now The Donald and his newfound passion all bore her fingerprints. Oh, and he couldn't forget the sudden pregnancy of Ol' Dill's thirteen-year-old feline. Thank you again, Florence Hormel.

And heavy rains continued to fall on the Skunk Creek watershed.

Hillbilly Armageddon

They finally buried the poor dead guy who had been floating down Skunk Creek after giving up on finding even a trace of an ID. None of Sheriff Sephus' inquiries had yielded the slightest lead, and after a couple of days, there was not much else to do. Unless they wanted to send him to the big city for an autopsy. No one really wanted to pay for what was said and done there, whatever that was. So Doc Karst did his own: "Dead, reasons unknown." Sheriff Sephus accepted it as performed and recorded: "Case closed." Albeit, a very strange one, Sheriff concluded.

A nagging thought presented to Sheriff Sephus' regret. Once before, when Sheriff had closed a potential murder case because of lack of evidence, he had been dead wrong. Two grisly float trip murders had become three because Sheriff had not believed his dear and deceased friend Lucas Jones about the first two. The demon lady with the yellow eyes and her sick sect had also gotten Lucas before being disbursed to hell. At least he hoped that was where she lived now.

So dunkin' in dirt, as Dinky Doodle used to call it before he ceased being Dinky and transitioned to The Donald, was about all Hardlyville could offer.

Pierce Arrow lent the cadaver a very old and bedraggled suit, a frayed white shirt, and a pair of jockey underwear Lettie didn't really like. Undertaker Bob found a used casket to lay him in. This seemed something of an oxymoron. Used casket? Undertaker Bob confirmed that, on rare occasions, the family of the deceased would have him or her dug up if they could not meet casket payments, burn what remains were left, and return said casket to the undertaker. He declined comment on Pierce Arrow's sidebar zinger about a casket repossession program seeming a little heavy-handed.

"Just trying to serve the people, dead and alive," was all Undertaker Bob could muster.

Doc Karst offered to insert two ping pong balls into the victim's empty scrotum at no charge. Seemed a more natural way to send the poor soul home to his maker, he mused. No one thought this was a good idea.

Pastor Pat conducted a graveside service, and Hardlyville bid a sad farewell to the stranger in their midst. All wanted to provide a gracious Hardlyville sendoff, in keeping with their reputation and tradition.

Pastor Pat returned to his office to pray for the stranger until Billious Bloom stopped by for her biweekly Ancient Religions class. Their studies took them to holy places—atop the communion table, the floor of the narthex, the bottom of the baptismal pool—in search of hallelujah moments, which were long and plentiful. Pastor Pat taught the course with passion and reckless abandon. Ms. Bloom was settling for nothing less than an A+ and reveled in what she had missed for many years.

Pastor Pat even had a biblically based theory for the stranger's missing equipment, which he shared with Ms. Bloom during a confession interlude between multiple consummations. Citing the gospel of Mathew, Pastor Pat quoted from Chapter 19, verse 12: "For there are some eunuchs, which were so born from their mother's womb . . . and there be eunuchs, which have made themselves eunuchs for the kingdom of heaven's sake." He could make a strong argument that the naked dead man was a eunuch, though he had really never heard of one in those parts. He was unsure as to whether this particular naked dead man was self-made or natural born, but his case was closed as the Bible said it was so.

Pastor Pat was always handy with Scripture. Ms. Bloom thought him brilliant, while Sheriff could only shake his head in utter befuddlement when he heard.

It was early morning when the ground began to tremble. Most Hardlyvillains were up and about, in steady rain, as usual.

Minutes before, upstream and east, a tidal wave of water and waste burst through the passages of the old religious sect's rock fortress as a mighty sinkhole, stuffed with Skunk Creek Ranch hog waste offload, exploded below and above, shattering subterranean karst and blowing the lid off surface springs. The ranch itself was spared the full force of a direct hit, but the pig barns and sewage lagoon were not. The barn structure collapsed on ten thousand squealing pigs and washed the whole fetid mess down what literally became Swine Branch.

Over the roughly eight miles to the merger with flooded Skunk Creek, pigs were thrown fore and aft, back and forth, up and down like porker rag dolls. Some escaped the killer current to wander the land in confusion, squealing displeasure and fear, but most were drowned, crushed, dismembered along the way—all in the toxic soup of their own personal waste.

Those that made it to Skunk Creek were soon swept full-bore into the streets of Hardlyville, stuffed with death. It was a nightmare of unprecedented proportions.

Deal Sealed

Lettie Jones' eyes blazed, and her lower lip quivered. Pierce Arrow had seen this look only once, and he knew not to go there.

"It is my body," she repeated to Pierce, "and I will use it as I see fit."

Pierce's thoughts raced backward to how they had gotten from there to here, and he could only shake his head in disbelief and wonder.

The Skunk Creek Ranch travesty had stunned and touched them all. The cataclysmic flood had been root shaking, the damage indescribable.

Cleanup had been long and painful, and the full community had pitched in. Sheriff Sephus and his occasional deputies had gathered hundreds of scattered pig carcasses in borrowed pickups and trailers and carted them far from town before igniting the biggest barbecue in all of Ozarkian recorded history. The foul odors emanating from the acrid smoke spoke to death and spoilage.

Skunk Creek would have to cleanse herself, flush the filth and waste through her system down to the big waters below. For the first time all spring, Pastor Pat prayed for more rain. It would take more than rain to undo the damage to the creek's ecosystem. Skunk Creek was pure no more, her relatively pristine condition sacrificed on an altar of dollars.

Smelly slime coated most dwellings in Hardlyville, inside and out. The tidal wave of pig shit and offal spared no resident, seven of whom drowned, two while trying to save a neighbor. It was the Hardlyville way, and no tragedy could change that.

Even Thomas Hardly's residence in ruins burst apart and was last seen floating in pieces downstream from its perch on a rise where Thomas and his beloved Petunia had sipped coffee and viewed beautiful Skunk Creek from a small balcony under a rising sun. Hardlyville was gutted from house to house, from history and tradition to gravestones swept away by the torrent. Amazingly enough, Lucas Jones' memorial still stood amidst the broken and stained tributes to past Hardlyvillains. Octavia Rosebeam's Roman figurine was left headless and without arms.

Pierce Arrow had wept when he first entered the *Daily Hellbender*. Beyond Lettie and the little one ready to pop from Lettie's belly, the paper was his heart and soul. His second floor office was spared, except for the stench. He sat down at his computer and begin to write the next day's editorial.

He had begun with a tribute to those who had died. He moved next to those who had survived and joined hands and hearts to reclaim their village. It would take all of the passion, energy, and hope Hardlyvillains could muster to ever find normal again, but they would do it. He continued on with stories of bravery and sacrifice during just the past forty-eight hours. It would take time to disinfect and salvage. It would take years to heal. It would take decades to restore.

Even if it took a lifetime, he was in it to the end, as were all of the friends and neighbors he had visited with. Hardlyville and Skunk Creek would be restored, the *Daily Hellbender* promised that. It was less likely, he observed, that his paper's namesake would ever be seen again in the Skunk Creek watershed—a small loss in the context of human history, yet a true tragedy in the flow of human development and Skunk Creek grounding.

He closed with the announcement that Candidate Arrow would immediately suspend his campaign for the House of Representatives until justice was done and Skunk Creek was protected from more corporate rape and pillage. As soon as Lettie delivered and recovered, he reported that they would travel to Washington, D.C., as a family and picket the president at the White House until he took action to atone for this terrible and unnecessary disaster. Pierce would not return until Skunk Creek was protected forever and Skunk Creek Ranch could never rebuild or resume operations. Never. Finally, he would initiate court action seeking to assure that the Skunk Creek Ranch's owners would be billed for all damages to people and place.

Pierce had proclaimed that everyone knew Skunk Creek Ranch was wrong, ten thousand pigs in the Skunk Creek watershed was wrong, the arms that had been twisted and the money exchanged in back rooms was wrong, and that Big Pork was wrong, dead wrong. They would not win this time, no matter how much money or how devious their plan to rebuild and resume CAFO operations upstream.

Pierce noted that he had researched how Skunk Creek might be protected going forward, once damage was determined and mitigated. The president of the United States has the power to establish wildlife refuges without Congressional consent. Given the sorry state of affairs in Congress and the pathetic representation provided by "Dr. No," Pierce Arrow reasoned that was the only practical path to protection. He and Lettie would lobby the president for executive action. They would not return until the president created the Skunk Creek National Watershed Wildlife Refuge. It was their personal promise to the citizens of Hardlyville.

The current resident of the White House was a somewhat liberal, ne'er-do-well bachelor who, among other things, proclaimed himself an ardent environmentalist and was somehow elected despite that claim. He was also very wealthy, courtesy of a successful family-owned business conglomerate, so he ran as a friend of business as well, citing his success in that arena. Some found him cute, some charming, some harmless, and he spent more money to eke out a victory than any previous candidate by a multiple of one-and-a-half times.

Pierce and Lettie had promised to take the crusade to the top, and they did.

The baby girl that had graced their presence healthily and happily in a neighboring community's hospital had no idea what she was getting into. Several weeks after her birth and Lettie's return to health, baby Mona was loaded into a leased RV with her parents and their neighbor's teenage daughter, Lil' Shooter, to serve as nanny, and headed east to the nation's capital.

Lil' Shooter, namesake of local businessman Rifleman and his wife Steele, didn't much like school anyway and was delighted to be part of such a grand adventure. She would be excused from senior classes at Hardlyville High School if she would Skype daily with Mr. Clavecal's American History class and share details of her experience, which would surely be richer than any textbook experience. Mr. Clavecal came from a liberal arts background and valued engaged learning above any curricular requirements. Only in Hardlyville, perhaps, but since many Hardlyvillains were self-educated themselves, most saw no harm in such a progressive approach to learning.

Rifleman and Steele were delighted that their daughter would likely avoid flunking out, probable pregnancy, and would be checking in daily, which was better than her current frequency of contact. Pesky Hardlyville boys had a thing for their daughter, who enjoyed their attentions, particularly camping out on the banks of Skunk Creek, far too much. Their fierce support of Pierce Arrow's anti-Big-Pork crusade sealed the deal.

It was not quite *Mr. Smith Goes to Washington*, but not far from it.

Pierce arranged to hook up the RV at a trailer park in Arlington, Virginia, just across the Potomac from their field of play. Lil' Shooter manned home base, while Pierce and Lettie metroed it to the front gates of the White House every morning. They joined a lively lady, who went by Crazy Mary, to walk the picket line. Her signs and causes changed daily.

Pierce toted "MR. PRESIDENT: SAVE SKUNK CREEK WATERSHED FROM BIG PORK" to Lettie's "SKUNK CREEK WATERSHED NATIONAL REFUGE." They wore matching t-shirts as well, with a sketch of a lovable-looking skunk sitting in a canoe on a beautiful creek. Crazy Mary loved the company and the attendant attention when it became known that this was a legitimate candidate for Congress, who had taken to the streets with his partner, not wife, but mother of his child. They even brought baby Mona along a time or two but soon realized that Lil' Shooter needed the responsibility of a child to keep her from grazing the D.C. scene. With the sweet smell of weed and an empty six-pack carton awaiting their return from a Mona picket outing instead of Lil' Shooter, they got the message. She said she had camped on the banks of the Potomac with some new friends when she checked in early the next morning. No, Lil' Shooter needed baby Mona to stay out of trouble.

Problem was that baby Mona was magic on the picket line. Lettie even had a t-shirt made that read "Babies Love Skunk Creek." It got them on the evening news. Channel 5 started covering the candidate's quest and the cute baby and babe who flanked him. A couple of special reports on the Skunk Creek environmental disaster and a Democratic candidate for Congress in a bright-red state picketing for access to the president finally got the White House Press Room's attention.

"All they want is a national refuge designation for some god-forsaken corner of the Ozarks?" the president asked the shapely lady lying next to him in a most natural state.

"Where's the Ozarks?" she mumbled back, trying to get just an hour of sleep before suiting up to become his principal aide again. It had been a long and amorous night.

He thought the Ozarks was somewhere down South but wasn't sure. He recalled a brutal movie about bones and drugs and thought that was the locale. Or maybe it was that one where the guy had to squeal like a pig. A cultural wasteland, no doubt.

He tickled her backside to break her doze. She complained that she was used up for now but would be back for more later. She promised. The president indicated that was not what he was interested in at that particular moment.

"Why not invite them up for a chat?" he wondered aloud. "Bring the baby too." What harm could come from opening the White House doors to a fellow Democrat and potential vote in the Congress? He asked Principal Aide to find out more about the fellow and report back as soon she could.

"Shower first?" she begged.

He smiled and nodded yes, assuring her that ten a.m. would be fine.

She sauntered into the Oval Office, where their previous night's adventures had begun, at nine fifty-seven, about the time they had started their fun twelve hours earlier.

"Interesting guy," she confirmed.

"Do tell," he nodded.

"Small-town newspaper editor, the *Hardlyville Daily Hellbender*, Pulitzer winner for his coverage of a series of murders by a religious sect deep in the Ozark Mountains, ran against that idiot Larry Larrsnist in the last election only to withdraw at the last minute because of child pornography accusations that were dropped without filed charges."

The president wondered why he would run again under such a shadow. His aide confirmed it was a hit job, orchestrated and funded by Larrsnist supporters, slander in its rawest form. A pork producer, banker, and chairman of the state water commission were in up to their asses, with the latter serving time for accepting a bribe and the banker's bank taken over by the FDIC. The banker accomplice had died of a heart attack.

"Why and what now?" the president wondered.

A major environmental disaster involving a hog CAFO, a creek named Skunk, and a devastated town full of Hardlyvillains, the aide responded.

"You couldn't make this up," chuckled the president.

"No, it was apparently a pretty bad deal, and this candidate named Pierce Arrow—"

"You must be kidding," interrupted the president.

"No, I'm not," the aide continued. "This Pierce Arrow has sworn not to return home, campaign or not, until his precious Skunk Creek is protected, calling for an executive order to make the whole sorry hog manured place a wildlife refuge."

What good that would do, the president couldn't comprehend. It's not like the federal government can rebuild a desecrated creek or restore decimated species. Damage done. But then again, maybe the symbolism would sell with some in that hostile state.

"That's about it," offered the aide. "Oh yes. Arrow's partner is not his wife, but that is their child. The woman's name is Lettie, and apparently her first husband was murdered by the leader of the religious sect. Their baby's name is Mona. Arrow is a bit frumpy, but baby and lady are cute as hell and have captivated the local press."

"Wow, you are good," confirmed the president with a smile.

"I know," was her response.

"And you do good research as well," he delivered with a pinch to her derrière.

That was one of his trademark antics that she detested but put up with because of the power and access it afforded her.

He called for his principal political advisor immediately and wondered aloud again what harm could come from meeting with this zealot and listening to his case. Plus, the little filly was not hard on the eyes. The advisor agreed on both counts, and Principal Aide arranged to pass a message to the protesters via a Secret Service agent, who handed the printed invitation to Lettie. She opened it and stared in disbelief. There, beneath a genuine Presidential Seal, was a signed, handwritten note.

The president of the United States was inviting Pierce, Lettie, and Mona for tea at the White House the next afternoon at three o'clock sharp. A black limo would pick them up from their standard picket line site. They should dress just as they do for protesting. Mona in her "Babies Love Skunk Creek" tiny t-shirt was perfect.

The invitees were ecstatic and smelled victory. Crazy Mary was pissed. She loved those kids, their giddy love and naiveté, but she had been walking the block for seventeen years and had never heard a peep from the current or three previous residents of the house across Pennsylvania Avenue. She forced a smile, nonetheless, and vowed to live vicariously through her sidewalk mates.

The principal press aide leaked to the media the whole arrangement, and with cameras buzzing and reporters shouting questions, Pierce, Lettie, and Mona, all clad in their finest Skunk Creek paraphernalia, entered the limo. Though they were only driving a few yards, an infant car seat had been installed for the occasion. The press waved goodbye and promised to await their return.

The president greeted them in the Rose Garden and blubbered through his prescribed list of pleasantries. His charm and charisma were infectious and persuasive. Only the principal aide and the wait staff were present, though a staff photographer slipped in to catch a photo or two of the president talking earnestly to his Skunk Creek guests. It would appear the next morning in *The Washington Post* and then be digitally disseminated regionally, including to the *Hardlyville Hellbender*.

The president asked them to talk about their beautiful creek, to which Lettie replied with tears in her eyes that it wasn't beautiful anymore. Presidential eyes watered as well, caught up in the emotion of the moment. Pierce added that an industrial pig farm, which never should have been there in the first place, had desecrated a near holy place and trashed a town of undeserving citizens.

The president expressed outrage and asked what he could do to help. Pierce explained that an executive order establishing the Skunk Creek National Watershed Wildlife Refuge would protect their precious creek and surrounds for future generations of Hardlyvillains, and that he was pursuing legal action against the perpetrators for damages and restitution.

The president nodded his agreement and asked his principal aide to research his options for intervention. He was a proven environmental activist, and this course certainly seemed a reasonable option. He asked for twenty-four hours to respond and promised he would be open and timely.

Pierce and Lettie were deeply touched with his interest and willingness to consider their request. Baby Mona cooed cutely. The president urged them to return to the picket line tomorrow so he could track them down. He kissed the baby and hugged Pierce then Lettie, a little longer and tighter. Pierce saw her jump slightly but counted it as nervousness. It had been an emotional and productive encounter that carried great promise, and that is what they shared with the waiting press. The principal aide issued a similar release.

As Pierce and Lettie toted Mona back to the RV, Pierce asked what had made Lettie jump in the presidential hug.

"I think the son of a bitch pinched my ass," she spat back in confusion.

"Surely not," was all Pierce could muster in response.

Lil' Shooter was evidently camping on the Potomac with her new friends again, so Lettie resolved to take her with them to picket the next day. It would be a big and important day, indeed, and she could Skype the whole thing to Mr. Clavecal's history class.

As this ragtag contingent took their positions next to Crazy Mary the next morning, all were abuzz with expectation. They refused comment to the press for fear of overstatement, but clearly were energized and inspired. Lil' Shooter loved the attention and the live coverage of her classroom Skype. Each network kept a cameraman in place for the promised presidential communication.

About two in the afternoon, a D.C. police car stopped near Pierce. An officer jumped out, shoved him against the car, and applied handcuffs. Lettie didn't see what was happening as she was distracted by a homeless-looking man, who whispered in her ear that she was to join him immediately in the unmarked car that pulled up on cue. The president of the United States wished a private conversation with her. Before she could react to the contradictions in his request, she was gently nudged into the front seat next to a Secret Service looking kind of dude, and only as they sped off did she see what was happening to Pierce. Lil' Shooter was screaming, and Mona was crying, and for all they knew Mom was being kidnapped. Before she could scream back, a handkerchief from the backseat sent her senses spinning, and she awakened in the Oval Office of the White House with the president of the United States smiling softly at her.

As Lettie began to regain her senses, she demanded to know what the police were doing with or to Pierce. The president assured her it had been a case of mistaken identity, and her partner was fine. The principal aide was on the scene, explaining the error to the press and assuring Pierce that Lettie was okay and currently with the president discussing the wildlife refuge issue. He had a brief window of scheduling opportunity for a meeting and didn't include Pierce because he couldn't wait for the chaos to settle and didn't want to make a big scene with the D.C. police.

The president handed Lettie a glass of water and suggested that she had passed out briefly from the excitement of it all. She knew better but didn't remember much. She stared coldly at her Commander in Chief, the only presence in the pretentious room.

The president observed that he had something that Lettie wanted and that she, in turn, had something that he desired. He had invited her there to strike a deal that honored the needs of both. Lettie sensed what was coming and wanted to throw the glass of water on his silk tie and fake-smile face. Instead, she listened.

The president reported that research had confirmed his ability to issue an executive order creating the Skunk Creek National Watershed Wildlife Refuge, subject to required regulatory due diligence. He had a press release announcing that grand development prepared for issuance the next day at three p.m. He was honored to be of service to the good citizens of Hardlyville and the precious water resources of the Ozarks. Was that what Lettie wanted? She nodded cautiously.

The president's part of the deal was this. He found Lettie very attractive. And while he would never interfere with a happy marriage, it was clear that, despite their happiness, she and Pierce were not married. He would ask only that Lettie return to the

Oval Office tomorrow at noon for a private lunch and sex. No marital infidelity there, just mutual pleasure. He prided himself on his ability to satisfy even the most finicky ladies and was confident Lettie would leave with a smile on her face. All would be done in strictest confidence—her partner, Pierce, would never know—and all the president would require would be an hour and a half of Lettie's time. And all of her body. He promised it would be worth her investment.

Lettie was struck dumb. What could this neanderthal be thinking? She grasped for words to respond but could find none.

Sensing her shock, the president quietly confirmed he would send a car to her RV park at precisely eleven forty-five a.m. the next day. Of course, he had figured out where she was staying. If she were to enter it and join him, the world would know of his aggressive and generous decision on behalf of the environment. If she did not, the press release would be destroyed, and no one in the world would be the better for it. It was that simple.

The president had escorted her to the Oval Office entrance, where a driver awaited. He pecked her on the cheek and pinched her ass while waving goodbye.

By the time Lettie was dropped back off across from the White House, the furor over Pierce Arrow's mistaken cuffing had died down, though the press was hovering. Pierce hugged Lettie, sensing her confusion, and refused comment on her behalf. All knew of the meeting with the president and were anxious to be the first to break the news of an outcome. Lettie could only shake her head. The press wanted to know if that was a "yes" or a "no." When she shook side to side, the press groaned, presuming a "no" she couldn't say. When she nodded up and down, the press cheered loudly, and Lil' Shooter jumped excitedly with little Mona in her arms. This confusing non-verbal exchange continued for several minutes with Lettie speechless, the press groaning and cheering with each competing head movement, and Pierce totally in the dark. One cameraman vomited from motion sickness as he tried to follow Lettie with his lens. Pierce finally put an end to the charade, pleading ignorance and asking for room to take his family back where they were staying. Several demanded to know where that was, a query he refused to acknowledge.

They had driven the RV that day since the whole family was transported. Pierce quickly loaded everyone in and sped off before the reporters could follow. He circled the Lincoln monument twice to make sure no one was following, then headed across the Potomac to their Arlington refuge. Lettie said nothing the whole way, and Pierce knew she was in deep thought.

They fed the baby and left Lil' Shooter to put her to bed. Then they walked slowly along the streets of Arlington. First, Lettie wanted to know if Pierce had been harmed in any way. He assured her not and that both the D.C. police and the president's principal aide were most apologetic for the mistaken identity. He was told a broad daylight armed robbery had taken place just around the block, and that the fleeing criminal fit his description to a T. Pierce had not even seen Lettie whisked away, and when the principal aide had confirmed her private visit with the president, he had felt a gush of trouble brewing, not unlike he had felt when the first bloated, dead hog had floated down Skunk Creek that dreadful day. Pierce Arrow had smelled a rat, a skunk, a dirty diaper, a three-day-old pile of entrails. The principal aide had assured him that Lettie would return shortly with very good news, but Pierce had stewed.

"Did he hurt you?" he queried.

"No," Lettie confirmed, and she then shared the details of their exchange.

"The president of the United States wants you to do what?" Pierce had screamed at the top of his lungs.

Lettie tried to calm him, but he was in the middle of a rage the likes of which she had never witnessed. He later confirmed he had never before experienced one similar. His face was crimson, and his heart felt explosive. Lettie continued to calm him with kisses and nuzzles as they sat on a park bench.

It was nearly thirty minutes later when Pierce was able to speak. He lamented Lettie's misfortune and treatment before promising to do something about it. As a man of the press, he knew this one would sell big-time.

"He'll just deny it all," Lettie observed, "and he certainly has more credibility than me with the national media."

"What else can we do?" Pierce pondered. Lettie's far-off look caught Pierce's attention. "You would never do such a thing," Pierce demanded as a statement not a question.

Lettie said she needed time and space to think and asked Pierce to walk her back to the RV. They did so in silence until Pierce could contain himself no more.

"You can't!" he ordered emphatically, repeating himself until she flashed him "the look" and pronounced the "It's my body, and I will use it as I see fit" ultimatum.

Pierce was stunned back into silence.

They barely spoke before crawling into bed together on opposite sides, their relationship in crisis mode.

And that's how they had gotten from there to here.

Neither slept much. Pierce was too pissed, and Lettie was processing too much information. She had once had a "one and done" with Sheriff Sephus, back when she was married to first husband and deceased town hero Lucas Jones. She had been young, aware of Lucas' several indiscretions, and curious about whether big was really better. It had been wrong, but their marriage had survived and thrived after mutual confessions.

This situation was different. She loved Pierce in a way she had never felt before. The thought of hurting him hurt her more.

And yet this was as important as any decision she had ever made in terms of timeless implications. If by screwing the president of the United States she could protect Skunk Creek for generations to come, she had to give the unthinkable serious thought. No one could advise her on this one. She couldn't even decide if it was a no-win situation because if she did it all of Hardlyville would win.

Lettie rolled out early with a kiss to Pierce's forehead and said she needed to be alone. She thought of first husband Lucas Jones' sacrifice for the children of Hardlyville. She had learned later that he had sexed the evil demon of a lady who had ultimately shot him to his death, willing himself to the impossible above pain and remorse, in the interest of others. It was a long story. Probably had to be there to understand, though she was glad she hadn't been.

How different was this tale of sacrifice? Why did it always come down to sex?

Lettie finally determined a course of action. She would screw the friggin' president of the United States in the interest of Skunk Creek and Hardlyville and beg Pierce's forgiveness. It was her only option. She returned to share her decision with Pierce.

Pierce Arrow's shoulders slumped when he heard her conclusion and accompanying rationale.

She would be ready at eleven forty-five for the president's car. She would dress like a lady, not a whore. She would carry her head high as she submitted to his intrusion and finish as soon as he allowed. She would do it for the future of Skunk Creek and Hardlyville and the generations to come. Like Lucas, she would sacrifice for her community through a single act of sex, but she would come back to her true love and believe in his capacity to forgive. She would beg for it.

"It is my body, my love," she concluded, "and I choose to give it all for the creek and the community we love so much." Her conviction did not keep back the tears.

Pierce sobbed briefly as well, then slowly nodded his head in affirmation. He could never have dreamed that one he loved so much would sacrifice so greatly for such a noble cause, and he couldn't hate her so much for it. He actually felt sorrier for her than for himself and admired her deeply beneath the hurt of the moment.

Lettie dressed quickly and professionally. She even buttoned the top button of her blouse. She looked beautiful. She stuck one of Lil' Shooter's condoms in her purse, kissed the baby, and winked at Pierce, promising to be back as soon as she could. He reached out and pulled her near for a moment, whispering his love for her. Then he pinched her briskly on the butt. She smiled back through tears and walked crisply to the waiting black sedan, standing as tall as her small frame would allow.

A New Banker in Town

While Lettie and Pierce were learning the ways of Washington, D.C., a new face appeared in Hardlyville. Actually three. And then more. This hadn't happened in such magnitude that anyone could remember since Thomas Hardly set out to establish a new village a century plus ago and his relatives and friends from Western Tennessee had moved in. Locals saw it as a big deal, particularly in the aftermath of the Big Pig Flood that had poisoned Skunk Creek and devastated Hardlyville. They figured the new arrivals were either hustlers trying to turn tragedy into a quick buck or optimists, which Hardlyville was sorely in need of in its time of trial. The new ones were accompanied by a small entourage of bank regulators from the Federal Deposit Insurance Corporation, who announced their acquisition of the Bank of Hardlyville and their intention to reopen and provide a full range of banking services within a week.

This did nothing to answer the question of scam vs. hope since the previous owner and president, Banker Bud, had ripped off the community, unbeknownst to most until his fatal heart attack. His secret real estate deals, clandestine cash withdrawals for Las Vegas "run and guns," and world-class pornography collection, which he used to defame candidate Pierce Arrow during his previous run for Congress, were filthy little secrets that finally surfaced in the wake of the banker's demise. He was a dirty little scoundrel, up to his groin in pigs and Big Pork, and as such shared responsibility for the Big Pig Flood and Hardlyville's current wallowing in hog shit and dirty muck. At least that's the way most saw it.

The citizens of Hardlyville were indeed ready for a return to community banking if it was fair, honest, and safe. They had survived on a cash machine for over a year, which operated only when it chose to. As a result, Hardlyville had returned to the bartering roots that had served it so well a century past.

A weekly farmers' market allowed neighbors to swap staples and stories to stay afloat. Spring rains had dampened spirits but not a love of bargaining, and deals were cut down to the last turnip.

Hardlyvillains were an entrepreneurial lot but missed the convenience of a community bank when all was said and done. Demands for loans had gone unfulfilled, to the inconvenience of some. Jimmy Jones had wanted to expand his weed field, but he couldn't exactly swap his only currency, weed, for more weed. Doc Karst had wanted to enlarge his small medical clinic to two beds but already gave away so many freebies he had little to offer.

An undependable supply of cash also made the traditional weekend poker marathons challenging. The Hardlyville town game of seven card, roll your own, high low poker, hosted by civic leadership, was open to a select group of citizens who could drop in any time during the thirty-six hour time slot between Friday supper and Sunday school. Many did, although bets began to take on a unique character. What used to be dollar, dollar, dollar morphed into six-packs, condoms, joints, screwdrivers, tomatoes, fresh frog legs, and such. Rifleman's wife, Steele, who replaced the deceased and shamed Banker Bud in civic leadership, even threw in an occasional bra her teenage daughter, Lil' Shooter, had outgrown or some of Rifleman's wood shavings for fire starter.

The Donald grabbed every bra he could get his hands on for his cross-dressing antics as Village Jester. He would generally swap a thimble full of his precious absinthe with winners of such booty. He preferred the small ones to the sisters' saggy hand-me-downs. Took three socks each to stuff one of them, he explained. Given the level skills of combatants, most winnings not consumed on the spot were recycled in subsequent bets.

Enter Hardlyville's new bankers.

One was a rather homely middle-aged gentleman, who was either beset with extreme shyness or mute. A nod of "yes" or "no" seemed the full extent of his vocabulary, though he carried a presence and calmness about him that belied great wisdom. One look into his eyes and one could tell he was sharing the truth, whatever that might be. Even confirmed cynic Ol' Dill trusted him after their first meeting. He was accompanied by a substantially younger wife, who was warm, energetic, loquacious, and seemed very caring.

New banker answered to Jamin Bennell, owing to several unusual circumstances. He was the tenth of his lineage to be named Benjamin, going back to rural England. Most reduced that to Ben along the way, or clung to the biblical Benjamin. Given his mother's intuition that she had, indeed, birthed a child of extraordinary capability, she refused to reduce him to the Bennell norm. Ben or Benjamin simply wouldn't do. That left Jamin, and thus it became.

Jamin and wife, Mabel, were relocating from small-town Colorado with their ten children of varying genders and ages. They evidently celebrated each year of their marriage with a newborn. Both had roots in the Ozarks. Both longed for a return to hills, crystal springs and creeks, temperate weather, ticks, chiggers, and copperheads. So Jamin sold his Colorado bank, got wind of the failed Bank of Hardlyville, bought it from the FDIC at a deep discount, loaded up the whole crew in an old school bus, and set out on a new adventure.

This unusual entourage also included a strange-looking man dressed in bib overalls and sporting a wide-brimmed felt hat that never left his head. He purportedly even bathed in it on those rare occasions that Mabel demanded a "cleansing of the air," as she called it. His proper name was Mr. Ott, but he always introduced himself as Captain Happy, owing to his sunny disposition and core belief that "every day is a great day until someone proves me wrong."

Captain Happy's self-pronounced personal mission statement was to spread levity and love amongst all around him. He also served as the formal spokesperson for the very quiet Jamin, whom he described as impeccably honest, absurdly intelligent, and abnormally shy. Captain's duties ranged from closing business deals to negotiating sexual encounters between Jamin and Mabel. When asked about the latter, he confirmed that Jamin was so shy he slept in his pants and dress jacket. So how did they manage ten children? Captain Happy observed wryly that some men shoot blanks, some real bullets.

Captain Happy's presence and role initially created great confusion as to who partnered with whom in the Bennell extended family. Ol' Dill surmised that the good captain took care of Mabel in that several of the children bore an uncanny resemblance to him. The Donald thought perhaps he was gay. Most couldn't care less. They were simply happy to increase their population and tax base by five percent in one transaction and to have a full-service bank again.

Jamin's first official banking act was to offer twenty dollars cash to anyone who opened a new account, which he funded from his personal kitty. This was probably illegal but considerably more functional than a toaster or beer cooler. The resultant bank run required that he declare a one day bank holiday so as to hire and train new account representatives. He created more jobs in one day than Hardlyville had experienced in three decades.

Jamin's second official banking act was to lend himself enough money to construct three dwellings in which to house the clan. This construction job injection into the community halved the current unemployment rate. Captain Happy cheerfully interpreted Jamin's marketing efforts to the community at large. All of a sudden, Hardlyville was booming in the aftermath of the greatest unnatural disaster in its storied history, and Jamin Bennell was a very popular, if silent, hero.

Jamin decided to go outside the norm in selecting his bank board of directors as well. He wanted an honest and diverse base of community input so as to better serve the citizens of Hardlyville. Since there was no minority representation in the community beyond the young black child, Otis, born of the now deceased Sabrina Hendricks, his applicant pool was small. There were a number of qualified women in town, so diversity by gender would become his focus. Sexual orientation was neither solicited nor approved, just ignored. Above all, Jamin did not want a good ol' boys white man club as his board of directors.

He started with Steele, Rifleman's wife and a much admired civic leader since arriving in town. She also chaired the Hardlyville Chamber of Commerce, as co-owner of the village's only manufacturing enterprise. She quickly said "yes."

Jamin then reached out to Tiny Taylor, owner of Greasy Spoon Grill and Bar. Tiny was an immensely popular Hardlyvillain, who won hearts with her vast assortment of fried food offerings. Finally, Billious Bloom, Hardlyville librarian and executive director of the Rosebeam Endowment, could bring substantial deposits to the bank. Both said "yes" as well. Three legitimate businesswomen was a real coup for Jamin.

To attain gender balance, Jamin named Captain Happy and asked Doc Karst and Postmaster Bond to join. All said "yes."

The first Bank of Hardlyville board meeting was a stemwinder. Jamin banged the gavel for order then sat in silence, waiting for someone to say something so he could nod "yes" or shake his head "no." Captain Happy knew the drill but chose to wait and see who might be the more aggressive board members.

After about five minutes, Steele raised her hand, to which Jamin nodded a vigorous "yes." Steele assumed that meant she had permission to comment and spoke of how proud she was to serve on a real bank board of directors. Others began nodding as well, to which Chairman Jamin began shaking his head in the negative. This confused and hurt Steele's feelings until Captain Happy explained that Jamin was merely saying it was not Steele who was proud but he himself with the quality of the board. Ice broken, Jamin passed out a strategic plan, complete with financial projections, and Captain Happy asked for board approval, which was granted. Jamin banged the gavel again, which meant the meeting was complete, handed each director a twenty dollar bill as board fee, and smiled them away. Each, of course, deposited the twenty in their newly-opened accounts, and deposits began to grow exponentially.

Jimmy Jones cleaned out his subterranean safe and brought the strangely sweet-scented cash in to deposit. He immediately became Bank of Hardlyville's largest depositor and quickly borrowed half the balance back to expand his weed field plot, earning the bank its first profits on a three percent spread.

Jamin greeted every customer personally with a nod of thanks, gaining immediate respect and trust. Community banking had indeed returned to Hardlyville.

Jamin also began to join weekend card games, but he preferred cribbage to poker. It didn't take long for others to take an interest in his cribbage board, and soon there were options for gambling, another first.

Pastor Pat felt a personal sense of responsibility for the Big Pig Flood. His entreaties to his God above had gone unanswered. Whether it was his prayers to stop the early spring rains or to divert the tidal wave of feces, waste, and pigs from his beloved Hardlyville, his God was clearly not on Pastor Pat's wavelength.

Pastor Pat knew he had sinned by renouncing his celibacy once again. He had gotten in trouble every time he had slipped before.

The horny wife of the board of trustees chair at his last church in Phoenix had taken him to heights he had never before ascended. When the board chair got wind of it, he used his personal friendship with a highway patrol officer to earn Pastor Pat four DWIs and dismissal from their pulpit. No question of the direct cause and effect from high in heaven.

His dalliance with the lead alto at Skunk Creek Church of Christ just after his arrival in Hardlyville had no doubt led to the death of Lucas Jones at the hands of the coven of evil and the demon lady with the blazing yellow eyes. His God had seen to that.

His "Good Samaritan" sermon to voluptuous French porn actress Florence Hormel had led to several otherworldly encounters over just a week and had undoubtedly caused the premature death of town matron Ms. Rosebeam in a tragic car accident at just eighty-three years of age.

And now this. He had no doubt introduced Billious Bloom to the joys of sex, rescuing her from virginity and unfulfilled desires, but, as always, his flock and community paid the price for his indiscretion. His God taught the linear relationship between bad decisions and bad outcomes, and the Great Pig Flood was clear proof of that.

Hindsight was always twenty-twenty. Four incredible partners and escapes from his reality as a man of God, and four tragic outcomes. It was clear that the chain of misfortunes, which echoed his bouts of lust, were linked celestially by a seriously pissed off Higher Power. Hindsight was also foresight, so the Bible said. He would have to look it up, but something about "now you see through a glass darkly" came to mind. He preferred a clearer vision of the future and would forego further earthly pleasures to that end, so help him God. He would pray for forgiveness and spiritual cleansing and put these pleasant memories behind him.

So he would have to call it off with Ms. Bloom. Not until he sinned one more time to commemorate the joy and pleasures that their frequent unions had wrought, but hopefully immediately thereafter. Or maybe after the encore. In his heart, he knew there must be a last one sometime and that he must return to celibacy if he was to be a good steward to the citizens of Hardlyville.

He crammed in three more incredibly risqué and rewarding commemorations, begging forgiveness after each, before finally succumbing to his fate.

Billious Bloom was heartbroken.

"Wasn't it good for you this time?" she whined.

"It was and has always been marvelous," Pastor Pat assured. But he explained that his focus on the divine Ms. Bloom had caused him to neglect the rest of his flock. He had prayed on it, and the guidance from above was clear. He must return to a life of celibacy without further ado.

"What will I do without you?" Billious had wailed almost as loudly as with her just fulfilled consummation.

He assured her she would find other lovers who could fulfill her needs and that he would miss that role in her life.

"But you've been the only one," she sobbed, "and it has all been so wholesome and right."

Pastor Pat expressed his pride in being the first to open the door but assured her there were other keys waiting to turn the tumblers. He particularly liked that metaphor. Pastor Pat acknowledged that Ms. Bloom had a lot of catching up to do given her three decades of abstinence, but he assured her it would be fun. He cautioned against rushing such a pleasurable project, against focusing on too narrow a target market, and against happily married prospects as he would surely hear of their indiscretions in confession.

"Will it make you jealous?" Ms. Bloom winked.

Pastor Pat blushed and gave her one last, deep hug.

"One for the road?" Billious grinned mischievously.

"What the hay," responded the good pastor and rode his wheel of good fortune through one last commemoration before sadly moving on.

Ms. Bloom, on the other hand, was a beautiful flower unfurling. She threw herself into cementing Ms. Octavia Rosebeam's Latin legacy in the community and around the bi-state area. As Hardlyville librarian, curator of the Rosebeam Collection of Rare Latin Books, and curator of the Rosebeam Endowment, Ms. Bloom was constantly on the go.

Ms. Rosebeam, granddaughter of Hardlyville Founder Thomas Hardly, had grown up absorbed by all things Latin, including a stint studying in New York City as a young lady. She returned to Hardlyville after being jilted by her Latin lover, under very distressing circumstances, to teach Latin to all Hardlyville High graduates until her recent death by auto accident. She left her collections, writings, and residence to the Hardlyville Library, along with an endowment sufficient to expand the eclectic collection.

Her textbook, *Coitus Interruptus,* had been utilized exclusively at Hardlyville High but, with Ms. Bloom's eye for promotional opportunities, was going into a second printing with plans for much expanded distribution. Ms. Bloom administered it all capably and with a passion befitting the subject.

She dabbled in men as she picked and chose, and at her own pace, generally following Pastor Pat's prescribed guidelines. A torrid but brief affair with the executive director of a large city history museum opened a whole new prospect list of potential funders, and her reputation as an astute collector of Latin antiquities drew many to her. She dreamed of Hardlyville becoming a destination for aficionados of all things Latin and knew Ms. Rosebeam would approve.

While she did not resume Ms. Rosebeam's regular Latin classes, she did reinstate the annual toga party as a Hardlyville Senior Class tradition, complete with a ceremonial dollop of Ol' Dill's white lightning in the foot-stomped grape juice.

Pastor Pat resumed serving his flock in a more evenhanded way, and he heard no tearful confessions that might implicate his former lover in marital indiscretions, which pleased him greatly.

It was about this time that a second naked dead man was found floating down Skunk Creek, adorned similarly to the first several months back, helium balloons and all. Empty scrotum as well. A singular episode had been confusing enough, but a second lent credence to a pattern, perhaps even a conspiracy. All of Hardlyville was soon armed and up in arms, demanding that Sheriff Sephus Adonis get off his fat rump and solve these frightening crimes.

The sheriff had never seen anything so weird in all of his years fighting crime and hadn't a clue as to where to begin beyond repeating his signature "shit, brothers" over and over again, a furtive chant in search of an answer.

As the sheriff pondered the bizarre murders, Billious bloomed in all ways Latin, and the bank moved forward in Hardlyville, little Lettie prepared to take one for the home team over in Washington, D.C.

Consummation

The president of the United States welcomed Lettie Jones to the Oval Office for the second time in two days. He wore a silk robe—emblazoned with a large red, white, and blue stallion—and gold slippers. He was definitely underdressed and probably overstated for a president, Lettie thought. He closed and locked the door behind them and motioned for her to sit on the couch next to him. His swarthy smile turned her stomach, but she held a firm face.

He offered her a watercress sandwich from a tray on the table and a chilled glass of Meursault. After all, it was a luncheon date.

Lettie declined on both counts. "This is a business deal," she reiterated and expressed her wish for consummation as quickly as possible.

The president nodded and handed Lettie a copy of the press release with the issue time of fifteen hundred hours. "My part of the bargain," he confirmed, noting that it was loaded and ready for automatic release at that exact time, even if their frolic was not yet complete.

She muttered a muted "thank you" and assured the president they would be finished by then. She could not comprehend the mind of one so arrogant. And to think, he was the leader of the free world. There was nothing free about this engagement.

She scanned the release, and it read as promised. His executive order would establish the Skunk Creek Watershed National Wildlife Refuge and initiate due diligence for sustainable financial maintenance support immediately. At least he could keep his word, if only when it suited his whims and pleasures.

Lettie began to unbutton her blouse, top down. The president stopped her and requested that she begin again, only this time facing him as he moved to his executive chair behind the large desk of state. He reclined with a smile, and she began again, top button first. She actually felt a slight surge of power for some very strange reason. She was changing history in the Ozarks.

She moved quickly to disrobe, and the president watched with lecherous eyes, moving to each new section of flesh revealed. He reveled in her small breasts, ogling them one by one and back again. He asked her to step back as she removed her skirt, stockings, and panties. He commented on her bald spot midship, saying that was just how he liked it.

"So did Lucas and so does Pierce," she muttered proudly to herself.

He asked her to put her heels back on and stand with her arms at her sides. He simply leered for at least five minutes. She felt goosepimples pop, either from the heathen gaze or the air conditioning.

He finally rose and headed toward her. He grasped her shoulders and planted a vicious kiss on her lips, which she refused to part. He persisted to no avail, promising he could make her feel better. She simply resisted.

He smiled, stepping back and removing his robe. He folded it carefully on the couch. He had nothing on beneath.

At first, she shied from looking, then, despite the gravity of situation, Lettie suddenly burst out laughing. She was face-to-face with the smallest erect penis she had ever seen. In that this was only the fourth in her entire lifetime, she could not be considered an expert, but it did not take a veteran penis watcher to catch the lack of everything—length, girth, breadth, depth. His was simply abnormal, and she laughed out loud again. For some reason, Barbie and Ken dolls popped from memory to playing out in front of her very eyes.

"What's wrong?" the president blushed.

"It's so little for such a big and powerful president," Lettie gushed.

This did not set well with the president, and he ordered her to bend over his executive desk and prepare to take her medicine.

"A mighty small dose." Lettie laughed to herself as she handed him a condom.

He frowned again. She insisted, though wondering how he could possibly keep it on board his tiny member. She then did as told and prepared to take one for Skunk Creek, not sure if she would even feel it. She sensed shame, sadness for Pierce, and yet a certain pride in her sacrifice for the greater good. She just wanted it over and done.

At that very moment, a shrill siren blared throughout the Oval Office. There was banging on the locked door. The president stared blankly through his lust to the flashing red light on his telephone.

"Oh shit," he muttered, "it's a national emergency." He raced to the phone, deflating into nothing even visible as he ran.

Lettie could only hope the emergency was not so horrid as to offset the relief she felt from being spared, if only for the moment. She hurriedly began to reclothe, quickly regaining her professional bearing. She heard the president shouting about Pakistan dropping a nuke on the disputed territory of Kashmir in Northern India and India threatening to retaliate on Islamabad. He screamed insults to both nationalities and cursed them for interrupting his life and his presidency.

There was something almost comical about a naked man commanding his chief military official to launch fighter jets and relocate aircraft carriers. The absurdity of the president of the United States ordering the nation to arms without a stitch of clothing on finally dawned on him, and he quickly reclad, grabbing a suit, shirt, and tie from his private closet.

Though not consulted, Lettie simply advised "don't fire." Fortunately, she now had a thirty-second video on her cell phone, with enough raw footage to bring down a presidency. Lettie didn't know whether to laugh, cry, or burp as a subtle smile crossed her lips. She could not wait to share this fiasco and her subsequent release from duty with Pierce.

"You owe me one," the president whispered as he pushed her toward the locked door to his office, pinching her bottom along the way.

What an asshole, she thought. She smiled back and was led to a waiting car for return to the RV.

Amidst the chaos and confusion of the next hours, several important things happened. India refrained from immediate retaliation, instead calling for sanctions on Pakistan by the United Nations. No superpower intervened on the side of either warring nation. The world rushed toward self-emulation, then back from the brink. Reason prevailed, if only for the moment. And finally, a press release establishing the Skunk Creek Watershed National Wildlife Refuge was distributed to all major media outlets. Thankfully, it got lost in the shuffle, and the president forgot to cut it off, losing any further leverage over Lettie amidst his other victories.

Lettie returned to Pierce barely three hours after she left him.

"That was a quickie," he observed.

"Quicker than you think. Traffic was awful," she responded with a smile that lit up the sky. She jumped him on the spot, and he responded with curiosity and affection once Lil' Scooter and the baby had been sent for a long walk.

"What in the world . . . ?" Pierce asked when they had come to a mutually satisfactory conclusion.

"It's an interesting tale," she had responded before drifting off into peaceful sleep.

"What the hell, Lettie?" was all Pierce could mutter. And it was only three o'clock in the afternoon.

Pierce lay next to Lettie for the next fourteen hours. He held her, she didn't move, and he didn't know why. He just held her tight. Except when he had to take a leak. When she awoke, the world had calmed and commentators were singing the praises of the president of the United States of America for taking immediate and decisive action to prevent a nuclear exchange.

Pierce asked nothing as Lettie emanated calm.

"I didn't sleep much the night before." She smiled. As she watched CNN repeat the news again, she suddenly laughed.

Pierce was confused as to what was so funny. The world had almost blown up yesterday, Lettie had fucked the president of the United States who knows how many times, and all she could do was giggle.

Lettie took a deep breath. "Mr. President has a pretty paltry little pecker," she began. It took her five significant laughing spells before she could get to the meat of the story, less or more.

"You're sure you are not making this up?" Pierce gaped in amazement.

"How could I?" Lettie gasped through another laughing binge.

"And you really didn't have to screw the beast?" Pierce asked again.

"No," Lettie responded, "and never will."

Pierce Arrow was ecstatic, aghast, inspired by Lettie's bravery, and astounded at their good fortune. He had to ask again whether she was making this up just to make him feel better.

"Pierce," she responded, "it was really only this long at full salute," extending her forefinger from her thumb. Then they both guffawed together.

"Want some proof?" she asked, reaching for her cell phone. The video of a totally nude Commander in Chief barking out orders to his minions in an unprecedented time of crisis set off another jag of laughter. Lettie's stomach was hurting, and Pierce was gasping for air.

Lettie stopped suddenly, as a wicked smile began to spread across her face. She had an idea to bounce off Pierce. What if Lettie asked the president of the United States to conduct a formal dedication ceremony of the Skunk Creek National Watershed Wildlife Refuge in Hardlyville? What if Lettie coyly acknowledged to the president that she indeed owed him one for his courageous and timely intervention? What if she promised to feel more secure and amorous on her own home court? What if she promised to share her secret loving spot where no one could catch them? What if she would promise to make it all worth his time beyond a quickie? What if she confessed that she was only teasing him about the size of his penis and promised that she would never do it again?

"You're not really going to do this, are you, Lettie?" Pierce frowned. "You stir this asshole up again, particularly under false pretense, he is likely to have you hurt. He is the most powerful man in the world, despite his presidential package shortcomings."

"Just trust me on this one," Lettie responded. "I have a plan that can't possibly fail, if I can get him to Hardlyville."

Phase one of Lettie's plan unfurled to perfection later in the week. Once the international fervor died down, the president sent an invitation to Lettie and Pierce to bring the whole family to the White House for a press photo op. He hadn't gotten what he wanted, but the press release for a new national wildlife refuge had garnered huge public praise for a president who could not only handle global crises but had his domestic priorities in line. The president would not miss an opportunity to pass on such a promotional opportunity, and while he had lost his leverage over Lettie, he was not through trying to consummate the deal as originally structured.

Lettie, on the other hand, was anxious to get her "what-if" agenda in front of the president while he was still in heat. She and Pierce had it all figured out.

The president welcomed them into the Oval Office once again. Select photographers and reporters gathered outside. He made a short speech at the door about his passion for all things natural and invited the family and press into the cramped confines for photos and questions. Pierce and Lettie were generous with their praise of the president's bold and timely action and, on behalf of the citizens of Hardlyville, said thank you with a capital T. Lettie hugged the president and kissed him on the cheek as Pierce peered proudly on, baby in hand, Lil' Shooter at his side. Cameras snapped all around.

As if on cue, baby Mona began to whimper.

"Hungry baby." Lettie smiled and asked the president if it would be offensive for her to nurse in the Oval Office.

"Of course not," the president excitedly affirmed, hustling the press and photographers out in the interest of Miss Lettie's privacy.

Again on cue, Pierce asked if the principle aide could give Lil' Shooter and him a short tour of the West Wing while Lettie nursed. The president was sputtering with enthusiasm by that time and waived them on their way. This left just the president, baby Mona, and Lettie, with her left breast prominently displayed in the exact same location where just days before she had shown her all.

Lettie opened with the confirmation that she owed the president "one." She shared the rest of her spiel, including the invitation to a dedication, with sincerity and warmth. She noted calmly that when she made a business deal she always delivered the goods, hers in this particular instance. The president asked if he could nurse her other breast, but Lettie declined, noting that was not part of the deal. He could only stare and lick his lips. She was certain that little pecker was at full attention. She even felt a little guilty about taunting him, but not for long.

Pierce knocked before reentering with Lil' Shooter. Both had gotten hung up with TV interviews and had finally given up on the idea of a tour. Lil' Shooter was particularly excited to be on TV. When asked what the most fun part of her visit to the nation's capital had been, she had smiled and said, "Camping with new friends along the Potomac with a little weed and some cold Bud." The interviewer had quickly tried to change the subject, but Lil' Shooter was on a roll, in the spotlight for the first time in her young life, and began comparing Eastern weed with Cousin Jimmy's back home.

"Commercial break," screeched the home based anchor.

As Pierce entered, Lettie flapped her left breast back toward her nursing bra, making sure to let it dangle free while she lifted little Mona for a burp before seductively restuffing with a wink toward the president. He was fifty shades of red by the time her dignity had been restored.

Lettie reported to Pierce that the president had kindly accepted their invitation to attend a wildlife refuge dedication as election day neared, as well as speak at a couple of Pierce's campaign stops. Pierce expressed genuine appreciation to the president for his support and attention, and especially for the executive order saving Skunk Creek. Hardlyville would welcome him as one of their own.

The president wished them safe travels home and thanked them for their patriotism, whatever that meant. He would join them in their quest to bring down that pest Larry Larrsnist and rid the world of his "no" votes.

They followed the previous post-game ritual, with the president shaking Pierce's hand, kissing the baby, hugging Lil' Shooter, who grabbed a quick selfie with the Commander in Chief, and then embracing Lettie a little too long. As they walked to the Oval Office door, the president reached back to pinch Lettie's behind and instead found Pierce's hand strategically placed to receive his good will offering.

As they walked to the waiting car, Pierce and Lettie high-fived and took a victory lap around the limo. Pierce accused Lettie of laying it on thick and having a little too much fun.

"El presidente was really revved up." He smiled.

Lettie nodded enthusiastically.

"The son of a bitch even pinched my hand," Pierce whined, showing her the red spot.

"You should see my backside after three visits to that idiot." Lettie laughed.

"I would like to," Pierce volunteered.

Lettie kissed his bruised hand well, and the merry band of protesters headed back to the RV to return to their beloved Ozarks as soon as possible, victory in hand, pinched or not.

Later that afternoon, the principal aide entered the Oval Office to find the president in heat.

"How was the little lady?" she asked.

"Missed my chance because of the threat of nuclear war, but she has promised to give me a second go," he responded. "Her body rocks."

The principal aide cast a disparaging glance at the president through a side wall mirror. She cautioned the president that they might have gotten a little ahead of themselves with the Skunk Creek Watershed Wilderness Refuge Executive Order. Seemed that the Department of the Interior needed to validate the environmental importance of any potential acreage before accepting administrative responsibility. There may not be enough invaluable assets left to protect and sustain after the wave of pig farm devastation.

The president simply said, "Make it happen. Twist who you need to. Sleep with the committee chair. Fire those who object. Pay off the usual suspects. I'm going to Hardlyville before the election to campaign for my good friend Pierce Arrow and dedicate the Skunk Creek Watershed Wilderness Refuge, invaluable or not. Miss Lettie's party is one party I will not miss. Call it a debt past due."

In the meantime, the president said he was desperately in need of relief and hoped Principal Aide was up to it. A push of a button under the president's executive desk locked the Oval Office door immediately.

When they had finished, and it didn't take long, the principal aide repeated her concern that maybe they had gotten a little ahead of themselves on Skunk Creek. The president repeated his orders to just make it happen and reconfirmed that he would be going to Happlyville, or whatever the name was of the godforsaken place where Lettie Jones lived, probably the week before election eve. He knew the importance of prime time good news during that critical polling period, and what could be better than protecting an environmental treasure with wilderness refuge designation and pitching in for a sure supporter of his programs if elected? All this in the heart and soul of red country. The president knew politics, and this was a no-brainer.

The principal aide asked if the president remembered the lobbyist for a major player in the pork industry who had generously provided to his last campaign. Sure the president did, noting that they supported that scumbag Larrsnist as well. But they had given the president's campaign more than a million dollars through various PACs and front men, considerably more than Congressman Scumbag.

"So?" the president wondered aloud.

Principal Aide confirmed those involved had a surreptitious holding in Skunk Creek Ranch, a large hog CAFO, in the Skunk Creek watershed. In fact, much of the damage inflicted on tiny Hardlyville seemed pork sourced, be it carcasses or waste. And Lettie's good buddy Pierce Arrow was committed to going after all involved for recompense.

While most Skunk Creek Ranch infrastructure had been destroyed in a massive sinkhole collapse and surface water eruption, the owners wished to rebuild on the existing site, had state approvals in place, and under no circumstance would support the president's creation of the proposed wilderness refuge. An urgent message to the president had arrived immediately after his press release. In fact, lobbyists were even more adamant in person with Principal Aide, stating that they would fight the president to his demise if he did not rescind his executive order. This was totally in his control, and politics was not a factor he could place blame on. Either "yes" or "no" within three weeks, the amount of time it would take to order materials for reconstruction and expansion of this great economic development project in an impoverished corner of the country. The president would be praised for his support of free enterprise and job creation.

President rolled his eyes and muttered an expletive. No Skunk Creek National Watershed Wildlife Refuge, no Lettie. No million dollar contribution, no big thing in the millions of dollars roiling around his campaign. No. He, the president of the United States, would stand by his word to pretty Miss Lettie, and she, in turn, would do the same. Perhaps some money could be raised to in fact buy out the Skunk Creek Ranchers and clandestine backers and send them packing. Principal Aide would look into that.

One more minor complication remained before Pierce and party could go home. As they stocked food and drink for the long trip, they heard a knock on the door. They were surprised to find Lil' Shooter and another waiting outside. They presumed she had been sleeping in the RV loft, as she often did when there was work to be done, but no, there she was at front and only door, introducing her friend Booray Abdul. Beyond spelling his name, Pierce was shocked but intrigued.

Lil' Shooter announced that Mr. Abdul was coming home with them to ask Rifleman and Steele for Lil' Shooter's hand in marriage. In person, which was the way they did it in Lebanon, and she wasn't talking Missouri. Pierce and Lettie were confounded and showed their confusion. They hadn't seen this one coming. Booray picked up little Mona and rocked her back and forth like she was his own. There was obvious recognition and affection in her coos.

"Oh my," was all Pierce Arrow could mutter, over and over and over again.

Lettie was more hospitable and began with the mandatory questions in a calm and supportive tone. Why? How long? How? Do folks know and approve? When? What next?

Lil' Shooter answered each dispassionately. Because they were in love. Ever since her first camping trip with friends along the Potomac. It was love at first sight. No, she was not pregnant. No, folks did not know. Yes, they will approve. Hope to tie the knot next week. Yes, they would remain in Hardlyville forever.

Pierce had recovered adequately to assume a more prosecutorial pose. Do you love her? Are you really from the Middle

Eastern country of Lebanon? Shi'ah or Sunni? Aware that there are no mosques in Hardlyville? Do your parents know? Do you have any idea of the cultural gap? How will you earn a living, forever?

Booray was equally dispassionate. Yes. Yes. Neither. Yes. No. Yes. Open a Lebanese restaurant with his wealthy parent's money. Forever, yes.

They then kissed each other with a passion not often seen in public.

"Oh my," again and again and again.

Pierce asked for time to huddle with Lettie. They hadn't a clue as to what to do next. Judge and jury reconvened with the obvious question of "What if we say no?"

"We'll hitchhike home, which will probably mean postponing the wedding for another week," was the firm response.

Pierce couldn't resist a final observation, that there had probably never been an Arab sandal set foot in Hardlyville, ever. Lil' Shooter observed that such commentary was probably racist as Booray wore Nikes. Pierce Arrow apologized and restated the comment, to which Lil' Shooter responded that it never entered her frame of reference as there was always a first time for anything and everything. Pierce tried to dig out of his hole by noting that he loved Lebanese food but wasn't sure about other Hardlyvillains. Booray offered to cook all the way home if allowed to join them and pulled forth a pouch of pungent seasonings, which Pierce could smell before the Ziploc was popped.

"Oh my." Only once this time.

Booray took this as a sign of progress.

Pierce insisted that they would at least need to call Rifleman before proceeding. Lil' Shooter insisted just as firmly that to do so would send the two of them packing with thumbs in the air immediately—that this needed to be a surprise. Lettie whispered something to Pierce, causing him to relent. It had to do with the power and resilience of young love.

"Come aboard," was all Pierce Arrow could mutter, and the very unlikely month in the halls of national power came to a close.

The first dinner on the road was unbelievable.

All Hail

All of Hardlyville was out to greet the returning heroes. They had seen their own on national TV, hugging the president of the United States of America, mugging with their Skunk Creek paraphernalia, and introducing their very own town, Hardlyville, to the rest of the country.

Pierce Arrow, Lettie Jones, Lil' Shooter, and baby Mona had gone to Washington, D.C., on an important mission, and they returned that day with that mission accomplished. And an additional guest.

There were a few Agenda 21 signs in the crowd, calling for Hardlyville to send all blood money back to Washington, but they were clearly on the outside looking in on a grand celebration. Skunk Creek and its watershed would be protected from further exploitation and greed, albeit after the fact. And the dirty little secret about failing septic systems throughout the community that would need to be repaired or replaced would emerge only with the implementation of protective measures. Maybe there would be some blood money available for that as well.

The Donald turned to Ol' Dill and asked who the Arab waving out the back window of the RV was. Ol' Dill thought he heard kabob and wanted to know when Tiny Taylor had added that to her Greasy Spoon menu.

"Squirrel, coon, or sucker?" he inquired further.

"You are hopeless," The Donald observed of his friend, without malice.

Ol' Dill assured The Donald that he was not homeless, and while small, it was adequate for him and his beloved dog, Muffle, except when Muffle got into the absinthe. The Donald could only shake his head.

Pierce saw Rifleman and Steele, proudly awaiting the return of their newly-famous daughter. Rifleman was armed, as usual, because he loved to fire rounds into the sky at any excuse for a celebration. Pierce could only shut his eyes as he stopped in front of the beaming parents. Lil' Shooter leapt out and hugged both with tears all around.

And then Booray burst forth, wearing a wrapped headpiece and Bedouin robe above his Nikes, knelt in front of Rifleman, and asked for Lil' Shooter's hand in marriage on the spot. Rifleman commenced firing rounds in the air because he couldn't think of anything else to do given the enormity of the question, sending Booray diving under the RV, robes and all. Steele fainted as the celebration sank into eerie silence.

Sheriff Sephus, who had been leading the procession, dimmed his flashing lights and quashed his siren. He ambled back to Rifleman, who was still firing, and wondered aloud if this was a little much, no matter how happy he was to have his daughter home. A couple of geese who had been on a casual flyby lay dead in the road, victims of Rifleman's barrage. Tiny Taylor noted where they had landed.

Lil' Shooter tried to explain to anyone who would listen why she had brought home an Arab from Lebanon to wed and settle in Hardlyville. Lettie stepped out and up to Lil' Shooter's defense, gaining Rifleman's attention. Booray crawled cautiously from beneath the RV, shaking dust from his robes, and again got on one knee in front of Rifleman, armed and all. Steele rolled her eyes once and fainted again. Booray promised to take care of their little girl, to give them many grandchildren and, seeing a dead goose to his left, pointed to it and promised a Lebanese dinner in celebration that they would never forget, waiving a spice sack wildly beneath Rifleman's nose. That got Rifleman's attention.

Lil' Shooter spoke of her deep and spontaneous love for Booray and assured Rifleman she was not pregnant but wanted to be soon so he could become a grandfather. Steele awoke as the last phrase was uttered and fainted again.

Pierce Arrow opened his eyes twice only to snap them shut each time, his reporter's instincts temporarily shuttered.

Rifleman finally invited Booray and Lil' Shooter to come home for a more private discussion, helped Steele to her feet, and thanked Lettie and Pierce for bringing their daughter home safe, if in a confused state. He promised Sheriff Sephus his ammo was gone and he would not reload unless the Arab attacked him. Lil' Shooter called him a racist, and Rifleman apologized to Booray on the spot, begging his patience as mother and father tried to play catch-up. He complimented Booray on his taste in women, if not clothes, which most in the crowd took as a hopeful sign. He even started to hum the theme song from the movie *Aladdin* as they walked away. Lil' Shooter started to call him racist again but backed down when Booray smiled his okay. Probably a good place to begin, he reasoned.

The homecoming celebration resumed as Pierce and Lettie proudly delivered little Mona to her real crib.

Sheriff Sephus Adonis headed straight to Pierce Arrow's house following the festivities, apologizing for barging in so soon but desperately in need of advice. Pierce was stunned to hear the second naked dead man story and, like the sheriff, felt this raised the stakes substantially. Same circumstance, same appearance, same anonymity, everything the same down to the very last detail, including what wasn't. And again, no indications of foul play or entry wounds related to missing parts.

Doc Karst had sent the cadaver to a big city hospital for a formal autopsy, which came back as empty as the poor soul's pouch. No missing person reports within a hundred miles, no unexplained crime scenes, no nothing.

Pierce promised to turn Lettie loose on the Internet as soon as she had time to reacclimate with the young ones she had left behind with Flotilla Hendricks while in D.C. Both Lil' Shooter and Booray had offered to help Lettie with all the kids so as to gain experience before launching out on their own.

"Letti should have time for research, and she's pretty good at it," bragged Pierce.

In the meantime, Pierce needed the sheriff's help in figuring out how to get to the bottom of Skunk Creek Ranch's role in the Big Pig Flood and devastation of Hardlyville. There was no doubt that their inventory had done the damage, but whether their role in precipitating the disaster extended to liability was a corollary question and central to Pierce's campaign to make them pay to restore Hardlyville and Skunk Creek to preflood condition.

Pierce Arrow shared that Jimmy Jones had provided some interesting information and postapocalyptic photographs. He couldn't tell all to Sheriff Sephus at this point, out of respect to Jimmy, but what he could seemed worth investigating.

One of Jimmy's clients, say for a certain agricultural product, got drunked up one night at purchase time and asked Jimmy if he knew why those pig farmers up at Skunk Creek Ranch had paid him and his boys to pipe a bunch of liquid pig waste from a full lagoon up to a big sinkhole and flush it on down.

"They paid well, but it didn't seem right, something they reinforced by making us do it at night in the pouring rain and taping cam over the pipes," he had said.

"This got Jimmy worried for reasons I can't confide," Pierce continued, "and he ended up at the ranch, poking around in the remains, where he uncovered a section of camo'd pipe, as seen in this photo. He also took pictures of the collapsed sinkhole and blown up karst passages that we discovered in our quest to follow the map. Utter devastation. Something caused a monumental eruption of hydro power that set loose a flood of epic proportions, destroying the pig barn and related infrastructure, breeching and splitting in half the gross waste lagoon, and sending thousands of swine to meet their maker." More pictures.

"Could Skunk Creek Ranch have caused the Big Pig Flood, as well as contributed the grist for devastation?" was the question on Pierce Arrow's mind.

Sheriff promised to swirl it all around in his mind. Just now, he had a death, or murder, or both to deal with.

This year's Bulrush Festival would feature Jimmy and Sally Jones and their new baby daughter, Girl, as well as Pierce and Lettie's little Mona—a twofer for the first time in celebration history. Pastor Pat had prayed long and hard over a decision and in the end did what good pastors are tasked to do: appease all. At least that's the way he saw it. Sure, Girl had been born first, but Jimmy and Sally would likely have more in the pipeline for later notoriety. Not so with Pierce and Lettie, he presumed, given the former's age and the latter's stable of babies. Both infants were ideally qualified for a starring role—given age, lineage, and parental church membership. Pastor Pat always preferred a male

Moses, for obvious reasons, but with none available and peace in the valley more important than tradition, he reached out to both sets of parents. Both said "yes." As for a second set of costumes, Booray offered to lend his Bedouin robe and head gear, and Pastor Pat could disguise the sexy gown Ms. Bloom had given him in a going away fiesta so not even she would recognize it.

Pastor Pat had, several years past, introduced the annual Bulrush Festival in late July to cover traditional spiritual downtime between Easter and Christmas and keep his congregants energized in the study of their Bibles.

Pastor Pat's favorite biblical tale was that of baby Moses, featured in Exodus. Moses' mother placed her infant in an ark of bulrush to save him from the pharaoh, whose daughter ultimately adopted him and unwittingly raised him to lead the Israelites to freedom from her father's enslavement. A true mouthful of irony that Pastor Pat felt deserved more adoration than traditionally received.

This midsummer celebration engaged the whole community, given beautiful Skunk Creek's seasonal perfection for a baby float trip ritual, and even earned regional acclaim. Every fourth Sunday in July, Pastor Pat would read Exodus 2:1-10 from the pulpit, as he would read from Luke's Christmas story five months later. Basket weavers would weave and seal an ark of locally grown reeds in which to place the chosen Moses for a short float from the bridge put-in to the waiting gravel bar and adoring parents a short distance below. Gentle summer water and flow levels invariably delivered baby safely and on schedule, while congregants waded alongside the tiny vessel to assure its arrival.

Sadly, Skunk Creek was not fit for a religious service by late July's Bulrush season. Waters ran over brown tinged rocks and gravel, and while the stench had dissipated, a strange scent and unholy aura lingered. No one splashed in swimming holes, took river baths, or caught fish to fry or crawdads to boil for supper the summer after the Great Pig Flood.

Pastor Pat would not be deterred. He asked Jimmy Jones to scout out streams around the county beyond Skunk Creek watershed that might serve as a temporary replacement venue. At least Pastor Pat hoped it would be temporary. Jimmy excitedly accepted the challenge because it earned him paid time off from Rifleman and a chance to fish new waters. It was particularly timely in that the famous Skunk Creek smallmouth topwater bite hadn't been worth the shit that lay beneath.

Jimmy found a site about twenty miles away which, while lacking Skunk Creek's prior water purity, was low and slow and without sour bouquet. It had a French name that Jimmy couldn't pronounce, so he just called it Moses Branch in honor of the occasion.

On the given Sunday of celebration, Pierce and Jimmy robed up, Lettie and Sally looked matronly in their gowns, and the babies were swaddled for placement in their respective bulrush arks. Pastor Pat arranged to borrow school busses from Hardlyville and other surrounding districts to transport the congregants to Moses Branch. All who wished were bused to the put-in immediately following the Sunday service. Fresh fried chicken and deviled eggs were passed around along the way, and all were in a festive mood on arrival.

The put-in was not exactly as Jimmy had described it. There was a river party going on. A large number of college students in various states of dress and drunkenness were killing the second of four kegs and having a grand old time doing so. Summertime in the Ozarks was good, with or without Moses and his clan.

Pastor Pat and Sheriff Sephus approached the festivities, sending underage freshman running for cover. Some took a deep breath and stayed underwater as long as they could. Others crouched behind small trees and weeds. At least two pretended to sleep or were already passed out. Sheriff Sephus noted all these details prior to advising the participants to hide their driver's licenses somewhere safe so they wouldn't lose them. The collective sigh of relief that met this pronouncement moved a couple of clouds overhead.

Pastor Pat explained the nature of his congregation's mission and the need to crash their party for just a short hour or two. He was greeted with smiles, offered a beer and a busty young lady who thought he was cute, and assured that his peeps would be welcome to party on. Rather than offend, and in the hope of saving lost souls, he accepted both offerings with a smile and a prayer as his flock waited in their un-air-conditioned school buses. On bended knees, his back to the busses, the good pastor chugged the Bud and blessed the young lady's breasts with a gentle pat before returning to the congregants to invite them to join the party.

It was soon a scene for the ages, with students and congregants of all bents joining hands and hearts, swilling beer and cheer, and stripping down and wading around the swaddled babes and costumed moms and pops to celebrate the baby Moses. Pastor Pat marveled at the true ecumenical essence of celebration and blessed all combatants.

Someone accidentally tipped over Girl Jones' ark, but a comely coed quickly scooped up the screaming infant, handed her to Sally, and kissed Jimmy, who she thought was cute, flat on the lips. This did not please Sally, who thought Jimmy lingered a bit too long in the embrace, leading her to rip off her robe and demand to be taken home. Unfortunately, she forgot that she had never put her nursing bra back on, earning cheers from all within range of the spectacle. She swiftly slapped little Girl on one side and covered the other one with a beer Jimmy handed her, causing The Donald to marvel aloud at her manual dexterity. Ol' Dill asked The Donald if he was referring to himself because he, Ol' Dill, certainly had sex more than annually.

"Only in your memory, old friend," The Donald muttered, earning a rebuke from Ol' Dill about using such big words to describe the simple beauty of a woman's breast.

Pastor Pat, who was nursing his third visit to the keg from an innocent looking colored plastic cup, quickly herded his smiling parishioners, most with similar looking vessels, bus-ward. He blessed the river partiers in leaving, thanking them for their hospitality and inviting them to service the following Sunday. Sheriff Sephus reminded all to find the driver's licenses they had hidden before they drove home, earning a long and rowdy round of applause.

Pastor Pat sat deep in thought most of the bus ride home. Several parishioners had whispered to him how much fun this year's Bulrush Festival had been and "might we celebrate next year with another river party?" While Pastor Pat had enjoyed himself a little too much as well, he did not want to lose the underlying message to frivolity, and he doubted that Moses had drunk much beer in his day. More importantly, he hoped and would pray that poor, sullied Skunk Creek would be fit to host a year hence. No. In the end, Bulrush Festivals were not river parties, and Skunk Creek's current demise was not an excuse for transitioning thereto.

The Little Girl with the Big Yellow Eyes

Lettie was so excited to be back with her precious toddlers Lucas, Jr. and little yellow-eyed Vixen, both sired by Lucas shortly before his death—the latter with the demon lady, literally on his deathbed. Both children were special in her heart, both coursed with Lucas' blood, and both had changed dramatically in the month she had been away. Flotilla had treated them as her own, paring them with her own grandson, Otis, her deceased daughter's out-of-wedlock African-American boy, while Lettie was gone. Both toddlers had swarmed to Lettie's arms with happy sounds and smiling faces. No love lost there, Lettie concluded thankfully.

Lettie was a little put off by Pierce's commitment to her doing some research for Sheriff Sephus immediately. She just wanted to hold her two toddlers and baby Mona and let the world turn. She had been through so much the past month that she wanted to play slow ball for a while. She had been spared the shame and pain of consummation with a despicable power monger in the name of Skunk Creek, but just accepting that outcome as inevitable at one point had dragged her down. She needed to breathe real Ozark air, make love with the man she loved for no more important reason than that she wanted to, and cling to her babies while they grew, one day at a time. No more causes for a while. Maybe nevermore. Except getting Pierce Arrow elected to Congress. Maybe.

Still, this research was important stuff, and she knew it. Hardlyville was in an uproar and with good reason. It wasn't just any year that two naked dead men came floating down Skunk Creek buoyed by helium balloons, sans testicles. Something bad was going down, and if she could be part of the solution, it would make the world safer for all of her babies.

Lettie held the little girl with the big yellow eyes close and thanked God for bringing them together. The story of how that came to be was one for the ages.

In fact, it all probably started decades back when Ms. Octavia Rosebeam, beloved granddaughter of the village founder Thomas Hardly, was raped in New York City by a beast of sorts who sported glowing yellow eyes. At least that is what Octavia tearfully claimed in a historical treasure-trove of letters discovered in her house after an automobile accident not long ago ended her eighty-three year run as the grande dame of Hardlyville. Lettie, Pierce Arrow, Sheriff Sephus, and Billious Bloom had personally presided over the readings of the letters before the aged, handwritten records had been committed to Ms. Bloom's care as curator for the Rosebeam Foundation. All of them had been moved by Ms. Rosebeam's horrid account of the travesty and her subsequent embrace of life as an old-maid Latin teacher.

She had, in fact, put the unexpected offspring of the brutal attack up for adoption directly from the delivery room, without so much as a glance or motherly touch, because of the intense shame she felt. She was told her child was a baby girl, but she could confirm nothing beyond the baby howls that soon died out behind the swinging door. Her letters to her parents were the only existing record of that tragic time in her youth, and she had never uttered the slightest hint of confirmation.

The rest of the story, from then to the precious infant in Lettie's arms, was well documented, including Pierce Arrow's Pulitzer Prize for reporting on the evil mess that ensued: a yellow-eyed demon lady; a murderous religious sect, secreted away in the Ozark hills; the violent rapes and murders; the plans to hurt Hardlyville's youngest; the brave last stand of Lettie's then husband, Lucas Jones; the raid by authorities to root out the evil coven, which ultimately cost Lucas his being, even as he gave life to another through consummation with the wicked witch, a selfless act of self-defense; the appearance of the beautiful little baby with the big yellow eyes on Lucas' grave; and Lettie's tearful embrace of the newborn as her own. Lucas Jones' last gasp had given Lettie a final piece of his earthly legacy.

The plot line was too twisted and bizarre to be true, but it was, and Lettie and all of Hardlyville knew it to be. As Lettie played it all over in her mind again, whirring like a grade-D horror film, she hugged little Vixen ever tighter. She had lost Lucas, gained Vixen, embraced Pierce, and with him created little Mona—all in the space and time of a couple of years. Her life's scorecard seemed oddly balanced in a tumultuous sort of way.

Lettie only knew that she wouldn't change a thing, as altering one detail would surely lead to the collapse of it all. Life was funny that way. Lettie was happy with her life as it was and looked forward to every day with a sense of possibility, not dread. She simply needed a dose of normalcy to get back into her flow, beginning that very day. Her little girl with the big yellow eyes grounded her and stoked her hopes for the future.

She gratefully tucked all in that first night home, including her exhausted husband, and pulled out the laptop. She really didn't know where to begin. She typed in "genital mutilation," even though nothing appeared to have been mutilated on the victims, and got nothing but horror stories about women from sub-Saharan Africa. She couldn't believe what was done to the very youngest in the name of tradition and domination.

She tried "male genital mutilation" next and found only the "Is circumcision a form of genital mutilation?" debate. None of it seemed relevant to her.

Next up was "men without gonads." Gonads was such a laughable sounding term to her. Female organs generally had official and sensual sounding names. Well, maybe not vulva. She laughed out loud. But gonads was definitely the most bizarre. Evidently from the Greek word "gone," with a little curly-Q over the e, it related to seed, which might make sense. One thing for sure, the naked dead men's gonads were definitely "gone."

This stab in the dark at least produced a non-mutilated outcome for men without testicles. "Testicular agenesis" is a birth defect which presents as a newborn male without testes. It happens once in millions of births but is a fact. Grown men with this condition show little hair growth, particularly in the crotch area. Hopefully, Sheriff Sephus could validate that condition or lack thereof on the cadavers in question.

"Anorchia" is the technical term applied to the empty scrotum condition, though "vanishing testes syndrome" is more descriptive. Lettie laughed.

"Probably shouldn't have laughed," she muttered to herself. "Those poor souls." Lettie even found Anorchia Anonymous, a national support group based in Denver, Colorado, for victims and parents of newborns with the defect. She found it interesting that, with all the human on human violence in the world, mankind kept trying to help and support one another in the strangest of ways.

This deep thought brought to mind a conversation she, Pierce, and Crazy Mary had while passing time picketing the White House. Pierce was trying to explain to Crazy Mary the ancient

Ozarkian art of noodlin'. It was a hard description to paint, even to one so far out as her.

"You say they take off all their clothes, jump in a creek, stick their bare hands into underwater holes in root wads and rocks, grab a twenty pound catfish in the mouth, and wrestle it to shore, just for the fun of it all? And they risk fines and jail time because it is illegal?" Crazy Mary was beside herself, jumping up and down, cackling like a banshee. She had never heard anything so preposterous, and Crazy Mary had heard a lot over the years, particularly given her choice of venue across from the president's house.

"So why do they call it noodlin'?" she screeched at Pierce.

"Some say because it is slang for stupid," Pierce responded, sending Crazy Mary into another frenzy. "They even have Noodlers Anonymous support groups," Pierce added.

That was the last data point Crazy Mary could absorb. She could see it now. A bunch of stark-naked men sitting in a quiet circle, lights low, some missing fingers, some sporting bloody wrist stumps, one rising slowly. "My name is Cletus, and I'm addicted to noodlin'."

They all three were gasping for air at this point, causing the D.C. police to ask if they were okay.

Humankind trying to support one another. It was sure like that in Hardlyville, Lettie concluded. Anorchia Anonymous. Who would have thought of that?

Lettie had clearly increased her knowledge of male anatomy by thousands of percentage points in the last hour. Guess that made her an expert on gonads, at least in a Hardlyvillain sense. Write a book? Start a speaking tour? Come on, corporate America or convention city. Bring little Ms. Lettie Jones, mother of many children and international expert on Balls, with a capital B, in to talk to your group. Only ten thousand dollars a pop and worth every penny. You want your sales force to be more aggressive? They need to understand the theory of testicular energy. How about the National Convention for Unemployed Black Jack Dealers? Betting they need a heavy dose of testosterone just to play Go Fish. And the National Association of Arachnophobics? Takes a full scrotum to step on big, ugly spiders. Fact is, most anyone who attended one of those gatherings could most surely use advice on something with a capital B.

Lettie was laughing out loud at herself in its most off-the-wall iteration. She was happy to be laughing at home again. No, she would leave the speaking tours and book signings to others, despite her newly gained niche of knowledge. The Internet is amazing, she concluded before shrugging her way to a final verdict.

So what did this have to do with anything other than make it even more bizarre that Hardlyville had witnessed two sitings of this rare birth defect in less than a year, and both specimens were dead? One in millions, in this case two in multi-millions, all in little Hardlyville, population somewhere between two hundred fifty-three and three hundred one kindred souls, depending on who did the counting. Lettie reported her findings to Pierce and the sheriff the next morning and resumed cuddling her babies.

Two dead anorchias. No reason.

Pierce Arrow and Sheriff Sephus pondered Lettie's research and knew not what to make of it. There now was a natural explanation for the condition of the two Skunk Creek cadavers, but no reason for the rest of it, including their deaths.

The knock at Doc Karst's door near midnight could only bear bad news. It was Tiny Taylor with a silk robe wrapped tightly around her smallness, tears leaking from her eyes. She apologized for the intrusion but wondered if Doc could come over to

Ol' Dill's place for a look-see. Tiny was sure the old geezer was gone. Doc didn't raise the obvious questions as to how she had come to that conclusion or why Tiny was so scantily clad.

All knew that Ol' Dill had a thing for sex, exaggerated or not. Most simply smiled their support of his fading dreams. Not Tiny Taylor.

Tiny's life as a wife had been varied and unsuccessful. Prior to moving to Hardlyville, she had been through four or five husbands, depending on who was asked, none of whom matched Ol' Dill in his enthusiasm for love and conquest. Tiny simply took a shine to Ol' Dill, despite being half his age, and those who watched closely could see the quick, gentle touch or slight pat on the rump in the Greasy Spoon Grill and Bar that bespoke affection.

In actual fact, there was a lot more to it. Ol' Dill had recently shared all with The Donald, who, in a post-amorous fit of inspiration, had told one of his lover sisters, which one he wasn't sure, who told the other, and both spread the word far and wide.

Seems that, on the first Thursday of every month, Tiny Taylor would call on Ol' Dill for the sole purpose of doing whatever it took to keep his love flame burning. Sometimes it was simply a kiss and snuggle bug in the old recliner. Others it was an exotic striptease to titillate the old goat's senses. And every now and again, they got it on, much to Ol' Dill's satisfaction and Tiny Taylor's sense of good will.

It all brought a smile to those in the community who were aware and earned Tiny Taylor unsung accolades for her benevolence. While there was no mention of the love word, all sensed its presence in the monthly ritual.

As they walked to Ol' Dill's house, Tiny asked Doc Karst if he was aware of their First Thursday tradition. Doc nodded "yes," and both blushed.

Miss Tiny confessed to Doc that, on that particular Thursday evening, Ol' Dill had been exceptionally energetic and adventurous, inspiring her to follow suit. Not once, but twice, the octogenarian had risen to the occasion, and both had found pleasure in their lust. As they had lain reveling in the afterglow, Ol' Dill had suddenly spasmed, stiffened, and lost all consciousness. Tiny tried to revive him but feared the worst when her mouth-to-mouth resuscitations went unnoticed. That was one of their favorite Thursday night games, and it never failed to elicit a response. She advised Doc that she was sure it was the big one, sobbing that she was really going to miss her playmate.

They opened the front door and walked hesitantly into the bedroom. There, sitting straight up and grinning beyond the corners of his mouth, was the old one himself, sipping a glass of his favorite homemade nectar. He pointed at Tiny, who was too shocked to speak, and pronounced her one hell of a woman. Doc quickly checked his pulse and pronounced him ready for more, to Ol' Dill's shrieks of delight. Tiny sobbed again, but this time in gratitude, and ran to put her arms around his neck. Maybe he should wait until first Thursday next month, Doc prescribed, and quickly exited. He really hoped they would.

Doc Karst could only smile at the strength of the human spirit and the power of sexual healing as he wandered home to wife Lois. He thought he remembered a song about that. Might could use a little himself if she was still up.

The village of Hardlyville—with all its ups and downs, backs and forths, and naked dead men without testicles floating down the creek—seemed always able to conjure up a little lovin' in the name of perpetuity. Doc loved his hometown for that.

Election Eve

Most of Hardlyville sat glued to their TV sets as election results began to roll in. Pierce Arrow had set up a large projection screen in the Hardlyville High School gymnasium, where he had launched his first campaign what seemed to be ages ago.

Much had changed, including his principal reason for taking on such a quixotic pursuit and his subsequent betrothal to Lettie, complete with new baby, Mona.

Big Pork had been flushed out of the Skunk Creek National Watershed Wildlife Refuge, but not before depositing destruction and despair and leaving scars, the anticipation of which had driven Pierce's near madness in the first place.

"Why continue?" he had asked Lettie, and she had responded that he owed it to his loyal Redneck Army, as they had come to be known, even if only for one term. Besides, he would surely return with much to write about after two years in the belly of the beast, probably a lifetime supply of editorial material. Lettie would man the *Hellbender*, and Pierce would operate out their home as much as possible—if they won and ran the rat Dr. No Larrsnist out on a rail. Getting rid of him was as important as anything at that juncture. At least the president of the United

States had so stated in a campaign appearance on behalf of Pierce in Hardlyville a week earlier. And what a week it had been.

As promised in Washington, the president had appeared on a Monday to formally dedicate the watershed refuge and rabble-rouse for Pierce.

His entourage blared into Hardlyville in the early afternoon—sirens singing, lights flashing, the entire village out to offer a presidential welcome. Hardlyville had never seen anything like it.

Pierce Arrow and Lettie greeted the president as he stepped from his rented limo to rebel yells and hollered praise all around. He was hailed as a hero, and he reveled in the moment. He embraced Pierce, hugged Lettie, and grabbed the quick butt squeeze that she offered up.

A podium had been erected on the front steps of the *Daily Hellbender,* and Pierce introduced the president as one of their own—one who cared for clean water, pristine creeks, and country life; one who had risked political fallout to establish the Skunk Creek National Watershed Wildlife Refuge and expel Big Pork from its confines forever. He also expressed gratitude for the federal funds allocated to Hardlyville for cleaning up the environmental disaster. Pierce promised to keep pursuing restitution from Skunk Creek Ranch and its foul benefactors but praised the president for jump-starting the recovery.

The president's dedication speech was short and sweet as there were other fish to fry. In fact, some wondered if he had even said anything.

"Seems to be in a big time hurry," Sheriff Sephus whispered to Pierce.

"He is," smiled Pierce.

In closing, the president declared that he needed an honest man like Pierce Arrow to help him run the country, and that Dr. No needed to go. This set off the Redneck Army, and Sheriff had to turn on his siren to quiet them so the president could finish.

The president assured all that he was finished, a man of few words who carried a big stick, which set Lettie to swallowing her giggle and coughing it back up so he wouldn't see.

The president offered that he would enjoy a quick tour of Hardlyville, and Lettie stepped forward to grab his hand and lead him away. He ordered his Secret Service agents to fan out around the perimeter of the village to assure security, baited Pierce's Redneck Army with another call to arms to rid the nation's government of Dr. No—setting off an even louder spontaneous Redneck Army demonstration—waved at Pierce and Sheriff, and followed Lettie, hand in hand, down a dirt path away from Main Street. Sheriff Sephus Adonis gave Pierce Arrow a puzzled glance, to which Pierce shrugged and smiled.

Lettie opened the door to the old village root cellar and led the president into the dark, dank confines. She whispered to him that it was time to get buck naked, grabbed what must be a blanket, the president reasoned, from somewhere in the dark, and urged him to wait for her there when he was ready. She stepped into the shadows, if there was such a thing in a pitch black room, and promised to return. A rustling sound and sliding zipper scratch confirmed disrobe. The president of the United States was beside himself with lust.

A smiling president returned to the podium and attempted a heartfelt thank you and warm goodbye over the continuing Redneck Army celebration. He called Hardlyville the most beautiful village he had ever visited and promised to return to celebrate Pierce Arrow's victory. He thanked Pierce Arrow for hosting and lovely Lettie for the brief town tour, pinched her butt in passing toward the limo, and whispered his gratitude for a woman of her word. She cringed a smile, then gave a real one to Pierce over her shoulder, rubbing her backside gently.

Inside the presidential limo, the president's principal aide congratulated him on a stellar performance, acknowledging that the timing and nature of this appearance should far offset the loss of Big Pork money at this late stage in the game. She offered that Dr. No and Skunk Creek Ranch were both toast.

The president was genuinely aglow in the back seat. He, of course, concurred with his principal aide's assessment, but more importantly, the president had gotten what he came for. Call it a promise kept, a debt repaid, a score settled. It hadn't been pretty, the president confirmed, just short and sweet, but oh my, how worth the wait, he beamed. And she had promised more, he literally gasped. Principal aide rolled down her window just in time to vomit on the side of the limo, blaming it on the twisty Ozark roads. She didn't know if she could ever sleep with the idiot again, no matter how much power and influence it afforded her.

Pierce and Lettie had returned to the campaign trail for one final push. They were optimistic about a win but, more importantly, content with any outcome as they considered it all win-win. They felt the president's visit and wildlife refuge dedication had provided strong momentum for the sprint to the finish line.

And that day they finally gathered with friends and neighbors to tally the score in the high school gym.

Banker Jamin, whom Pierce had gotten to know and respect in his brief time back home, was brilliant with numbers and took on the task of scorekeeping for Pierce Arrow. The race would be won or lost in the two biggest towns in the district, and Pierce had invested his heart and soul in both.

With every update, Pierce's numbers ebbed then flowed. As in his previous futile campaign—in which he had been slandered, backstabbed, and falsely accused of a felony—Pierce had solicited no money from donors, nor spent funds on promotion. It had been he and his Redneck Army, one-on-one, two-on-two, mano-a-mano against the well-funded Larry Larrsnist, and that mid-count results were so tight was a victory in itself.

Ol' Dill stayed up beyond his bedtime and was pacing back and forth along the foul line. The Donald became Dinky for an evening to try and add a little comic relief. He dressed as a high school cheerleader, complete with pompoms, oversized buzzums, and a big bow in his blonde wig. He paraded around the court perimeter leading "We love Pierce" cheers and egging on the Redneck Army. Lettie finally asked him to tone it down a bit so they could hear. Dinky promptly flipped his short skirt up and presented Miss Lettie a great big pink backside, which sent the whole crowd into fits and shrieks. Lettie blew Dinky a kiss and returned to Jamin's side. He had noticed a discouraging trend and called for Captain Happy to interpret his numbers to Pierce.

He deduced that, while Pierce Arrow was holding his own in the metros, he was being trounced in several key rural towns in the northern part of the district. They had not borne the brunt of the Big Pig Flood, had no sense of loss or source of misery, and several even questioned in their exit interviews if it had not been anything more than a big publicity stunt. That was not an undercurrent Pierce had picked up on previously, and it concerned him. His friends and neighbors in the Ozarks were not beyond conspiracy theories, witness Agenda 21, and if this one had taken root in rural venues beyond his own, it could hurt.

Metro voter turnout was high, which Jamin thought was good. He extrapolated a projected turnout from current levels, front loaded rural results because country folks go to bed early, and formulated a likely .0005 margin of victory, subject to .0001 slippage or gain, all in his head.

This translated into a fifty vote margin of victory, give or take ten votes each way. Pierce was stunned by the tightness of the race and couldn't help but wonder if he had spent a dollar or two here or there if it would have helped. He kicked himself for even thinking about it. His intentions in this race had been pure, and there were a lot of folks out there who respected that.

Ol' Dill simply couldn't keep his eyes open any longer and lay down in the free throw lane. Tiny Taylor gently laid a blanket over him and returned quickly to her fried ice cream cart, where another large line had formed. There was a festive air about as few sensed the razor-thin margins either way.

Pierce weighed in his mind whether he would ask for a recount if he lost by fifty votes. He concluded that he would not. He was sure Larrsnist would if he were on the short end, and that big money would slip under any table it could to find a vote or two. No, truth be known, Pierce Arrow didn't give a fig whether he won or lost on this last stride to the finish line as his principal goals had been met. Only Lettie had the slightest sense of the inner peace they shared. She left twice to go home and nurse baby Mona, only to return to a continued deadlock. Gridlock in Washington was infuriating, but the deadlock in his home district was intriguing.

Midnight turned to one, then two in the morning, and there was still only a thin shadow between the contender's votes counted. Amazingly, most Hardlyvillains stayed put, some sleeping in rigidly erect poses, others curled together as water snakes mate. That had gone on as well. Earlier in the evening, Jimmy and Sally Jones had snuck off to the men's locker room for a memorial tryst on dirty towels, not unlike the third or fourth time they had hooked up long ago. They just never had been able to get enough of each other. No one cared or seemed to notice.

Pierce and Lettie walked among the Redneck Army, thanking each individually, then walking through to thank them again. All

Pierce could think of was that phrase from his misbegotten, radical political youth: Peace, Love, Dove! He didn't fully understand it then, and he still didn't, but it somehow captured the simplicity and innocence of his campaign.

Suddenly, at three forty-three a.m., Lettie saw the time on the screen, NBC called the race for Pierce. Their computer based projections whirring turnout, weighting subtrends, even stalking Facebook exchanges and Twitter tweets, confirmed a fifty-five vote victory for liberal Pierce Arrow in a bright-red district. Banker Jamin had been right on the money utilizing only his brain. CNN followed seconds behind, noting the obvious impact of a popular and reelected president's visit to tiny Hardlyville just the week before. Billious Bloom claimed an assist as she and Lettie hugged.

Wow, thought Pierce as he hugged the shy banker, lifted Lettie to the sky, and mugged with the Redneck Army, high-fiving and posing shamelessly for selfies. *There is justice in this corner of a cynical world,* he concluded.

Rifleman was so excited, he began firing celebratory rounds through the Hardlyville High School gym roof until wife Steele could disarm him. Deaf Ol' Dill slept through it all until he awakened to take his bihourly bladder bleed and demanded to know what all the ruckus was about.

Pierce walked to the hastily erected podium, hand in hand with Lettie, and leaned in to the microphone.

He accepted the people's verdict with humility and grace. He promised to listen to those very people and serve them in the national arena as best he could. He said he would remain home, caucusing with his constituents, as often as possible so he could represent their voices in the national dialogue. He reminded all that he was beholden to none other than them. He owed no one anything except the voters. There had been no donations, cash or in-kind, to report. Just the heart and soul of volunteers and the fervid belief that honesty and energy could beat Dr. No. It, and they, had. He confirmed that he would serve one term only, and he hoped that perhaps another from the Redneck Army would step up to carry on. He smiled silently in remembering Lettie's offer of sacrifice in the name of Skunk Creek and praised in a loud voice all who had stood strong and tall, each in their own way. The Redneck Army awakened to collective joy and raised the roof of HHS, holes and all.

Dr. No, on the other hand, charged fraud and demanded a recount.

Unregistered voters had sneaked out of the hills and voted two or three times in friendly polling places, screamed Dr. No at five a.m. He said he would fight this fraud to its death so that the district could have true representation. He also announced he would file a personal lawsuit against Pierce Arrow himself for the slander and misrepresentation that had prevented his landslide victory.

Big Pork licked its chops and began to pony up, even before the count was complete.

That said, Pierce Arrow was the new duly elected representative of the most famous "No" district in the U.S. of A.

"God Save the Queen," pronounced Ol' Dill as he took his six o'clock leak and returned to Tiny Taylor's blanket in the lane, just along the free throw line.

Tiny was still selling fried ice cream cones to the occasional Redneck Army veteran who was still awake. She closed shop with a victory salute to Pierce and Lettie and led Ol' Dill to his home. Though it was not the first Thursday of the month, he was feeling rested and lucky and wondered aloud if Ms. Taylor might stay a while.

Another amongst the most unusual days in Hardlyville history.

Diversity Training

Given the doubling of diversity in Hardlyville with the addition of Booray Abdul, civic leaders determined it might be appropriate to provide their youth with formal diversity training. In that Hardlyville High School could not afford a superintendent and barely a principal, curriculum was influenced by civic leadership, aka the Hardlyville Junta. Steele was particularly vocal, as the newest addition to leadership, that graduating Hardlyvillains needed to be more in touch with the outside world and the many colors and religions it contained.

Her future son-in-law, Booray, was case in point. He had been viewed more as a curiosity than a threat since his arrival and generally treated with respect. She always wondered what was said behind their backs and, in fact, was told third-hand about one neighbor who began sleeping with his shotgun under his pillow, in case there were any terrorists in the neighborhood. Booray seemed comfortable in his own skin and adept at fitting in. Steele had to admit to liking the young man and admiring his courage for following the lady he loved into the heart of the infidels. Their betrothal had been rescheduled for the coming spring to perhaps allow Booray's parents to join in the festivities all the way from Lebanon.

The remainder of the civic leadership team—Undertaker Bob Klunkerokatus, Postmaster James Bond, and Mayor Josephus Dudley—saw no harm in Steele's advocacy if it didn't cost any money. They had served loyally as civic leaders for years with no compensation because no one in town seemed to care. Steele had been chosen to replace deceased Banker Bud because of her ties to Rifleman's business and her love of seven card, roll your own, high low poker, which was played most every weekend and always at civic leader meetings. Steele also served as director of the local Chamber of Commerce, another phantom post in that there were only a couple of small enterprises in town. This fragile and inconsequential coalition of community leaders stayed out of people's business and, as such, contributed to keeping the community running smoothly on all cylinders.

A diversity initiative would be different and perhaps even start Hardlyville on a more progressive path into the future. The mayor warned that this could be "risky business." He had once seen a movie of that same name, which was the source of his statement. As usual, no one paid any attention to him. His sole official duty in life was to smile and mouth platitudes. He followed with something about "an Arab in the hand is safer than two in the bush," spitting his homemade cliché between smile-clinched teeth. He then voted for the diversity training initiative as long as he didn't need to have anything to do with it. The vote was unanimous.

As they discussed who might lead diversity training at HHS, focus turned to who would do it for free. What if they simply added it to the existing job description of Ms. Bloom, who also served as town librarian and curator of the Ms. Rosebeam Foundation, devoted to spreading Latin culture? There was clearly a branch of diversity already imbedded in her leadership portfolio. Steele agreed to approach Ms. Bloom with such a proposition.

Billious Bloom seemed thrilled with the challenge. After considering it further, she also asked for permission to add a sex education component to her responsibilities. She had often regretted not knowing about sex as a teenager and blamed her long drought from pleasure on her lack of proper education in school. Steele thought this was fine and reasoned that Latin, sex, and diversity somehow went together, though she wasn't quite sure how. She had great confidence in Ms. Bloom's ability to provide linkages that high schoolers could relate to.

When Billious Bloom asked about compensation, Steele advised that every effort would be made to find funding in future budgets, but for now there was none, unless Ms. Bloom wanted to raise a little money on the side. She had been very successful in raising money for Ms. Rosebeam's foundation and could surely find a few dollars more to pay for sex ed and diversity training.

Billious accepted on the spot and began preparing her syllabus. She knew she had to make things simple enough to understand but exciting enough to keep attention. An example might include the question of why every race, and even every ethnic subset, had different hair. She could point to her own flaming-red mane as evidence of something, though she wasn't sure what.

As for sex, she would probably start with birth control. Something like "the penis goes in where the baby comes out" to establish a quantitative link between the two. And by dressing the penis in a raincoat the baby would stay put until the participants could afford he or she. Simple and understandable.

One mistake Ms. Bloom made was inviting HHS alumnus Jimmy Jones to speak to her sex ed class. After all, Jimmy had a job, a business on the side, a lovely wife, and a beautiful daughter. *What a role model for seniors*, she reasoned. What she didn't know was how Jimmy had gotten from there to his current properity.

She became aware of her mistake when Jimmy opened his lecture on sex education by confidently writing in bold letters on the chalk board "PMP." He asked if anyone knew what it meant.

A hand in the back announced that them was his initials, Paul Michael Peters. Jimmy congratulated Paul on his observation but asked him to put PMP in the context of sex for purposes of the discussion. Paul allowed that he had never had sex before but was game to try if pretty little Janie in the front row wanted to hook up after school. The class roared, Janie blushed, and Jimmy laughed that Paul was on the right track. Ms. Bloom gave Jimmy Jones the horizontal finger across the throat caution.

Jimmy then proceeded to elaborate on his theory. He explained that PMP was the first principal to understanding sex: Practice Makes Perfect. Miss Bloom fainted on the spot.

While she was being ministered to, Jimmy shared the details of his preparation for marriage and challenged all to enjoy sex as much as possible before old age and babies sapped their energy and drive. He concluded by urging them to always wear a rubber, just like his Uncle Norvel had taught him, and earned a standing ovation as a shaky Ms. Bloom pushed him gently out the classroom door.

While Billious Bloom could actually relate to Jimmy's PMP principle given her dearth of prior experience and only recently awakened sense of enjoyment, she knew she had only fifteen minutes to regain control of her class, and perhaps her career.

She could hear it now at the ringing of the class bell.

Bobby asks Matilda if she wants to go practice a little sex "like we learned in class today." Sure, Matilda nods, adding that her dad is always pushing her to make perfect grades in math so she can become an engineer and make lots of money. "Practice Makes Perfect" sure makes common sense.

And around the dinner table that night when Mom asked Cletus what he learned at school today? Ms. Bloom could only imagine the shriek that might greet the principle of PMP taught in sex education.

No, Billious Bloom had to get her arms around this quickly. The senior class in sex education was abuzz with laughter and the possibilities flowing from officially sanctioned sex. Paul Michael Peters had even shoehorned in next to pretty little Janie with his class calendar to schedule a practice session. Her blush had turned ashen.

"What Mr. Jones really meant," Ms. Bloom began, "was Parthenon, Mona Lisa, and Pineapple. The original PMP Principle. Nor did he complete the formula. PMP equals what?"

She had the class's attention and pounced. This was an equation to be solved before class tomorrow for fifty percent of everyone's grade. They could work in teams—no pairs, mind you—and could utilize the Internet for research, but the answer was due in twenty-four hours. And if she learned of anyone having sex that night, she would award each participant with an "F." This last bit of news shut down Paul Michael's advances and caused him to retreat into his shy shell again. He did ask if he might be on Janie's team. She blushed again, nodded "yes," and immediately recruited two of her female classmates to join her and Paul immediately after class in the computer lab to begin their research.

Ms. Bloom had clearly stemmed the tide, if only for a night. She offered a final clue: Fibonacci, a twelfth-century Italian. Might be a good place to initiate research, she hinted as the bell rang and students looked around at each other in confusion.

Thank God Ms. Bloom had just acquired a book written by Fibonacci entitled *Liber Abaci* or *The Book of Calculations* for the Ms. Rosebeam collection. Fibonacci, considered to be the most talented Western mathematician of the Middle Ages, popularized the Hindu-Arabian numeral system in Europe. His book formed the basis for the current Western number system and reached beyond simple numbering to abstract mathematical concepts related to beauty in art, architecture, and music. *Why not sex?* she reasoned.

Her students, at least those who did their homework, would learn of the Fibonacci Sequence, wherein the sum of the prior two numbers in a sequence would yield a geometric progression that approximated the "golden ratio" relationship embodied in the Greek number phi, a basic mathematical building block that had been applied through time to the arts. Some even reasoned that the "golden ratio" extended to nature and natural growth patterns in pineapples, seashells, and plant forms evolved to maximize growth efficiency. After all, Fibonacci's initial case study involved something about how many rabbits could fit into a fixed space in one year given some basic assumptions about procreation rates. In that rabbit sex formed the original basis for the Fibonacci Sequence, surely sex deserved inclusion in the "golden ratio" theory along with other arts.

Thus, Parthenon (architecture), Mona Lisa (art), and Pineapple (nature), could substitute well for Jimmy Jones's original PMP principle, and sex (humans) would be a logical addition in interest of equality and plurality. Hence PMPS. The "equals" in the formula could be Beauty, hence the solution to the Bloom Principle: PMPS = B.

While Ms. Bloom didn't totally get it all, she could muddle through a redirection of Jimmy Jones' PMP principle to a kinder, gentler application of sex education. Maybe something like "practicing" safe sex with 1.6180339887 (phi) partners before marriage was the "perfect" solution to why, how, how many, and other juvenile questions long unanswered about sex by adults. It was certainly more fact based than "just say no." And obviously, it was okay for any young lady who wished to remain a virgin until marriage to stick to her guns, but that was up to her, not societal vagaries. Further, it was okay to round up to two. It all fit together rather well.

Ms. Bloom would see what her students' research on Fibonacci revealed, then connect the dots with PMPS = B. That it would be a heavily weighted question on their final exam would lend substance and credibility to her guiding principle. And if most of her class would use raincoats and limit actual intercourse to a bogus mathematical formula, she would have accomplished her aim of exposing seniors to sex in a logical and controlled fashion, a privilege she herself had been denied.

In addition, she could share with them a beauty in sex that extended far beyond procreation. PMPS = B. A new and progressive take on sex education that would be too complicated for most parents to get pissy about and would provide enough freedom and choice to allow students experimentation beyond "no," which had no relevance to most teens. A new take on phi and the "golden ratio," which some scholars argued was a formulaic take on beauty itself, would be based on sound mathematical and real-life principles.

As Ms. Bloom congratulated herself later that evening over a glass of Super Tuscan on making lemonade out of lemons, she again gave thanks for *Liber Abaci.* She had actually enjoyed cavorting around Pisa, Italy, with the self-proclaimed descendent of Fibonacci—a happy, if slightly rotund, gentleman nearly twice her age, who was also a superb lover. Their negotiations for one of three original edition copies to be added to the increasingly famous Ms. Rosebeam collection of rare Roman books had been long and pleasurable, and her knowledge of all things Italian had spiraled in almost a Fibonacci Sequence of geometrical increase.

That Ms. Bloom had even gained access to the possibility of such a prize spoke to her persistence and creativity. She was gaining international acclaim for her fundraising acumen and nose for ancient treasures. That she was a relatively beautiful and sexy middle-aged lady with flaming-red hair and an air of independence that matched didn't detract from her core skill set. Billious Bloom was having the time of her life and putting tiny Hardlyville on a cultural map that couldn't comprehend its existence.

It was also true that no one in Hardlyville ever asked about Billious Bloom's background or credentials anymore. Unlike before, it was all just assumed to be proper and appropriate for her grand responsibilities as curator of the Ms. Rosebeam Foundation and executive director of the Hardlyville Library. She, like

Sheriff Sephus Adonis, had become larger than life.

What was certain was that no one who took Ms. Bloom's inaugural course on sex education would ever forget it. At least some, maybe most, would honor safe sex when they practiced, and to many "perfect" would be a term applied to serious relationships. Practice makes perfect. Maybe Jimmy Jones hadn't been that far off with just a mathematical tweak or two.

She smiled to herself as she finished her wine, wondering if this lesson would go down with the famous Ms. Rosebeam lecture on *coitus interruptus* as one of the landmark memories in Hardlyville High School history.

Ms. Bloom's course on cultural diversity also got an unexpected real-life boost.

Booray Abdul and Lil' Shooter's pending betrothal became the most anticipated social event in Hardlyville since the visit of fabulous French bombshell Florence Hormel.

As the two star-struck lovers began thinking about how to honor their respective cultures in a memorable marriage ceremony, they reached out to several in the community, beyond the parents, who might possess the wisdom and wit to meld Bedouin and Hillbilly. Ms. Billious Bloom was one with whom they consulted.

Booray and Lil' Shooter had postponed their marriage in the hope that Booray's parents could come to Hardlyville to make the celebration complete. His parents were finally able to commit to a date and agreed to stay for two weeks with Rifleman and Steele and the kids. The time of arrival was drawing nigh, and plans began to percolate.

Booray initially had trouble grasping the concept of a "shivaree," which seemed to be the key organizational component of a Hillbilly wedding. He didn't understand why Hardlyvillain males would drink Ol' Dill's finest the entire day of the celebration, come beating on the door of the rental unit where the newlyweds would spent their first night of wedded bliss, maybe even shooting a round or two through windows and doors, before dragging the groom out, stripping him naked, and throwing him in Skunk Creek. It all seemed so barbaric. And while it wasn't the potential interruption of consummation that bothered him, in that he and Lil' Shooter were well consummated at that point, it was the Arab principle of privacy that was being violated.

Lil' Shooter assured Booray it would be swift and painless. Besides, it would be historical in that she was quite certain there had never been a naked Arab in Skunk Creek before. Booray worried he would get so cold he wouldn't be able to perform his manly duties on the night of their marriage. It was a matter of pride and custom to him. Lil' Shooter promised to make it worth his while the day before and after, and far into the future.

Lil' Shooter, on the other hand, didn't think much of the Bedouin traditional wedding meal—a whole roasted camel stuffed with several sheep, who in turn were crammed with chickens and fish. Booray assured her he was not making it up, pulling up Bedouin Wedding Feasts on the Internet and even sharing photos. "Gross" was about as enthusiastic as Lil' Shooter could get. Booray promised that his parents would provide the camel if the village would contribute a couple of sheep, chickens, and fish.

Given their respective reservations, Booray and Lil' Shooter decided to consult directly with Ms. Billious Bloom, Hardlyville's acknowledged expert on matters of diversity and cultural tradition. Ms. Bloom agreed to serve as official wedding planner if her senior class in diversity and sex education could be involved every step of the way. Ms. Bloom promised them a formal wedding plan in two weeks, representative of both Arab and Ozarkian cultures, after consultation with her class, who would be involved in the final presentation.

On schedule, Booray and Lil' Shooter appeared at HHS for the first time together since Lil' Shooter's honorary graduation the previous spring—honorary because she didn't have passing grades but earned credit on the strength of her stellar representation of HHS students in Washington, D.C., her senior year. Her "selfie" with the president of the United States served as her senior picture.

Ms. Bloom asked several class members to present the results of their research to their clients.

First up were those students who had looked into Bedouin wedding tradition. They spoke of large outdoor celebrations that lasted anywhere from two to five days with tribal dancing and lively music, all wrapped in the finest traditional clothing. No one had found a single mention of "spirits" in all of their research.

The bride was generally clothed in an ornate red gown and covered with an elaborate headdress. The spice saffron was dabbed on the bride's cheeks, ears, and neck. Booray nodded enthusiastically at the latter, noting that he had plenty left in his spice sack.

The ceremony itself generally took place under a tent, and one researcher had found that, on occasion, the groom would dash in on a prize Arabian stallion, leaping to the ground next to his bride, nattily attired in Bedouin robes and a turban. Booray nodded his approval again.

There was a price, or dowry, due the family of the bride. Tradition dictated the nature and magnitude related to the groom's family wherewithal.

To Lil' Shooter's dismay, the stuffed camel feast stood the test of student research and brought cries of dismay from most in the class. She was also a little concerned to learn that a traditional ceremony was read by an imam from the Koran. She wondered if Pastor Pat even had a copy.

Next, Ms. Bloom introduced the researchers who had looked deeply into Hillbilly wedding tradition. They confirmed that the "shivaree" custom had evolved from the French "charivari," though the former was celebratory and the latter punitive. The French banged pots and pans and generally raised hell to protest marital aberrations, like a widower remarrying too early or a father marrying his step-daughter. Shivaree meant celebration and, from what most reported, damn near anything went. Crashing wedding night consummations was certainly fair game, and *coitus interrupts* was deemed the pinnacle of success. Anything from gunfire to dynamite was allowed in announcing the groom's procession to dunking, with or without clothing. Alcohol was clearly the drink of choice, preferably a variety of white lightning or moonshine.

Ms. Bloom congratulated her class on the thoroughness of their research and commented on the challenges of integrating cultural traditions and interests. That said, her class had recommended the following wedding plan:

> ✓ Bride and groom would wear traditional Bedouin garb—Lil' Shooter clad in red with headdress, Booray in traditional robes and turbin. He would arrive on one of Jimmy Jones' horses, bedecked in ribbons, borrowed jewelry, and other such finery.
>
> ✓ The wedding ceremony would take place at noon on the day of choice under a large tent set up in Jimmy Jones' weed field, the largest acreage available for a gathering of this type in the county.
>
> ✓ Pastor Pat would conduct from the Bible and the Koran with assistance from the elder Abdul.
>
> ✓ A special night of lively music and dancing would follow the ceremony, complete with the Ayyahah, an Arab traditional dance, and a square dance called by Doc Karst, who was renowned for his calling throughout the county.

✓ Ol' Dill's finest moonshine would be served in great abundance. Rifleman and Steele would foot that bill.

✓ Booray's family would be responsible for the camel roast, including provision and field dressing of the poor beast and stuffing it with sheep, chickens, and catfish, provided by the community in honor of the momentous occasion. Steele would coordinate the community gift.

✓ A dowry would be provided at the discretion of the groom's family. Perhaps a live camel would suffice.

✓ Booray would provide saffron and deliver and administer it to the bride on Jimmy's dashing steed.

✓ A shivaree would be organized and delivered by Rifleman, father of the bride, no holds barred.

Booray shivered at the final piece, but both he and Lil' Shooter marveled at the class's melding of culture and history into a contemporary celebration. They expressed their appreciation to the class and Ms. Bloom and charged off full of energy and excitement to deliver the goods.

The ceremony proceeded as planned, with a few minor exceptions.

The issue of the camel came into play the moment Booray's parents—Abdul Abdul and his beautiful wife, Kiri—arrived by rental car from the big city airport. They were accompanied by Booray's two sisters, Obi and Uvi—one older, one younger, both stunning in appearance.

All were greeted with an open and loving community embrace, although Ol' Dill was confused. He pressed The Donald about the father's name, like which was his first and which was his last name.

"Both," confirmed The Donald.

"They came by boat?" asked Ol' Dill, supposing they had travelled by paddleboat up the mighty Mississippi then a john boat up Skunk Creek to Hardlyville.

"You deaf old bull," laughed The Donald.

"Bull," screeched Ol' Dill, proud to have finally gotten it. "Bull Abdul is a fine Middle-Eastern sounding name," he observed and rushed forward to shake Bull's hand and tell him how much he liked his son and his name.

Most standing nearby thought Bull was probably Abdul Abdul's nickname and addressed him as such the remainder of his stay.

Paul Michael Peters stood deep in the crowd but not so far away as to not be smitten by Booray's younger sister, Uvi Abdul. It was love at first sight, and though he didn't quite yet fully understand Ms. Bloom's sex ed formula, he wanted to give it a try. Pretty Janie from the front row of class didn't seem interested, so he would definitely give Uvi a go if he could just figure out how to get to her to explain PMPS = B. He waved wildly and, thinking she was smiling at him, blew her a kiss. His mad and immediate obsession led down paths over the next two weeks that he could never have anticipated.

And the camel, oh, the camel.

"Where in the world will we get one?" asked Abdul Abdul, anxious that his obligation not go unfulfilled and tarnish his honor.

Booray hadn't really thought about that and, despite not having seen one of the sorry beasts since arriving, assumed they could be bought at market like in the homeland. Lil' Shooter suggested that Booray consult with Jimmy Jones as he was somewhat of a wheeler-dealer. Booray agreed to do so once his family was settled in at Rifleman's and assured Abdul Abdul things would be okay. Rifleman and Steele were the perfect hosts, and all, even the two beautiful sisters, agreed that it was a blessing that Booray and Lil' Shooter had brought them together.

The next day, Booray and Jimmy gathered to talk camel. Jimmy thought there was a wild animal commercial enterprise about fifty miles away and agreed to drive there with Booray to negotiate an acquisition. They paid the fifteen dollar entrance fee to drive around amongst the many fenced beasts, finally locating a small herd of camels.

Jimmy had done a little research the prior evening and found that dromedary, or one-humped Arabian camels, generally went for from five thousand five hundred dollars to eight thousand five hundred dollars. Abdul Abdul had wired in funds from his Lebanon bank to the Bank of Hardlyville, and Banker Jamin had been happy to collect a small fee and arm Booray with a large wad of hundred dollar bills.

When they approached the proprietor about a purchase, he smiled and said it just wasn't possible with all the federal and state regulations. When Booray flashed his wad of cash, the proprietor added a quick, "however . . . perhaps you could pay to rent and subsequently lose a camel," getting him off the hook and simply making them appear stupid. "Such a transaction would require a large deposit," he added. How large consumed the better part of a day.

Amongst the cultural similarities between Hillbilly and Arab tradition was the art of bargaining. The proprietor started at one hundred thousand dollars, noting that there were no other camels within a five hundred mile radius—beyond large city zoos—and he was sure that with the price of gas it would be cheaper to pay a little more up front than waste precious time and petrol searching far and wide for a beast in similar good health. Besides, they could always return the borrowed camel and the deposit would be returned, less a stipend for wear and tear. Jimmy noted they could fly one in from Saudi Arabia for that price, grabbed Booray's arm, and headed toward his truck and trailer.

"Whoa!" shouted the proprietor, asking what price Jimmy had in mind.

Jimmy scratched his goatee and suggested five thousand cash. And back and forth the two warriors went, with Booray joining in with a strategic "no" at critical moments.

"So just how much cash you got?" the proprietor inquired.

"Seven thousand two hundred," Booray lied.

The proprietor shook his head and concluded it was a shame Booray couldn't come up with seven thousand five hundred because they might be able to deal. Booray asked for a moment to look around the truck for some spare hundreds and shortly returned to count out the final price. All smiled, shook hands, loaded an emaciated-looking dromedary into Jimmy's horse trailer, and parted as best friends.

A minor problem remained. Booray feared Hardlyvillains would not attend the wedding celebration if they learned that the main course was stuffed camel. Jimmy agreed. They would have to secret the beast away for several days, stuff and cook the camel off-site, lead with the sheep, chicken, and fish stuffing, and only carve the camel as the final course. Some might still retch, but most would have had enough of Ol' Dill's finest to believe it nothing more than a large oxen. The high schools students who knew better had agreed to remain silent on the subject.

Jimmy suggested letting the camel roam with his horses for several days, and if anyone noticed, which was not likely, he would explain that he was considering getting into camel crossbreeding.

All went according to plan as the magical date approached. Sally took young Girl out to see the camel. Unaware of its fate, Sally and Girl fell in love with the beast, and vice versa. While the camel would spit at Jimmy, Booray, Abdul Abdul, and any of the family who ventured near, it would slather young Girl with camel kisses, give her bareback rides, and kneel down for easy mounting every time it caught sight of her. Girl Jones thought the camel was simply the coolest thing she had ever met in her young life, and Jimmy Jones knew this spelled trouble for him.

Hardlyvillains gathered several sheep, chickens, and grabbed a few large suckers as their contribution to the celebratory meal. Ms. Bloom and her class helped with all the preparations, from sewing outfits to decorating the large tent that would be erected in Jimmy Jones' field the day of the event. Pastor Pat worked on details of the service with Abdul Abdul to assure both Islamic and Christian needs were met. And Paul Michael Peters stalked beautiful Uvi.

Uvi feigned disgust but actually found the young fresh-faced teen in the bib overalls kind of cute. Her culture did not permit her much contact with males beyond family reach, and she was flattered with Paul Michael's attention. The only time they came in close proximity was at the bank one day, and Uvi noticed Paul Michael drop a wadded piece of paper near her feet as he blushed uncontrollably. She scooped it up and later opened it in the privacy of the bathroom. She was confused yet intrigued by the formula contained therein: PMPS = B. Being quite adept at math, she attempted the solution of the equation time and time again without success. If she could just get a grasp on several of the variables, she believed she could intuit the rest.

When Abdul Abdul took the family for a fried squirrel breakfast at Tiny Taylor's Greasy Spoon, Paul Michael happened to be there with his father. He considered Uvi's appearance an omen of good things to come, and she used the opportunity to scribble a brief note on her paper napkin and drop it at Paul Michael's feet as her family exited to friendly smiles all around. Obi noticed and later asked Uvi what was going on. Uvi confessed her interest in the young man in the bib overalls and Obi, who was somewhat bored with life in Hardlyville given the lack of attractive gents her age, agreed to serve as liaison for a get-together. Uvi's note had simply asked what M, S, and B represented.

With the wedding ceremony fewer than forty-eight hours away, Jimmy knew he had to do something about the camel. It would break Girl's heart to learn it had been consumed at the wedding feast. So he kidnapped it, grabbing the beast just after midnight prior to the day of its execution, and led it, spitting and all, to a cave on the far side of his property. When Sally brought Girl for her daily visit, Jimmy explained that he had lent the camel to a friend to show his children, and it would be returned after the wedding. This dried Girl's tears for the time being.

When Abdul Abdul and Booray showed up later in the morning to butcher the poor beast, Jimmy pronounced that evidently some Hillbilly had slipped in under the cover of darkness and stolen the camel. Abdul Abdul was stunned.

"No Arab would ever steal a neighbor's camel," he asserted, angry and dismayed.

Jimmy noted that this was the Ozarks, and when the family got hungry, anything was fair game, even if you didn't know what it was. He observed that Abdul Abdul had fulfilled his part of the bargain. His honor was upheld, Bedouin tradition fulfilled, even if not consumed, so why not just focus on roasting the sheep, chicken, and fish, and spice with the soul of Lebanon? Abdul Abdul reluctantly agreed, and preparations for the feast resumed.

Jimmy asked Booray if he wanted to practice his racing dismount on Jimmy's horse. Booray scoffed at the idea, noting that he had ridden fast horses and driven fast cars all of his life.

"Piece of cake," he predicted.

Pomp and Ceremony

The wedding day bloomed fresh and beautiful. All of Hardlyville was abuzz with anticipation. As the sisters had their hair done, Paul Michael, who followed Uvi's every move, wandered into the beauty shop under the false pretense of looking for his mother, dropping a wadded piece of paper at Uvi's feet as he retreated in full blush. Uvi excused herself to use the ladies room, grabbed the scrap, and read it behind locked doors: PM(Mona Lisa)PS(Sex) = B(Beauty). Uvi blushed out loud, felt a sudden rush of excitement, returned to her chair, and handed the note to Obi, who promptly exited for the ladies room. She returned wearing a large and radiant smile and patting the breast beneath which her heart lay.

Sheep stuffed with chickens, fish, and handfuls of Lebanese spices had roasted through the night over a large charcoal pit in the corner of Jimmy's field. Abdul Abdul had taken the first watch, Booray the second, and both smelled of smoke, spice, and a faintly sweet underlay. Unbeknownst to either, Jimmy had contributed a large bouquet of weed to the coals before retiring to bed himself. Both men scrubbed and scrubbed but could not shed the evidence of their handiwork.

"Want a quickie to fulfill your manly duties on betrothal day?" Lil' Shooter had asked Booray as he returned from the shower. Both were aware of tradition and the unlikely wedding night consummation, given shivaree revelry.

Just then Uvi rushed in without knocking to seek Booray's permission to add another platform guest, a Mr. Paul Michael Peters.

Booray shrugged a "sure" with some confusion, and Uvi returned to write a formal invitation. Obi would deliver the message, having previously learned from Ms. Bloom where Paul Michael lived down by Skunk Creek.

Paul Michael was struck dumb and palsied when he opened his front door to find beautiful Uvi's stunning older sister holding forth an envelope. Obi explained that they wished to invite Paul Michael to join the wedding party at noon under the grand tent of celebration. She offered no further explanation and extended her hand in friendship. Paul Michael dead fished it and nodded "yes" in shock and joy, his face the color of boiled beets. Obi added as she waved goodbye that a Bedouin robe would be provided to cover whatever Paul Michael chose to wear.

Paul Michael's hands shook as he ripped open the envelope to find a note written in the most precise script he had ever seen, addressed "Dear Pomp," which Paul Michael took to be Lebanese for Paul Michael Peters. In actual fact, it was Uvi's term of endearment for the shy lad, and Pomp would last a lifetime. As his mom and dad asked what was up, he stripped naked and jumped into the day-old cold water of the bathtub. His parents could only shake their heads in wonder at their son's sudden interest in bathing. It wasn't even bath day.

Meanwhile, Booray got his quickie to uphold tradition and honor, and Lil' Shooter even claimed to enjoy it. Life was good and about to get better.

Kiri, Obi, and Uvi dressed Lil' Shooter in the ornate red gown, infested with bingles and bangles sewn in by several of Ms. Bloom's students, as Steele looked on proudly. They had some difficulty securing the ornate headdress but finally trussed it down with a strand of bailing wire. Lil' Shooter looked stunning.

About eleven o'clock a.m., Booray headed out to meet Jimmy and his farm horse, also festooned with a variety of trinkets. Only Jimmy was aware of his plans for a dramatic ride-in entrance, so most assumed he was off to relieve nervous energy and would meet them under the tent where they gathered with Pastor Pat at eleven forty-five, as scheduled. A huge crowd grazed about to witness the spectacle. Paul Michael snuck toward the tent shyly. Uvi had her eye out for him and waved him into the wedding party, where a Bedouin robe two sizes too big was wrapped about his overalls and a turban placed on his head. He was instructed to stand on the bride's side of the aisle, across from Uvi, who flirted with him constantly and unmercifully.

"Where is Booray?" Abdul Abdul asked with some concern.

Lil' Shooter could only shrug and assure him things were okay. They always had been between her and her Arabian suitor and would be at that moment of truth.

At precisely noon, a trumpeter from the HHS band blew a series of loud and unrelated notes in an attempt to establish a Middle-Eastern kind of romantic feel. That was also the cue for Booray to dash in, sweep his unsuspecting bride off her feet, and circle the crowd twice, warbling a high-pitched Arab war cry, before returning to honor the Christian side of the equation.

As Jimmy cleared a path through the large circle of Hardlyvillains, Booray showed off his equestrian skills by rearing the old farm horse time and time again, something it had never experienced but apparently found exciting. Path cleared and "wheelies" complete, Booray charged in at full gallop, braked directly in front of beaming Lil' Shooter, and scooped her with one arm onto his lap just as the farm horse reared with great joy and threw both to the ground. The stunned wedding party quickly helped the bride and groom to their feet and slapped the dust from their attire, while the entire village of Hardlyville roared in laughter and approval. A small group of Agenda 21ers, who had been banned to the fringe, waved signs warning of "terrorist infiltration" and "interracial marriage," but few paid attention.

The ceremony itself was brief and to the point. A few prayers and chants, followed by the obligatory "you may kiss the bride," led Booray to first try and lift, then jerk at Lil' Shooter's headdress. She screamed in pain. He tried again, only to find it unmovable. Booray looked in confusion at his father, who could only shrug. Finally, Kiri remembered the bailing wire fix and rushed forward to remove it and help her son lift the heavy headdress off his wife to be's head, wiping tears from Lil' Shooter's eyes.

"She's crying," The Donald warmly observed to Ol' Dill in their front row seats, where they had been sitting since six a.m. to assure a good view.

"Trying to do what?" responded Ol' Dill, knowing only that at least one article of clothing had been removed and adding that he sure hoped they wouldn't strip down and do it right there in front of everyone.

"An old Bedouin custom," egged on The Donald.

"Beddin' her in public?" gasped Ol' Dill before acknowledging that maybe he could learn a new position or two from watching a "feerner" do it.

The Donald could only nod and wink at his sister friends sitting next to him.

Kiss complete, Booray and Lil' Shooter Abdul were introduced as the "newlyweds." The crowd surged forward to offer congratulations and attack piles of roasted meats. No one missed the camel. The table containing small paper cups of Ol' Dill's finest was constantly under attack as the crowd got rowdier and rowdier. The proud father-in-laws celebrated each in their own fashion. Rifleman fired round after round in the air, as was his celebratory custom, until Steele was forced to disarm him. Abdul Abdul kept kissing Lil' Shooter on alternating cheeks, time and time again, until wife Kiri disarmed him as well with a swift kick to the groin.

Meanwhile, Obi had gathered Paul Michael and Uvi under each arm and quietly led them into the woods, where she spread a blanket and invited them to talk. Paul Michael was tongue-tied, so Uvi spoke first. She was, of course, interested in solving the complex equation that Pomp had presented to her before they moved on to anything else.

As he stammered through Ms. Bloom's theory on sex and beauty that he had learned in sex ed, Obi reached for his hand, lifted it gently to Uvi's small gown-covered breast, and let it linger there for a moment before replacing it in his lap. Pomp passed out on the spot. Uvi revived him with a light kiss on his cheek only to see him lose consciousness again. Both Obi and Uvi were giggling when Pomp awakened the second time.

Obi explained what had just happened to Pomp, and that in the Middle-East young ladies were protected and kept separate from men. That would be the closest to a sexual experience he would ever have with Uvi, formula or not, unless he were to move to Lebanon and join the long list of suitors awaiting her marital consideration several years from now. She further noted that Uvi was a virgin and would remain such until her betrothal, lest her marital value be diminished. Dowries were still a big deal, and virgins warranted top-tier compensation.

Paul Michael asked why Uvi liked to call him Pomp. Uvi explained that Pomp was the first English word that had come to mind that day he waved wildly at her from the welcoming crowd. Anyway, it seemed relatively close to the sex ed formula, which she again asked Pomp to solve for her in final form. When Pomp explained more clearly this time that the Parthenon, Mona Lisa, Pineapple, and Sex were joined to form Beauty in Ms. Bloom's theory, and that the golden ratio of phi allowed aspirants 1.618 sexual partners, which could be rounded up to two, before marriage, if undertaken with protection. Uvi smiled that she would always remember Pomp in this light with great tenderness. She added that she wished she could apply Ms. Bloom's theory to Pomp, in that she found it more mathematically pleasing than Arab tradition, but she simply could not do that to her parents or lineage.

Pomp, emboldened by his most recent lesson in sex ed, asked Uvi if he could touch her clothed breast just once more before parting. She declined but allowed him a peck on her cheek. He swore he would answer to nothing else but Pomp for the remainder of his life in honor of his first true love.

Back at the tent, the celebration was in full stride. Native dances from both sides of the ocean were being enjoyed and participated in by many who remained. Ol' Dill's finest was a bottomless paper cup. Pastor Pat had a new crush. Kiri, Abdul Abdul's wife, was the most beautiful creature he had ever seen on his God's earth. He would later beg God's forgiveness for lusting in his heart, but for now all he could do was dance with her, hoping against hope that she would not seek to tempt him. She didn't, but she enjoyed the attention of a genuine man of the cloth.

Jimmy decided they might as well go ahead and shivaree in broad daylight because he had an unusual twist to add. They could always do it again tonight if anyone was still standing, which he counted unlikely given what he had seen to that point.

Jimmy gathered the boys at the edge of the woods, passed out joints, moonshine, firearms, and sticks of dynamite to prime the pump, pulled a couple of pickups around, and led the frightened camel to the front of the procession. The boys gawked and guffawed. Their shivaree stood to be one unlike any other in the history of the Ozarks.

Jimmy went first, the camel reluctantly following on a leash. The boys loaded into pickup beds and sat quietly, stoned and starry-eyed in the shadows, awaiting Jimmy's call to action. What remained of the crowd parted as Jimmy led the beast straight to Booray, who was taken by surprise. Jimmy presented the reins, ordered the camel to kneel, and suggested to Booray that he take his wedding gift for a quick spin.

As Booray mounted up, Jimmy whacked the camel on its backside, shouted "shivaree," and fired his pistol into the air, signaling to the boys to charge. And charge they did, screaming like banshees from their pickup truck beds—shooting into the sky and tossing sticks of lit dynamite right and left. The terrified camel took off at a near gallop, Booray hanging onto its hump for dear life, Bedouin robes flowing in the wind.

Wedding guests ducked, ran, hugged their sweeties, hid under tables, and otherwise sought protection. In the midst of a do-si-do, Pastor Pat grabbed Kiri to shield her from the onslaught, pressing her supple body next to his. Abdul Abdul ran after his purloined camel and terrified son. Ol' Dill didn't hear a thing.

The pickup truck drivers herded the frightened beast toward Skunk Creek. Everyone now knew where this was going except poor Booray, who was still just recovering from the indignity of having been thrown from a farm horse. The camel was bleating and spitting and running as fast as its cloven hooves could carry it. The crowd, now recovered from its initial shock and fear, surged behind—far enough to avoid the occasional dynamite stick, close enough to share in the joy of the chase.

The scene was straight out of a movie: dashing, costumed Arab hero clinging to his camel while chased by a hostile mob in battered pickup trucks, hurling ribald remarks and dynamite, firing round after round skyward; the newly betrothed screaming for each other; the crowd closing from behind; the raging river ahead. As the terrified camel charged into Skunk Creek full-bore, it realized the error of its ways and braked urgently, tossing Booray over its hump and headfirst into the chilly waters to float downstream, bobbing up and down, robe trailing in the current.

Jimmy Jones had forgotten to ask if Booray knew how to swim, and when it became apparent he didn't, Jimmy was in the water pulling Booray up for breath and dragging him to shore. The camel took off running and wasn't seen for days.

The next morning, all agreed it had been a never-before-seen magical day for Hardlyville and the newlyweds. Pierce Arrow's coverage in the *Daily Hellbender* preserved the entire fiasco for generations to come in photos and editorial comment. Sheriff Sephus Adonis sagely observed that this day provided further evidence of a Hardlyville that was rapidly progressing into the twentieth century.

"Twenty-first," corrected Ms. Bloom.

Back, Again

Shortly after the momentous wedding celebration and months after the second naked dead man had floated by, a third carcass appeared, similar in every detail—naked, dead, helium balloon floatation devices attached to all appendages, empty sack. As the sheriff pulled the body ashore for Undertaker Bob and Doc Karst to examine and dispose of, he noticed tiny writing in red ink on one of the balloons. The note was so small he couldn't be sure it was even a message. He pulled a small magnifying glass from his Swiss Army Knife and began to read aloud. Pierce Arrow took notes and photos for the *Hellbender*.

Written in tiny red letters were the words "I will have my revenge on this town with no balls. Each and every one of you."

There was stunned silence and disbelief all around. WHAT?

Dead men? Empty scrotums? Decorative balloons? Times three? A town without balls? A genocide against each villager simply because they happened to be Hardlyvillains?

Pierce wanted Lettie, Sheriff wanted sex, Bob wanted a body to preserve, and Doc wanted a valium, which he prescribed for all on the spot. Each sat on the gravel, awaiting further orders. From each other. There were no words to be said.

After an hour of silence and shivering in fear, they caught up with their newly spinning world.

"It has to be her," Sheriff muttered to a pale Pierce Arrow. "The demon lady, the devil woman, the lady with the graying ponytail. She's back."

They were all in deep shit now, deeper than the excrement piled high by the Big Pig Flood. Deeper than the sewage lagoon that had spawned a tidal wave of waste and destruction. Deeper than the ruse that crooked clean water authorities had used to permit Skunk Creek Ranch for ten thousand pigs. Deep . . . deep . . . deep . . . deep . . . and deeper.

Sheriff asked Pierce, Doc, and Undertaker Bob to keep all of this to themselves until he had time to think. Pierce said he had to tell Lettie to see if she could tie her prior research into anorchia back to this conclusion. Sheriff Sephus nodded in the affirmative. He needed all the help he could get.

Empty Sacks and Frazzled Leads

Sheriff Sephus Adonis had sought outside help in identifying the second cadaver with little to show for his efforts. A formal autopsy at the big city hospital had revealed no confirmable cause of death—no identifiable natural causes, no bruises, no wounds, no toxins. APBs and national ID search nets came up blank. The victim was an unknown, unidentifiable, unviolated, unfortunate, empty-sacked man who was simply dead.

Given the level of threat to Hardlyville this third time around, including the implied extermination of all Hardlyvillains, the sheriff called his friend who headed the state highway patrol and was promised full logistical and crime solving support. They had last worked together in the partially successful raid on the evil coven, which led to its dissolution but cost Lucas Jones his life and allowed the escape of the evil lady who led the coven. And now she was back. Sheriff and the chief patrolman had great respect for one another, and he pledged whatever energy and resources were needed to stop and apprehend her.

Again, a formal autopsy produced nothing, cause of death indeterminable. However, a national DNA screening revealed a match in Denver, Colorado. The name, address, and contact information were secured and pursued through the local police. Nothing. Apartment empty, furniture and clothes in place, refrigerator empty, no known friends or family of the same surname, no cell phone, no means of transportation. At least the poor soul now had a name and address. Just nothing else.

As Pierce Arrow, Lettie Jones, and Sheriff Sephus discussed possible links to Denver, it dawned on Lettie that Denver was the city where she had discovered the national anorchia support group. She wondered aloud if the poor testicle-shy victim could have lived in Denver for that very reason. And perhaps the other two victims as well. Could this be a path worth wandering down?

Sheriff Sephus' follow-up with the Denver police yielded about as little as other efforts to date. They didn't even know of the organization initially, and in trying to follow up, found members secretive and unwilling to answer even rudimentary questions about their mission, membership, or meetings. "No," was the common refrain. There was no way to know if there were any missing members because of their focus on anonymity. There was no desire to publicize their organization to the world beyond victims of anorchia, who were understandably a secretive lot in themselves. There were no official spokesmen or communication lines beyond the website, which was vague, at best.

Hmmm, thought Lettie as she inquired on the website whether she might make use of the organization's support services in light of her young son's sad birth defect known as anorchia. She needed help for him and her family in dealing with his rare condition.

Two weeks later, Lettie Jones sat aboard a flight to Denver, Colorado. She had been contacted by e-mail within twenty-four hours of her inquiry with directions and meeting times. By whom was a mystery. No names, no words of sympathy or support, no request for confirmation of attendance.

As she walked into the dimly lit conference room of a seedy motel just off West Colfax Avenue, she felt tension and suspicion rise around her. As her eyes adjusted to the low light, she determined that she was one of two females among the twenty or so attendees. A voice welcomed all to an occasional meeting of Anorchia Anonymous and invited participants to share their stories in complete confidence and trust. After five minutes of silence, Lettie rose and began.

"My name is Lettie Jones. My young son suffers from anorchia," Lettie lied and continued on, sharing the family heartbreak and concern for him when he comes of age. She sought counsel and advice, not sympathy. Lettie felt duplicitous but strangely saddened by the burden those present must bear. No one else spoke for an hour, implying that they were all regulars who must have shared their stories previously. There were no responses to Lettie's request.

As attendees began to drift into the shadows one by one, the other woman moved to sit by Lettie. She patted her hand gently and with understanding. She asked if Lettie would like to grab a beer on her way home, and Lettie nodded in the affirmative.

They walked wordlessly for several blocks before turning in to a small bar. The woman introduced herself as Kay and confirmed that her son suffered from a similar fate. She asked the age of Lettie's child, and as Lettie described Lucas, Jr., who was really quite normal, she felt guilt creeping into her cheeks. They talked for two hours over two beers as Lettie probed for information beyond the poor lady's son.

Lettie finally confessed to feeling uncomfortable in her first meeting of Anorchia Anonymous. Her bar mate explained that it was likely because she was a woman. Women were welcome but rarely attended. Most first-timers never returned.

There had been an exception off and on over the past year that in the end had heightened the anxieties of all. Lettie's antennae twitched. Apparently, a mysterious lady, purporting to be grandmother to an anorchiac child, attended five or six or meetings in all. She always dressed in black, concealed her hair under an oversized baseball cap, hid her eyes behind dark glasses, and spoke in a gravely kind of voice. Oddly, she had a sensuous air about her as well. Kay saw her leave with several different men over the months and did not remember any of them returning, with one exception—Ed.

Ed hadn't spoken at a meeting since, and the dark lady had not been back. Lettie knew she was on the trail.

Kay needed to get back to her son. As a single and underemployed mom, her babysitting money was limited. She did agree to meet Lettie for dinner the following evening to provide further support before Lettie's departure home.

Lettie reported all to Pierce by phone. He urged her to be careful and stuff her guilt in the interest of obtaining information vital to the protection of Hardlyvillains.

"Here we go again," moaned Lettie, adding that she was not Wonder Woman.

That drew a laugh from Pierce, observing that at least it wasn't her body on the altar this time. Lettie wasn't so sure but said nothing.

Kay and Lettie huddled over an early supper the next evening as Lettie pressed forward on how and when Kay was going to explain anorchia to her son. It was a painful discussion for Kay, who, in the end, said she didn't know. Had Kay ever asked Ed how he came to know of his condition? Kay indicated she had met with Ed on several occasions and found him open, helpful, and surprisingly hopeful. That is until recently, when he had locked up like a cheap safe. Lettie wondered if Kay knew how to contact Ed, and she confessed to not only knowing that but that they had, at one time, been intimate. Lettie was stunned. She apologized for getting personal but wondered how a victim could perform a sexual act. Kay smiled at the memory but declined further comment. She only lamented that Ed had suddenly lost interest, almost coincidentally with the last meeting attended by the strange grandmother—if, indeed, that's what she was.

Lettie knew she had to talk to Ed before she returned to the Ozarks and pushed Kay for his phone number and address. She promised her interest lay only in discussing how to break the news to her son. Kay nodded, recorded his contact information on a napkin, and wished Lettie good luck in getting him to visit with her. Lettie thanked Kay from the bottom of her heart for all of her counsel and promised to stay in touch by e-mail as their lives evolved and sons aged.

Lettie took a cab to the inscribed address in a prosperous looking neighborhood, walked to the front door, and rang the bell. A somewhat good-looking, middle-aged man peered through drawn curtains and shook his head "no." Lettie begged him with all the sincerity she could display—hands in prayerful position, eyes showing desperation.

She held her breath as the drapes closed and seconds passed. The man cracked the door, chain attached, and asked what she could possibly want at this late hour. She said it was a matter of life and death, and only he could help. It involved a strange lady who attended Anorchia Anonymous meetings and was suspected of damaging and unnatural behaviors. Lettie said she had found Ed through Kay.

Ed blushed deeply, then assumed a panicked look, asking if Lettie knew the lady in question.

"She murdered my husband," Lettie shared with tears streaming from her eyes.

Ed slowly unleashed the chain and opened his front door, adding in passing that she had almost killed him as well.

When Lettie left Ed's house at about two in the morning, she had closed the loop on the naked dead men murders and was desperate to return home as soon as possible to warn Sheriff Sephus of what was to come. Lettie hugged Ed goodbye and mentioned that Kay missed him and hoped they could reconnect sometime. He nodded in the affirmative, escorting Lettie to the cab he had called.

Sheriff Sephus Adonis and Pierce Arrow sat transfixed as Lettie shared her findings.

She laid it all out up front. The evil lady with the graying ponytail and yellow eyes had infiltrated the national Anorchia Anonymous chapter with the blatant motive of murder and intimidation. Murder was a random event. Intimidation was targeted specifically to Hardlyville. Her choice of victims of anorchia was both bizarre and cruelly brilliant in its message and end game. And more frightening yet, Lettie summarized what the evil lady planned for all Hardlyvillains once she got their attention and stoked their fears. She then filled in the blanks with Ed's story. And yes, she added almost preemptively, men without testes can have sex, particularly if they choose to pursue hormone therapy.

Ed said he had noticed a strange lady—dressed in black, covered head, and sunglassed eyes—about a year earlier. She had sat through two or three meetings before rising to share her dilemma as the grandmother of a young toddler stricken with anorchia. Her story was unusual, as was her appearance at a meeting in that most participants were male, she and Kay excepted. She never once used a name, claiming shame, and was allowed her privacy. She was a seemingly attractive, athletically built, middle-aged woman, who spoke with a deep voice and always maintained an air of superiority. She garnered sympathy, and it didn't take long for several men to strike up post-meeting conversations. Ed himself felt drawn to her in an erotic and sexual way.

Ed remembered a particular gentleman, whom he did not know, leaving a meeting with her and never rejoining the group. While Ed did not attend every meeting, it did not strike him as unreasonable that this had happened on several occasions, particularly in light of his near-death experience.

Ed had found himself strangely drawn to the mysterious grandmother, beyond feeling sympathy for her story. He sensed she shared the attraction as well. One post-meeting evening, he had accepted her invitation to join her for a beer and discuss how he had coped with his condition as a young boy and even as a man. It might be useful for her to share with her grandson as he began to grow into manhood. Ed had accepted her offer with a strange sense of excitement and surge of desire.

Ed didn't often drink much but was surprised as to how woozy he felt after half a beer, almost as if in a trance. Grandma insisted on grabbing a cab and getting him home. He evidently passed out in the car and came to in a garbled state, naked, and with the grandmother sporting the body of a twenty-year-old mounted on and riding his erection for all she was worth. His condition allowed for extended usage, and she was insatiable. It was her eyes that frightened him most. They glared yellow in the darkness of his bedroom, and he feigned sleep out of abject fear. She finally seemed to have had enough, climbed off him, dressed quickly, reclothed him, called a cab, and carried him over her shoulder to the vehicle when it arrived. Too much to drink, she had informed the cabbie.

He continued to mask his returning clarity as the lady hoisted him up a flight of stairs to a third-story apartment. Her strength was abnormal, and her apartment had a wild stench to it. She lay him on her bed and used him again, muttering between sighs and growls of satisfaction that he would not feel a thing when his time came, that he would strike terror in the heart of a pitiful, putrid little village and its idiot inhabitants far beyond his last breath, and that once she had their full attention, she would wipe out Hadlyville or Bardlyville or some kind of ville to the last breathing soul for what they had done to her and her congregants.

After she had finished her second go-round, he heard her reach for a towel, dab it in a foul-smelling liquid, and bring it to his mouth. Just as his ability to hold his breath expired, her cell phone rang, and she released the pressure enough to allow Ed to breath in the fetid but undoctored air of her apartment. She paced back and forth around her bed in an agitated state, still naked and swinging a long gray ponytail with each jerk of her head. When she retreated to squat in her bathroom, Ed leapt to the cold wooden floor, dashed to the front door, and fled down the steps to the street below, still naked himself. He threw himself into a large plastic garbage container, tossing the contents street side except for one large bag that he placed on top of his shivering body.

Soon he heard her rush by, snarling and venting her anger to the empty street. She used otherworldly terms and tongues, finally drawing the attention of a passing police car. She quickly apologized to the officer, who stepped toward her from his open car door, explaining that she suffered from PTSD after losing her husband less than a month earlier to suicide and was possessed with dreams of how she might have saved his life. She must have been fully reclothed as the questioning officer made no mention of nakedness. He asked whether she needed to be taken to the hospital, an offer she declined stating that she had just medicated and would be fine. The officer asked if her eyes were okay given the sunglasses in the middle of the night. She said she needed them to sleep as any speck of light disturbed her, and she had forgotten to take them off after her dream. Ed heard the officer escort her to the apartment building, the slam of a door, and the sound of the police car pulling away.

Ed crawled from the garbage container, tore two garbage bags open, dumped the contents and wrapped himself in their filth and smell, and headed for the shadows, trembling in fear and from the cold. He said it took him three hours of sneaking and crawling through dark places to reach his house and gain entry through a broken window. He threw on clothes, grabbed his wallet, phone, keys, and fresh clothing, and drove to a nearby motel to shower and regain his senses. His near-death experience had left him shaken and shocked to the bone. He scouted his house clandestinely for the next forty-eight hours, fearing that the lady with the demon eyes might return, but he finally gave in to the need to go home. The police were out of the question. They would never believe what had happened to him.

He had remained reclusive, generally behind locked doors, never resumed contact with anyone from the outside world, and never said a word at another Anorchia Anonymous meeting, or beyond, until Lettie had knocked on his door late that night. His confessions to her set him to trembling uncontrollably again. Her confirmation that the evil lady had left Denver to harm tiny Hardlyville provided some comfort that his life might regain a degree of normalcy, and his expressed intention to resume contact with his prior lover, Kay, left Lettie with some hope for his future stability.

Sheriff Sephus Adonis was speechless beyond "shit, brothers." Pierce Arrow could only hold Lettie tight to the point of near suffocation and thank her for her courage. All recognized the need for urgent action.

The next day, Lettie received an e-mail from Kay indicating that Ed had reached out to her and wanted to at least discuss how they might resume a relationship. Kay thanked Lettie for whatever she had done to facilitate this welcome turn of events. Lettie smiled slightly. Humankind supporting humankind. Sometimes it worked.

The Garden

The next day, as Pierce Arrow sat stewing in his *Daily Hellbender* office, contemplating what next, Jimmy Jones rushed in, not bothering to knock. While Jimmy caught his breath, Pierce complemented him on a shivaree unlike any in Ozarkian history—one that would stand in time as both memorable and singular. Jimmy nodded his thanks then begged Pierce to come the garden with him immediately. He had what he believed to be important information to share.

Jimmy and wife Sally had discovered the garden by following an ancient map from town founder Thomas Hardly's time. It was a crude, handwritten sketch that had gotten Thomas Hardly brutally murdered and had surfaced by accident amongst a treasure-trove of old letters unearthed in Hardly's granddaughter, Octavia Rosebeam's, closet shortly after her death a few years past.

The garden itself was indescribable. Jimmy and Sally were the only souls to enter it since who knew when. The garden's subterranean isolation from humanity's fingerprints and footprints had allowed it to remain a pure Ozark natural wonderland. Creatures and fauna long gone from surface streams and springs thrived in its cold, pristine waters. Even the iconic hellbender, in all of its misshapen glory, found peace and refuge in the stream that almost seemed to run backward at times deep underground.

Jimmy and Sally Jones had reported their discovery to Pierce Arrow after a memorable frolic in wonderland, one that resulted in the conception of their daughter, Girl. Pierce had cautioned them to keep their secret to themselves. He knew what would happen to paradise if the waiting world got wind of it—it would be lost to study, greed, exploitation, degradation, paradise indeed lost. He also cautioned them to never return for fear of someone else discovering their secret. This was one request they could not abide, though they did not abuse the privilege. They were beyond secretive when rolling away the large stone, dropping the long rope down the narrow rock gateway, and even dusting away their footprints from the immediate premises with branches.

Jimmy and Sally had, in fact, returned twice over the past year. First, to christen baby Girl in the holy waters, and then to commemorate her conception with an encore in hopes of a similar outcome. Both times they had spent the entire day. Both times they had left the garden exactly as they had found it. On neither occasion had they uncovered another 1803 minted silver dollar as they had on their initial visit.

Jimmy had later raced to the garden in the aftermath of the Big Pig Flood with great fear and trepidation. He knew that the violent eruption of buried hog waste had soured other springs and sinkholes, seeping into the water table as well. He had feared the worst as he rolled away the boulder guardian and descended by rope into the dimly lit landscape below, vague back lighting another mystery that hinted at natural light from some unknown source. He was greatly relieved to find the garden unchanged and untouched by the tragedy above and around. He could not understand how it had been spared but reasoned that its water source must be deeper or more distant. Its flow had always seemed counterintuitive, and perhaps that had saved it from devastation.

Jimmy shared all this with Pierce, embarrassed that he had defied his orders, yet proud to be able to confirm the garden's continued perfection. He then confessed to a visit just yesterday and a discovery which concerned him greatly.

He had gone to the garden to think and because something or someone had told him to. He didn't know which. Every time he paid a visit, he felt his dear deceased Cousin Lucas near, and that alone inspired him to think deeper, breathe slower, and love longer. Jimmy Jones knew that Lucas, who had been murdered in the rock amphitheater just above by the devil lady, was still there for his buddy. This time the Lucas vibes were serious. *What in the hell,* Jimmy thought, *could Cousin Lucas be calling me out for?*

Jimmy descended into the dark opening to the garden to find nothing but the paradise that had always been there—deep, pure, pristine. Nothing in history or nature amiss there. "Thank God," Jimmy offered, but he still felt dread and was not sure why.

Upon his return to the surface, he was compelled to look around. Recalling the futile trip in search of the map destination he had taken with Pierce Arrow and the sheriff years before, he returned to the rock fortress-like outcropping that had sheltered the evil coven and the high priestess before their discovery and dissolution. Again, he wasn't sure why, just a strange and nagging sense.

Jimmy had ascended the dominant rock amphitheater and walked to the rear of it where a down-sloping, narrow passage led to a waterfall that now barely trickled and carried a brown tinge and faint sulfur odor. Shitty fingerprints of the Big Pig Flood.

As he stepped behind the water curtain, he was stunned to find part of a deer carcass, bones stripped of meat, and a skin stretched to dry between two large sticks. He shivered with the memory of a similar scene when he, Pierce, and Sheriff had explored there before.

It had been the lair of the devil woman, the high temptress, the evil bitch who had murdered Cousin Lucas Jones in cold blood. It had been where she had hung out for months in hiding, waiting to deliver Lucas' baby girl, conceived at the moment of his death, before placing it on his grave in a woven wooden basket. The sweet little girl with the big yellow eyes had become the darling angel of Lettie and Pierce, and her wicked mother had gone free. Perhaps she had returned, reasoned a panicked Jimmy, bolting to the surface and his waiting pickup truck.

Pierce joined Jimmy in shaking at the thought as Jimmy's story unfurled. They both ran to Sheriff Sephus Adonis' office, Pierce lagging behind and drawing deep breaths. The "closed" sign on the sheriff's door midafternoon messaged that he was entertaining a guest in his back conference room, but there was no time to waste. They banged at the door in desperation, finally earning the disheveled sheriff's attention as his occasional visitor Holly Howell slipped by them with a nod and a sly smile. Pierce apologized profusely for the interruption as Sheriff shrugged it off, regained a semblance of dignity, and invited them back, swiftly kicking a bright-red thong under a cabinet in the corner.

Jimmy spilled out his tale of probable terror.

"It's her," was all the sheriff said, scratching his broad belly. He then added a couple of "shit, brothers."

Terrorist Attacks

"We've got to go back," Sheriff hesitantly confirmed, wondering aloud if they should go it alone or bring in the big guns.

Pierce reminded Sheriff that she likely wanted to kill them all, from what Lettie reported, and that implied attacking the water or food supply.

"Could be poisoned air or explosives too," observed Jimmy.

Could be anything, they all concluded.

Sheriff suggested a quick trip back to her den of iniquity. Immediately. If they found her alone, they would try and apprehend her. If there were others, they would regroup. Perhaps they would stumble onto something that she might be planning to use. Whatever, time was of the essence. Jimmy volunteered to drive. Sheriff Sephus deputized both Jimmy and Pierce and armed them with shotguns. Pierce didn't much like anything about guns, but he dutifully accepted the weapon, handling it more like a venomous snake than protection.

Their trip back in time, where they had ventured months before following the map that only Jimmy was later able to decipher, was long and unproductive. It took a long time to get to the rock fortress, but there was nothing there.

As they retraced Jimmy's steps to and behind the waterfall, senses alert and guns off safety, she watched from the shadows. There was no trace of any human touch—no deer carcass, no gnawed bones, no skins or antlers, nothing but raw dirt and slick rock.

Jimmy was dumbfounded. What had happened in the past twenty-four hours? His fears immediately turned to the garden. Yet he couldn't go there, even if it was only next door. He had promised Pierce. All Jimmy could do was shrug and shake his head. They explored several other passages to no end.

Jimmy knew the same thing had happened to Cousin Lucas on a gravel bar years before, a tale with no root or something like that Lucas had called it—one that Sheriff Sephus ignored to the peril of all. What you saw was not what you got. He could not risk calling out the good sheriff, who was his mentor, friend, and protector.

"What in the hell is going on?" he moaned to himself.

Then he apologized to Sheriff Sephus and Pierce Arrow for dragging them out on a wild evil witch chase. They headed home.

She smiled from a dark cavern corner above, completely shadowed, and watched them exit. It was so simple to cover her tracks, so pleasing to see their confusion, so hard to not laugh out loud at their ignorance. It was her gift of cunning that never stopped giving.

She patted the large, cold metal barrel that stood next to her, covered with red Xs and danger signs. Little did the idiots know what awaited them, their families, their children, and their friends. Their dogs, their cats, their pet raccoons. She would exterminate Hardlyville the way Reverend Jones had wiped out the Peoples Temple in Jonestown, Guyana. There would not be one Hardlyvillain left alive. It would be a gradual and painful death for most before they knew what struck them. Genocide, patricide, infanticide were but big words to describe her revenge.

Their backward, self-contained subculture of an already deplorable human condition was no more than a laughing stock—from fat sheriff to village idiots, from overwrought editors to weed-sucking symbiotic cretins. She would punctuate that truth, revenge complete.

Sheriff Sephus called his state highway patrol friend to seek logistical support and reinforcements. It would take several days to marshal enough resources to form a protective cocoon around Hardlyville until the evil one could be nabbed or determined to be gone again.

In the meantime, he ordered occasional deputy Cletus Bumrum to stand guard over the village's new community water tower, funded with the president of the United States' dollars as part of his Skunk Creek Watershed Reclamation Initiative that preceded establishment of the national refuge. Sheriff Sephus chose water as the most important and most vulnerable of Hardlyville's assets to protect. First and foremost.

Community and individual wells that had provided sweet, clean water for generations had been soured and degraded beyond recognition by the Big Pig Flood. Boiled, borrowed, and bottled water provided only temporary supply. Government relief funds allowed deeper aquifer access, reliable sourcing, and storage of "the good stuff," as the mayor described it. It all inched Hardlyville toward a return to normalcy.

Cletus was honored to have been chosen to protect this village treasure until reinforcements could arrive and was sworn to secrecy. He was a classic, large, raw-boned specimen of a Hardlyvillain hillbilly, who could hear a twig break at twenty paces and shoot lights out from one hundred. Sheriff Sephus would share early watch duty with Cletus, and Booray Abdul would provide support in the early morning hours.

First night out was overcast and drizzly. Cletus bid the sheriff goodnight as the clock turned to a.m. and sat back against an oak to await Booray's arrival. Cletus heard a light rustling and zeroed in on . . . a deer, foraging along the edge of the woods. Shame it wasn't season, smiled Cletus, relaxing as the deer slipped back under cover.

She slipped off the deer skin, made her way on silent cougar pads behind and around the water tower as only she knew how, slipped in next to Cletus' tree, reached quickly and silently around, and slit his throat. His gurgling last gasp soon died.

She dragged Cletus and his rifle deep into the woods and returned with a large container of colorless crystalline salt. She hoisted the heavy load to her shoulder, climbed the metal stairs to the top of the tower, disengaged an inflow connection, dumped the solids into the depths, and reconnected the whole apparatus. She would do the same thing the next night and even the next until potassium cyanide spread its deadly poison quickly and silently through the village water supply. Hardlyvillains, young and old first, the rest shortly thereafter, would begin to turn a ruddy red as their filthy bodies ceased to process oxygen, their feeble minds became more garbled and confused than normal, their breath shorted, and coma and cardiac arrest ended their worthless little lives. Shouldn't take more than forty-eight hours at the most. She shoved dust over Cletus' shed blood, hoisted the empty container to her deerskin-covered shoulders, and returned to her lair.

Booray had overslept. Lil' Shooter got to feeling amorous about bedtime, and in the privacy of their new postnuptial rental unit, they frolicked into the morning hours. Awaking, Booray had suddenly jumped up with a soft Arab curse, thrown on his clothes, and bolted for the door. Lil' Shooter, thinking she had done something wrong, burst into tears. He reminded her of his promise to Sheriff Sephus, grabbed his rifle, kissed her strongly, and promised to return for more at daylight if she was still awake. Young love is resilient, he smiled.

Upon reaching the water tower, he shouted his arrival, not wanting Cletus to shoot him dead. He was confused to find himself alone, no sign of either Cletus or the sheriff. He was also surprised to catch a whiff of bitter almonds, more in keeping with his homeland than the Ozarks. Booray didn't know what else to do but settle in next to a tree and try to stay awake. He fell sound asleep after thirty minutes.

Sheriff Sephus Adonis tapped Booray on the shoulder just after dawn, causing him to jump up and discharge his rifle into the woods. Sheriff gently admonished him for his dozing, but he was more interested in knowing where the hell Cletus had gone. Booray could only claim ignorance, to which the sheriff nodded in agreement.

Sheriff wondered if Cletus might have gone coon hunting during the early morning hours and promised to find a more reliable replacement for that night's watch. State patrol reinforcements should be available beyond that. Booray begged for a second chance, which Sheriff begrudgingly promised. Sheriff picked up a faint strange odor in the air but failed to mention it to Booray, who raced home only to find Lil' Shooter sound asleep. He quickly joined her.

Sheriff sought out Dan the Man Rutan to stand guard over the Hardlyville water tower for twelve hours. Dan the Man was known for his proficiency with a handgun, which was his deer hunting weapon of choice. There was no one quite like him in the county in that regard. Rifleman swore he once saw him pistol shoot a cigarette out of buddy Ed Bock's mouth from thirty yards, but the sheriff couldn't quite grasp that one. Sheriff knew Dan the Man to be a solid, reliable, if quirky, character and was pleased when he agreed to stand in for missing Cletus for a full night's watch. If the sheriff could just count on Booray Abdul showing up roughly on time about midnight, he should have it covered. Sheriff swore Dan the Man in and began the early night shift with him about seven p.m. He had sworn Dan the Man to secrecy, not wanting to panic villagers with his concerns about the water supply.

She watched from the deep woods, biding her time.

Sheriff Sephus wasn't feeling up to par and headed for home about ten p.m., confident in Dan the Man's competence and reliability to keep a trained eye on the water tower.

When Booray Abdul showed up five minutes early for the second shift, he again found no one around. He further wondered why the smell of bitter almonds seemed stronger tonight, but he passed on trying to understand either deviation from the norm. Little did Booray know that a mere two hundred yards away two blood-drained bodies were beginning to decompose in the deepest of woods and brambles.

Ol' Dill let his mutt Muffle off leash, as he usually did on their early morning stroll. Muffle darted into the deep woods, which was not what he usually did. Ol' Dill wondered if Muffle had gotten into the absinthe but let him be and headed home. Muffle returned two hours later with Dan the Man Rutan's blood splattered pistol in his mouth.

Sheriff Sephus Adonis had checked in at the water tower about eight a.m. He was feeling better until he found Booray alone and asleep. Again. Suddenly, the sheriff felt a jolt of concern. He shook Booray awake, expressed his displeasure, and asked where in the hell Dan the Man Rutan was. Booray apologized and shared his lack of knowledge with the sheriff. Dan the Man was nowhere to be seen when Booray had arrived five minutes before midnight, just like Cletus the previous night. Something was amiss. Booray asked the sheriff if he smelled anything out of the ordinary, and Sheriff acknowledged that he did, something like rotten nuts. Booray nodded in agreement.

"Almonds," he clarified.

As they sat scratching and contemplating, Sheriff Sephus caught a glimpse of Ol' Dill running toward them, waving a pistol and followed by a number of Hardlyvillains. As he neared, the sheriff ordered him to drop his weapon or face return fire. Sheriff wondered if the old coot had finally slipped his senses and reached for his service revolver. Ol' Dill hollered something about what the dog dragged in as the sheriff took aim at the old man's pistol hand. Booray was aghast. It was about then that the sheriff noticed blood on the weapon and Ol' Dill's hand. *What the hell?* Sheriff thought and dropped aim.

Ol' Dill began to explain that Muffle had run off in a crazed state during their early morning walk and had returned a couple of hours later with a weapon in his mouth, dropping it at Ol' Dills feet. It had discharged upon contact with the ground, drilling a hole through the front door. As Ol' Dill picked it up, he noticed bloodstains and, assuming he had been wounded, passed out. When he awoke, likely from the licks of terrified Muffle, he concluded that it was someone else who had been shot and ran immediately through town looking for the sheriff to report a murder. As a crowd gathered, someone noted they had seen the sheriff heading toward the water tower, and the whole entourage took chase after Ol' Dill as he headed that way.

Aimless Bevel, self-proclaimed leader of the local chapter of Agenda 21ers, strode forward to ask the sheriff what was going down. His small, energetic, and paranoid group of followers believed that the U.S. Government, aided and abetted by the United Nations, was out to steal their personal property and usurp the natural rights that went with it, all in the name of sustainability.

In actual fact, Agenda 21 refers to a non-binding, voluntary action plan endorsed by nearly two hundred independent nations, including the U.S. of A., at a 1992 U.N. conference on the environment and development held in Rio de Janeiro. Right-wing political hacks around the world had denounced the plan as a covert attack on individual property rights and ownership by environmental extremists and foreign enemies hiding behind the cloak of the United Nations.

Aimless Bevel himself was a shadowy character, prone to come and go without purpose or reason, which rendered him a perfect leader of a similarly themed group. Sheriff Sephus didn't even know where Aimless resided or if he had a home base at all.

Aimless saw several things that concerned him and demanded that the sheriff take action immediately. There had obviously been a cold-blooded murder in Hardlyville, as proclaimed by Ol' Dill Thomas. There was a brand-new U.S. of A. Federal Government funded water tower standing where none was needed, probably on land grabbed by a United Nations subcommittee. There was the sickening smell of rotten nuts in the air, probably emanating from the "ferneer" in their midst. There was a probable Arab terrorist standing right next to the sheriff that he, Aimless Bevel, demanded be arrested and incarcerated immediately to protect the women and children from murder and rape. A small stir of support emanated from corners of the crowd. He had touched several subterranean nerves in his senseless diatribe.

Sheriff Sephus looked on in disbelief and anger. He ordered the crowd to disburse. Some did, some didn't, and there was an angry tone to those who remained. Booray cringed behind the hulking bulk of Sheriff Sephus, shaking in his Nikes.

Aimless offered that he had a rope in his truck if anyone wanted to join him in dispensing justice. Sheriff pulled his service revolver, pointed it directly at Aimless Bevel's forehead, and ordered him to get his ass out of the way of real justice. Aimless crept to the rear of the crowd, and Sheriff asked for volunteers to form a search party for Cletus Bumrum and Dan the Man Rutan. He feared the worst for them as he recognized the bloodstained weapon as Dan the Man's own customized revolver, complete with his initials carved in the handle.

It took fewer than two hours before both bodies were discovered, stacked on top of one another, throats slit all the way back to their respective spines. Sheriff was shocked with the brutality of the act and had a strong sense of who done it.

State patrol reinforcements arrived to surround the water tank, setting rumors to flying. Doc Karst had several elderly patients stop by to complain about breathing problems. He blamed it on allergies. That is until one of The Donald's live-in sisters also flushed a ruddy-red color.

Sirens and red flags went off in the back recesses of Doc's mind. A quick read on poisons revealed that ingestion or inhalation of any cyanide derivative inhibits the processing of oxygen in the blood and can lead to convulsions, comas, and death. Doc concluded that something in Hardlyville was poisoning her citizens.

When Sheriff Sephus heard Doc's theory, he sounded every alarm, siren, and loud noise he could to bring the community together for emergency action. He ordered a quarantine of the village's water supply and immediate cessation of usage. He asked neighbors to warn neighbors. State patrolmen requested bottled water from surrounding communities on an emergency basis and immediate access to a team of analysts to evaluate the safety of Hardlyville water.

Sheriff withheld mention of the yellow-eyed demon lady, but he assigned three troopers to full-time protection of Lettie's little girl with the big yellow eyes.

Meantime, Aimless Bevel gathered a small posse of Christian, God-fearing men, who headed to Rifleman and Steele's house with a hanging rope. All knew that Booray and Lil' Shooter had fled there earlier in the afternoon after Bevel's previous threat. Rifleman had armed all in his clan, and when bullets flew, it was several of Aimless' men who fell.

When Sheriff Sephus Adonis heard shots, he raced toward the sound—full siren blaring, Pierce Arrow riding shotgun. One of Aimless' men shot at the sheriff's car and was dropped by Rifleman as soon as he fired. Sheriff was struck head-on and slumped over the wheel as his car crashed into a tree and burst into flames. Pierce pushed Sheriff Sephus through the driver's door, which had thankfully popped open on impact, and crawled out after him, trying to assess the damage to his friend.

Pierce hollered at Rifleman to call Doc Karst. Aimless Bevel sounded the retreat for his remaining men, who hopped into their pickups and drove quickly out of town. At least three dead, several wounded, including the sheriff, the town water supply poisoned, vigilantes and a devil woman on the roam, and trust shattered for a beloved and terrified Arab transplant. All in five minutes. And right after two previous and brutal cutthroat murders. Hardlyville would never be the same again.

Doc arrived to confirm that the sheriff's wound had been to his shoulder. Mind, body, and prize package remained intact. Doc stemmed the sheriff's bleeding and salved superficial burns, Undertaker Bob carted away three dead Agenda 21ers to add to the pile in his tiny mortuary, analysts quickly confirmed the cyanide-poisoned drinking water supply, and all of Hardlyville drank bottled water. The state patrol provided order, and citizens hugged one another for comfort as dusk fell with a resounding thud.

Pierce and Lettie slept with tiny Vixen between them, Pierce with his shotgun leaned reluctantly next to the bedstand, ready and loaded for bear, not knowing what threat could possibly present itself next.

Booray Abdul curled in a ball next to Lil' Shooter, pondering whether to stay or go home to Lebanon. The nation.

SHE

She watched the chaos unfold with eagle eyes from a rise beyond Rifleman's property. A smile curled the corners of her lips, and her eyes flashed bright yellow.

She regretted that the poisoned water could not have percolated a few days more to magnify its damage, but in terms of fear, she had tripped the town trigger, dented its psyche, shattered its naiveté, and split it wide apart. Not bad for a one woman wrecking crew.

She would allow Hardlyville to roast in its juices for a bit.

Maybe the fat sheriff was dead. At least a few of its sorry citizenry were. Maybe they would run the little Arab out on a rail. Maybe the supercilious little editor would have a stroke. There surely was time for all of this in a town without balls.

She reveled in the brilliance of that metaphor. She had enjoyed pursuing such a bizarre messaging code for cowardice to share with this sorry excuse for a town. The poor guys without gonads had been surprisingly pleasing to her, and she had sent them on their way in glory. Win, win, win.

What next? she pondered.

She would return some day for her daughter, to raise and train as she herself had been. It would have to be before the child was corrupted by the Goodie Two-Shoes surrogate who claimed her as her dead husband's spawn. What an idiot he had been, though not a bad ride, as she recalled. Certainly more pleasing than the fat sheriff. She laughed. It would also need to be beyond diaper training as she wouldn't enjoy messing with that. One day the window of opportunity would open, and she would be there to crawl through it. She would reclaim, rename, and retrain her daughter in the ways of her world, legacy assured. But not just now.

Her den was abandoned, her connection severed, and she would move on until the time was right. She contemplated hooking up with those idiots with the rope, maybe a new group of believers—disciples of hate, sex, and her omniscience. They certainly had proven their loyalty to the first fundamental commandment of her creed.

Still, she enjoyed being alone to worship herself. Pleasure was not hard to come by, as most men and some women were as malleable and disposable as the principles to which they professed adherence. No, she was better alone for now.

She would return to spread terror the next time she got to feeling real pissy. She stood slowly and loped off into the hills beyond Hardlyville.

Picking Up the Pieces

Sheriff Sephus Adonis' first order, issued as his shoulder wound was being cleaned by Doc Karst, had been to deputize Jimmy Jones and send him with a squad of state patrolmen to the evil one's den. He was sure that she would be gone, but it was a loop that needed closing.

Next had been to issue an APB for Aimless Bevel and his band of miscreants. They had moved beyond protesting Agenda 21 in all of its toothless wonder to attempted lynching and murder. He wanted them in custody in the worst way.

Finally, he asked to be taken to Booray Abdul as soon as he could be moved.

When Pierce Arrow was finally able to load Sheriff Sephus into his car the next day, he drove him over to Rifleman and Steele's where Booray and Lil' Shooter were hiding. He had to stand in line.

Ms. Bloom's Diversity and Sex Education class was in session in their living room. This had been Ms. Bloom's decision immediately upon hearing of the lynching attempt, and her entire class unanimously endorsed her call. They needed to comfort their dear friend from Lebanon and reassure him that all of Hardlyville treasured his citizenry.

The class house call brought Booray and Lil' Shooter to tears. Ms. Bloom asked her students to sit in a circle around the shaken young couple. Then, one by one, they expressed their horror at the threat to Booray's life and their support for him as a valued member of the community. Pomp went so far as to ask him to ask his whole family to move to Hardlyville. Beyond his self-serving desire to see Uvi again, and perhaps even be added to her long list of suitors, he spoke of the strength and depth that could be added to the community at large. Ms. Bloom looked at Steele with a proud smile, knowing that such magnanimous thoughts would never have surfaced twelve months past. Steele mouthed a "thank you" to Ms. Bloom, who returned her salute.

Sheriff Sephus Adonis and Pierce Arrow listened with pride, wonder, and amazement. Tiny Hardlyville was doing what it always had done with tragedy—recognize, mourn, then move forward, not back. Hardlyville was not a wallowing kind of place.

When the students had completed their circle of embrace, Sheriff Sephus added his words of embarrassment, condolence, and resolve. He promised such barbaric behavior would never be tolerated while he was sheriff and promised to bring the sorry culprits to justice. Hanging was too good for them. The last comment brought a shiver to Booray.

Booray and Lil' Shooter embraced everyone in the room and promised never to leave their friends. Booray doubted that his family would consider abandoning their roots and relocating, but he would certainly share the outpouring of community spirit and good will with them.

Pastor Pat, who had joined the gathering mid-circle, added a truly ecumenical blessing to bring closure to a very special moment in Hardlyville history. He tried not to look at Ms. Bloom for fear of feeling good old lust again, but the closing circle of hugs required their embrace, and they clung together conspicuously longer than the others.

"Old embers die slowly," whispered Ms. Bloom, finally breaking the clutch and leaving Pastor Pat in a condition that brought a chuckle from Sheriff Sephus, who had long been aware of their secret liaisons.

All of Hardlyville rallied around the survivors—Booray and the wounded sheriff—after burying Cletus Bumrum and Dan the Man Rutan with full community honors. Jimmy Jones dropped off some medical marijuana, as he labeled and packaged his best stuff, to both with wishes for a quick recovery. A bottle of Ol' Dill's finest was also part of the path to their recovery. While Sheriff Sephus was fully aware of the contraband nature of both offerings, he graciously accepted while looking the other way. Sometimes it was the thought, not the legality, of kindly gestures that mattered.

Banker Jamin even established a special savings account, calling it simply the "Hardlyville Heroes Account." He paid an extra one percent in interest to anyone who would leave their cash in his care for over two years, and he would lend it back to anyone creditworthy at one percent less than normal loan rates. "They gave more than they took," was the marketing tagline developed by Captain Happy.

Another feature was to allow any Heroes Account holder to borrow his or her money back any time during the two-year term at funds cost, meaning the loan cost them nothing. His only constraint was that one had to be a village resident to qualify for the Heroes Account. Jamin hoped this would induce some to move to Hardlyville because of its progressive nature as a community. Jamin was pro-growth all the way. Some did.

Obviously, Banker Jamin was making money somewhere else in his banking operation or he would have eventually gone broke. And Bank of Hardlyville grew like a stand of kudzu.

Pierce Arrow and Sheriff Sephus concluded that it was in the best interest of community recovery to leave the she devil out of the whole discussion. They both knew that she was the provocateur behind the evil that was planned and delivered, but Aimless Bevel presented as a much less threatening and more easily definable bad guy. Why plant the seed of unrequited evil in the community's fragile psyche when an idiot, albeit a very mean one, could carry the bull's-eye of scorn on his sorry back? Sheriff knew they could bring him to justice.

Neither Pierce nor Sheriff was sure about the whereabouts of the evil woman, or even where to begin looking for her. They would simply have to remain vigilant in the event she might strike again. Jimmy Jones was the only other man with an insider take, and he agreed to remain silent and watchful. Lettie was less sure and feared openly for little Vixen. But she remained quiet. All knew that an evil one who could kill innocent birth-defected men to merely send a message of fear and intimidation to a village, and then set out to exterminate every last resident, was more than a shadow lurking on the horizon. But for now, they would sweep it all under the community rug.

National press coverage followed Pierce Arrow's editorial lead in demonizing radical right-wing property rights movements. This was where he wanted them, and the village, to go.

Pierce wrote mountains of material. He mourned the loss of life, both those unknowns lost to bizarre and intimidating messaging and the brave villagers defending their fellow citizens. He wondered how the extremists, who had been killed in the lynching attempt, could lose their way to such a fanatical focus and endgame. Threaten a village with bizarre death messages, wipe it out with poison water, then lynch its only face of color? What could drive such hatred and bile? Were the property rights miscreants simply out to seize property, or was their purpose a deeper one? Were they set on establishing their own cruel culture on the backs of a simple, hardworking, and God-fearing, at least most of the time, citizenry? Was there substance in their actions or just random hatred?

Pierce argued substance and control, as sick as it was, and in the end, a much more frightening specter. There was method to their madness. He condemned fringe extremists, who preyed on innocents with violence and intimidation, and called for them to be brought to justice. And he called on anyone who could possibly help find Aimless Bevel to speak up now before he and his pitiful posse of vermin could harm again.

Not once was the evil she—the demon lady with the piercing yellow eyes, who had instigated the whole sick drama—mentioned. Pierce Arrow hoped she would take note of a community's unwillingness to bow and kowtow to intimidation and evil—if, in fact, she could even read or intuit.

As Pierce wove together in his writings Hardlyville's brave but violent history—from the brutal murder of founder Thomas Hardly over a mysterious map, to an evil coven of religious fanatics led by a strange and murderous woman, to the Great Pig Flood and the devastation of precious Skunk Creek, to the attempted genocide by a group of all too human property rights radicals—he forged a common conclusion. Hardlyville as a concept, and as a reality, was heroic, with a shared heart and soul—a throbbing, beating pulse of a place. He focused on the village's resilience, almost a cultural even, dare say, an ethnic bond that defied logic and common societal norms. Almost a "we are all unique pieces of a whole." Independent, ornery, laughable, and lovable. Knock us down, you'll bring us together. Hurt one, you hurt the rest. Threaten our individual way of life, threaten each and all.

Pierce Arrow was a damn good writer, and he knew it. He had the nation's attention because of the whole Skunk Creek National Watershed Wildlife Refuge process, how it was earned on the front steps of the White House, and the president of the United States' subsequent commemorative visit. Hardlyville was indeed on the national map.

The president even called Pierce from the Oval Office to share his condolences and offer encouragement. He would fly to Hardlyville soon to mourn their losses, celebrate their resilience, and bring more government assistance to assure no future tampering with the village's water. Pierce had anticipated this presidential philandering and, with Lettie's help, sought to encourage it, all in the interest of Hardlyville and its future, of course.

Pierce praised the president and his affection for a small town in the far-off Ozarks. He knew that this was all from the president's heart, as there was no political gain in such small potatoes. He thanked the president for his concern and promised his personal support for the president's current environmental initiatives being debated in Congress.

Pierce then asked the president if he would like to say "hi" to his friend Lettie. Pierce could only imagine what was going on in that dirty little mind as he handed the phone to a giggling Lettie. And did Ms. Lettie ever lay it on thick. She asked the president to come back to Hardlyville for a visit soon. She had missed him. Her partner was okay but simply couldn't take her where the president had.

After one particularly sensual riff, she confirmed that Pierce was in the other room and could not hear her whispered affections. Pierce, of course, could hear every word, from bountiful breasts to wanton kisses, gagging from ear to ear as the president of the United States promised Lettie what new tricks he would bring to her root cellar on his soon to be announced visit. Lettie cooed her concurrence and blew him a kiss in parting. Pierce was doubled over in laughter. Billious Bloom would be ecstatic.

Love in the Air...Real

The knock on the door got louder. It carried an air of immediacy. Sheriff Sephus Adonis wondered why some people just can't understand a sign that says "closed" on the sheriff's office door—a thought he shared with his partner of the moment, a middle-aged spinster who paid the sheriff a visit every other week or so. As she quickly reclothed in the back conference room, the sheriff hollered that he would be available in a minute, with a hint of irritation in his voice.

He unbolted and flung open the front door to his office. He was speechless.

There, standing directly in front of him, was a small, middle-aged, African-American female, prematurely graying at the temples of her close-cropped hair, dressed in jeans and a sweatshirt that read "Cleveland Browns."

"Airreal," was all the good sheriff could sputter, which he did at least three times.

"Some things never change," smiled the attractive stranger as Sheriff's recent guest slunk through the door with a muttered "thank you" directed toward the sheriff.

"Shit, brothers" preceded a question of how she had ever found him, followed by a fourth "Airreal."

"Not hard to track down a legend, Wilbur," she answered.

Sheriff invited her into his conference room, offered her a chair, and sat staring at her—flushing, bewildered, and obviously embarrassed. Neither moved for the next two hours as a lifetime of catch-up ensued.

Their reminiscence spanned about twenty years.

It began in high school in Cleveland, Ohio, when Sheriff Sephus Adonis was known as Wilbur Burris and carried the nickname Burr. He had moved to Cleveland from very rural Ohio to begin his freshman year and had progressed from Hayseed to Burr quickly.

"Burr, you were a big guy," Airreal laughed. "A really, really big guy."

She had been his first girlfriend and he her first lover, if backseat consummation qualifies as such. The memory that he had nearly squashed the life out of her brought giggles from both. That he had learned the art of love quickly and gently was a compliment she shared with affection.

"Still big, and still learning," Sheriff joked.

Sheriff lamented the hundred pounds he had gained since their last reunion. There had been several of those in the years during and after college at Cleveland State, but nothing stuck. Airreal had thought the transition to Sephus Adonis was a bit presumptuous but admitted in passing that it was well earned and beat the hell out of Wilbur when it came to whispering sweet nothings.

Airreal asked why the sheriff's arm was in a sling. He responded that he got shot in the shoulder by a bad guy, and that if he ever caught up with him . . .

Before he could complete the sentence, Jimmy Jones wandered in unannounced to offer more detail on his visit to the evil one's lair with the state troopers. He began spewing before sensing that Sheriff Sephus had company, trying to process why the sheriff didn't have his "closed" sign posted as he usually did when entertaining a guest in the back conference room. He went bug-eyed when he saw an attractive, middle-aged black lady about the size of Tiny Taylor seated across from the sheriff. She even had all of her clothes on. The final shocker was the big grin on the sheriff's face and the blush that enveloped it.

Jimmy stammered an apology and began to back out until the sheriff rose to introduce Ms. Airreal.

"What's your last name these days, hon?" he added, which did not sound very Sheriff Sephus like.

Airreal confirmed she had returned to her maiden name after several married names had slipped into unhappiness or boredom. "Airreal Flambeau" she proclaimed proudly, reiterating her second generation West African roots.

Sheriff Sephus confirmed that he and Airreal had been an item on several occasions long ago, and that her beauty and spirit had lived well through time. This set Ms. Airreal to blushing, which added to Jimmy's bank of knowledge in that he didn't know black people could do so. Of course, she was only the first or second he had ever met.

Sheriff advised Airreal that Jimmy was a young and successful entrepreneur with a fine family, and that he had a long and colorful Hardlyville lineage to live up to.

Jimmy excused himself, fearful of any elaboration, and headed toward the front door as Airreal thanked Wilbur for the compliment. This stopped Jimmy in his tracks.

"Wilbur?" he snorted. "Sheriff Wilbur? You must be shitting me," he croaked, apologizing immediately for his lack of tact. "You must be one hell of a little woman," Jimmy said in parting, digging his departure hole a little deeper.

Sheriff could only smile and wave him away.

Jimmy ran straight to Pierce Arrow's office with the news of Sheriff Wilbur's unusual visitor, and it took Pierce only five minutes to visit and confirm it for himself. He tried to say "Sheriff Wilbur," but burst out laughing before he could even spit out the "ur." Pierce apologized profusely and politely extended his hand of welcome to Airreal while dialing Lettie on his cell with the other hand and leaving a message that she needed to beat it to the sheriff's office as soon as possible.

The whole village was in an uproar within the hour as Jimmy spread the word far and wide. Booray Abdul soon strode proudly into the sheriff's office to welcome another person of color to Hardlyville. Ms. Billious Bloom and her entire class on diversity and sex education went straight from the classroom to Sheriff Sephus' office for a "real-life case study on racial relations," as Ms. Bloom put it. Pomp, who had not been at loss for words since Uvi had blessed him with a new name and first heartthrob, pronounced Ms. Airreal as simply too beautiful for words—and definitely for the portly sheriff. The sheriff's office could not begin to accommodate the entire class, so the students calmly and politely took turns welcoming Ms. Airreal to Hardlyville as Ms. Bloom smiled on proudly. Her efforts were bearing fruit and sparking societal progress.

Airreal was overcome with the attention and genuine kindness and accepted it in the spirit offered.

Ol' Dill was next in line, sharing that he had heard through the grapevine that an Asian or Croatian-American had come to Hardlyville to visit the sheriff, and he wanted to personally welcome her with a jar of his finest moonshine. He also wanted to witness for himself a little lady who could handle Sheriff Sephus' reputed largess, asking Airreal if it hurt. Airreal was quick to note that "only the first time," which would have been the case with any young man. She also noted that size was overrated and that reputation often overreached reality. She added that "the sheriff was a tender man." Ol' Dill seemed confused by her answer but noted that he appreciated her candor. He also hoped she would stay a while.

Sheriff Sephus, or Wilbur, finally whooshed everyone out and put up the "closed" sign so he could find out what Airreal had in mind with her surprise visit. "At it again" was all anyone in town could figure.

Airreal confessed that the real purpose of her visit was to rediscover the sense of grounding that Wilbur had always provided. She was tired of failed marriages and half-assed affairs that had left her emotionally spent and, on one occasion, battered and bruised. Beyond that, she didn't have a clue. She had no preconceived outcomes, no goals or objectives, no agenda to share. She simply wanted to be in the presence of her first real male friend.

Sheriff was deeply touched. He was also speechless. He began the only place that could register, with how beautiful Airreal had remained. He confessed to a racing pulse and pounding heartbeat. It was not the most romantic reaction Airreal had ever raised, but it was as real and true as the last four letters in her name. She could feel it.

He asked if she would be staying long and if so where. She just shrugged. He asked if it would be too forward to suggest that she stay with him for as long as she could put up with a "set in his ways" bachelor who didn't keep a very clean house. She just sat and smiled.

"I was afraid it was too forward," confessed a disappointed Sheriff.

"No, no," she turned her head slowly.

The confused sheriff indicated he understood her negative reaction to staying with him and suggested maybe his friends Pierce Arrow and Lettie Jones could put her up for a while. This sent Airreal into gales of laughter. Sheriff was near tears.

Airreal was finally able to stop and catch her breath. She said forcefully and emotionally that she would be honored to stay with the sheriff until she could figure out the "what next." She was confident Sheriff could help her with that. He always had.

Sheriff smiled broadly and promised to respect her privacy, to which Airreal smiled back a "not too much," she hoped.

News travelled quickly around the village that Ms. Airreal had moved in with Sheriff Sephus Wilbur Adonis, that they were former lovers and soul mates, and that every former visitor to the sheriff's back conference room should stay away until it became clear as to the "what next."

The "what next" did not take long to materialize in full village view. Sheriff Sephus Wilbur Adonis shared with Pierce Arrow that he had asked Airreal to marry him. They had been first friends and lovers, should have tried it back then—though it probably wouldn't have worked because of Sheriff's wild oats and Airreal's streak of independence—but it had always been meant to be. The sparks that were flying now confirmed that. Sheriff had promised Airreal a true reformation in every way—from weight to sex to shared versus self-centered focus—in his marriage proposal, and she had accepted after seeking and receiving twenty-four hours to consider.

Pierce wondered if Sheriff and Ms. Airreal were rushing things a bit. Fewer than two weeks between liftoff and touchdown. Sheriff could only smile and confirm that it had been a busy two weeks. They were sure of and committed to a shared course for the remainder of their days.

Pierce could only shake his head at their determination and resolve. It had taken him months to wake up to his love for Lettie—wasted months, for certain. He knew how significant a factor luck was in a marital experiment. Sometimes they worked, sometimes not. He had been on both ends of that spectrum. But one constant seemed true. Starting as friends provided a firmer foundation than infatuation. True luck was when both were in play.

Pierce hugged Sheriff and congratulated him.

"When will the festivities begin?" he followed.

"Tomorrow," Sheriff pronounced with dignity. Why waste time beyond the twenty-five years already invested in denial? Pastor Pat would be his next stop. And Sheriff added that he and Ms. Airreal would be downright honored if Pierce and Lettie would serve as best man and matron of honor, no costumes necessary. And maybe Vixen could be the flower girl. Pierce could only nod vigorously before running home to share the stupendous news with Lettie.

Pastor Pat reacted with shock . . . and joy and, as always, promised to be ready to rock-and-roll at the appointed time, even the next day. It would be an open ceremony, everyone in town invited—lacking the historical and cultural grounding of his most recent extravaganza with Booray and Lil' Shooter, but personal and customized to two middle-aged young lovers without further time to fritter away. They knew what they wanted, how they wanted it, and when.

The wedding vows were brief and to the point.

"I, Sheriff Sephus Wilbur Adonis, take you, Airreal Flambeau, as my friend, lover, and wife forever. I promise to be faithful, to have sex with no other, to use the back conference room only for real business, and to lose one hundred pounds over the first three years of our marriage."

"I, Airreal Flambeau, take you, Sheriff Sephus Wilbur Adonis, as my friend, lover, and husband forever. I promise to be faithful, to never get married again, and to gain ten pounds over the first three years of our marriage."

Sheriff's kiss was short but passionate.

Jimmy Jones hollered for a shivaree, but when the sheriff pulled his service revolver and drew down on the crowd with a comment about "in your wildest dreams," Jimmy's challenge hissed like a stuck balloon.

Pierce Arrow was the first to reach his dear sheriff friend and was greeted with an enormous bear hug that Pierce worried would crack a rib. Lettie went straight to Airreal to welcome her into the Hardlyville family.

Sheriff grabbed Airreal's tiny hand in his big paw and led her through the crowd, announcing in a loud voice that they had some important monkey business to take care of. They high-fived all along the way to the patrol car. Sheriff opened the back door for Airreal, hoisted her in the air toward the cheering crowd, laid her gently in the backseat, set his siren to blazing, and spun out toward his no longer lonely house. The couple was not seen again for three entire days, during which time not a single crime against property or person was committed within the Hardlyville city limits out of respect for her chief law enforcement officer and his new bride.

Ol' Dill boasted that he once had shacked up with an amazing young lady for an entire week, coming up only for air and an occasional bite to eat and sip to drink. The Donald asked politely if they had consummated, to which Ol' Dill confessed that only he had become quite constipated, and to the point of a dangerous bloat. There was more information in this brief exchange than The Donald could possibly begin to process.

When the sheriff finally emerged to resume his law enforcement duties, his fat face bore a glow of exhilaration that no one had ever seen before. He was also seven pounds lighter, though few could tell it. Sheriff Sephus Wilbur Adonis was, at last, a happily married man, and the average shade of the Hardlyvillain demographic palette had deepened ever so slightly.

The Deal

They drove slowly through town in a new gold Lexus, so as to not kick up any dust for fear of dimming the sheen. The driver leaned out the window to ask a passerby where the Bank of Hardlyville was located. "Straight ahead," he pointed. In three different directions. The driver shook his head and inched on.

The stoplight showed green, so the driver pushed on through to the bank, which lay on the south side of the street.

It was a brand-new stoplight, and it had caused a furor in Hardlyville. The Donald proclaimed there wasn't no one who was going to tell him when to stop and when to go. Not even his lively, sweet-lovin' sister friends. While The Donald didn't buy into all of this Agenda 21er stuff, this was a blatant attack on property rights. "It's my foot, my car, my bicycle," he reasoned, and for someone to tell him when he could and could not use them as he wished was probably a violation of his constitutional rights. It was clearly more damn government overreach—government, in this case, being Hardlyville's civic leaders.

Again, it had been Steele, businesswoman and chair of the local Chamber of Commerce, who had led the charge. Ol' Dill had nearly run her down on several occasions as she attempted to cross the street. She knew it wasn't intentional, but he just couldn't see much anymore along with his deafness. Last time, he had clipped her behind and waved merrily to her in passing. She had reported the incident to Sheriff Sephus Wilbur Adonis, who just shrugged and indicated it probably didn't qualify as a hit and run. Besides, he had tried to take Ol' Dill's keys away several times before and backed down when Ol' Dill begged him not to rob him of one of three remaining pleasures in his life. The others being Tiny Taylor and his finest mash. Sheriff simply couldn't do that to a Hardlyville icon who would probably soon be gone.

Steele still felt it was time to slow down traffic in the interest of public safety and progress. It was the latter term that scored votes with other civic leaders. All were proud of Hardlyville's progress of the past months. The Big Pig Flood, as disastrous as it had been, had triggered a succession of baby steps into the current century—from government relief funds to the national wildlife refuge, to national notoriety, to the presidential visit, to a new banker in town with a board of directors that included women, to new Arab and African-American citizens. And on and on. Hardlyville was on the move. Forward. Even the recent Agenda 21er threat had been dispersed. And though not without loss and suffering, the village had won that battle and simply could not be stopped in its tracks anymore. Yes, a new traffic light, though disconcerting for some, would be another step in the right direction. Civic leader approval had been unanimous. Community acceptance had been halting and far from universal.

A few rebels sat at the green light until it turned red. And then ran it. There was rarely any traffic, so such rebellion carried little risk but provided a bold statement of principle. Ol' Dill could not only not see well, but he was close to color-blind with what little registered on his visual radar, so the light made no difference whatsoever in his behavior. Most simply viewed the light as a curiosity and enjoyed red and green for the color each added to their daily toil.

The gold Lexus pulled up to the Bank of Hardlyville's front door and disbursed its load of slick, suited businessmen and women, two of each. They were making an unannounced call on Banker Jamin Bennell. They were from the big city and knew that in most small Ozarkian towns most significant transactions began with the local bank president.

Introductions completed, the delegation leader, a she, indicated that they wished to purchase Hardlyville and lease it back to the community in a win-win deal for all.

Banker Jamin leaned forward in his spare executive chair and rang for Captain Happy to join them. The business delegation evidenced surprise when a tall, slender man with bib overalls, wide brim hat, and the faint odor of a barnyard slipped in and pulled up a chair. He announced that he, Captain Happy, was there as a representative of the bank board of directors to facilitate communication. The delegation leader nodded and pulled out a rolled document resembling a site plan. Banker Jamin motioned toward the board table, and all relocated around it, the guests playing musical chairs to avoid sitting next to Captain Happy. Finally, the delegation leader stopped and moved over right next to the good Captain, extending her hand in welcome and in the hope of closing a business deal. Captain Happy returned her gesture and stuck a large wad of Red Bull chewing tobacco in his mouth before packing it firmly in his right cheek. Jamin remained locked in his forward leaning position, all ears.

The delegation leader announced that they were from the investment banking firm of Lolly, Gag, and Maggot, LLC, PC. She spent the next five minutes reviewing the firm's mission, credentials, successes, and references.

"They just want everyone to get rich," Captain Happy interpreted to Banker Jamin, who nodded for her to continue.

She recounted the incidents of the past few months that had put Hardlyville in the national news, expressing admiration and enthusiasm for the community's grit and resilience, both of which were extremely marketable in a nation generally gone cynical.

Captain Happy took note that she was an attractive sort of female, in a formal but provocative way. He was flattered that she had been attentive toward him and wondered if she might have the hots for a true man about town. He casually undressed her with his eyes, roaming from coiffed blonde hair past red painted lips to supple figure to slender high heels and back up again, drawing a dagger-like stare from the snooty goon seated next to her. Captain Happy winked at him and returned to the conversation. It was not every day in Hardlyville that an attractive young damsel took note of the captain.

The delegation leader launched into a string of "what-ifs." Her voice had a professional but slightly singsong cadence to it. This was not her first oral presentation, Captain surmised.

✓ What if the community that is and has been Hardlyville for over a century would share its inspirational story?

✓ What if that story could be aggressively marketed to the masses as a destination, an opportunity for a personal brush with a timeless and hopeful lifestyle?

✓ What if people would pay for the privilege of wandering through Hardlyville as observers and students of everyday life in the village?

✓ What if nothing would change for a normal Hardlyvillain, except an occasional stranger wandering up to ask a question or seek a story and more cash in his or her pocket?

✓ What if these strangers would be willing to pay for the right of observation and access, with half of each admission going into city coffers to invest in a new and even more progressive Hardlyville?

✓ What if investors would be willing to develop a first-class motel for guests to return to each evening after soaking up a day of Hardlyville life, with half of a proration of each night's rent going directly into the bank account of each Hardlyvillain on an annual basis?

✓ What if the village of Hardlyville would sell itself to a consortium of buyers for a million dollars and agree to rent the venue back for ten thousand dollars per year on a thirty-year lease, with an option to repurchase for a dollar at lease end?

She noted in passing that of course Bank of Hardlyville would make the construction loan at a market rate of interest and handle all operating accounts. The bank would further provide an account for each Hardlyvillain to receive their share of lodging profits.

In short, such a transaction would provide both long-term economic security and immediate cash flow to the community, as well as each and every Hardlyvillain. It would be good for community banking as well.

Banker Jamin's mind whirred around the numbers.

The one million dollar purchase price would compound into a major endowment over thirty years from which periodic draws could fund debt service on major infrastructure improvements as planned for or needed far into the future.

His calculations also implied the following results, with fifty percent average occupancy of a two-hundred room hotel at reasonable nightly rents (i.e. fifty dollars), a ten dollar daily ticket price for two hundred daily visitors, and a three hundred days per year operating cycle:

✓ The city of Hardlyville would net three hundred thousand dollars annually in additional operating funds.

✓ Each Hardlyvillain would receive an annual deposit into their personal bank account of twenty-five hundred dollars, regardless of age, gender, race, economic status, or state of mind.

The delegation leader added that investors would also receive a fair and attractive annual rate of return after covering operating costs.

"Win-win," she repeated.

Was this selling out a precious heritage and history in exchange for generations to come of economic security? Banker Jamin wasn't sure but knew that such numbers warranted serious consideration—first by civic leaders, then the citizenry at large.

Banker Jamin thanked the delegation leader and the investment banking firm of Lolly, Gag, and Maggot, LLC, PC for their interest in tiny Hardlyville. He asked how much time the community might have to consider such a creative proposal. "Twenty business days," was the response. Banker Jamin promised an answer of some sort within that time frame to the phone number highlighted on the delegation leader's business card.

The delegation pulled away as slowly as they had arrived, gently rolling through the green facing traffic light. Ol' Dill plowed into the right rear bumper, bouncing off and carrying on. He cursed whomever had gotten in his way and hoped they would drive more carefully in the future.

The Process

Banker Jamin requested a special session with the civic leaders that very afternoon. As he explained the proposed deal and details thereof, there was excited murmuring around the conference room.

The progressive arm of the Hardlyville Junta, Chamber Chair Steele and half of the mayor, wanted to know what could possibly be wrong with a transaction that generated a million dollars from an abstract entity to fund a Hardlyville endowment, provided lodging infrastructure at no cost to the village, and put major dollars into every Hardlyvillain pocket, employed or not. Steele even reasoned that a new motel would give her and Rifleman a romantic place to sneak off to from time to time for a little good lovin', far away from the rifle stock manufacturing line in their living room. Doc Karst nodded enthusiastically at that thought. Undertaker Bob wondered if he might be able to rent a room or two to store cadavers if Hardlyville ever had another gun battle. Postmaster PB wondered what kind of mail delivery volume it would generate.

Banker Jamin's quiet stare into the wall in front of him finally got the Junta's attention. Captain Happy explained that Jamin wasn't so sure. He intuited from Jamin that the concept probably made sense, the initial numbers looked pretty good, and the impact on Hardlyville, particularly his bank, could be quite profound. It was just this whole selling out thing that troubled him. How can one sell something one doesn't own? Sure Hardlyville belonged to them all in an ethereal sense. When asked what that big word meant, Jamin whispered to Captain Happy something like "vague or wispy."

Banker Jamin looked at Hardlyville as larger than the individual lives lived therein. It was history, hope, and individuals, past and present, melded into a whole that far exceeded even his capacity to quantify. Hardlyville was resilient, heroic, cathartic, flawed, and grounded. Can you sell that? At what price? And at what cost to village core values? A million dollars? Ten million dollars? Ten trillion dollars? Zero?

This deep-thinking Jamin was not something often on public display. Mabel loved this side of him, found it sensual and erotic, and usually ended up pregnant after one of his profound mind-bendings. It always threw Captain Happy, who knew Jamin better than anyone, and much preferred the calculating wizard of numbers to the meditative guru of granola.

Jamin broke his trance with a trip to the urinal. When he returned, Jamin was all business. He recommended to the civic leaders that they hire a qualified consultant, preferably one with Hardlyville roots, to assess the quantitative side of the deal. Postmaster PB thought he remembered that Flotilla Hendricks' son Chuck was a big-time CPA somewhere in the Midwest and certainly had the rootstock to stay grounded.

Jamin also believed a small group should be appointed by the civic leaders to look at the soft side of the equation. What would sell out mean to the legacy of Hardlyville? He thought Pierce Arrow might think deeply enough to lead such a discussion in a very public venue, with significant input from a few old-timers like Pastor Pat and unofficial town historian Billious Bloom.

A formal report should be issued to the community without civic leader endorsement and put to a vote without sidebar campaigning. There was much to do in a very short time if that was the process the civic leaders chose to follow, he concluded. He, Jamin, would contribute in any way they deemed productive, including the funding of any consulting engagements.

Despite early enthusiasm for the project, no civic leader took issue with Banker Jamin's recommendation. Doc Karst would seek out Flotilla's son, Steele would approach Pierce Arrow, Undertaker Bob would organize a voting process, and the mayor would smile and provide a personal platitude for each day of the process. He launched with "each day is a new one" to get things going.

Hotshot CPA Chuck Hendricks was delighted to offer his analytical services, particularly when advised that the Bank of Hardlyville would compensate him generously for his services. He was excited to return home after all of those years and amazed at what Hardlyville had survived and was becoming. He had not been back since sister Sabrina's tragic childbirth demise years before, partly because he was embarrassed by his roots and wished to hide them from the partners in his firm, but mostly because he had been preoccupied with a failed marriage and a nasty child custody battle. He was Flotilla's golden son and did not want to burden her with his failures. With input from mother Flotilla, he quickly organized and convened a financial impact committee that included Tiny Taylor and Jimmy Jones, among others, and they set out to verify the numbers Jamin had crunched in his head over fifteen minutes and look for holes in the deal.

Pierce Arrow cautiously accepted the role of chairing the soft issues committee with help from Pastor Pat, Billious Bloom, and The Donald.

Pierce was vaguely supportive of Hardlyville's transition to a more progressive community, but something about selling out rankled his inner workings.

Undertaker Bob put together a small committee to organize a community vote.

All of Hardlyville took note of the flurry of somewhat secretive activity, not sure what was going on, but they trusted a *Daily Hellbender* editorial that promised there were exciting opportunities on the horizon that the community would be asked to weigh in on very soon.

After ten days, Jamin asked that the Lolly, Gag, and Maggot, LLC, PC delegation return to Hardlyville to answer a number of important questions and meet personally with Hardlyvillain leaders involved in the analytical process. The original delegation, including the attractive female leader, arrived the next day, this time in a Hummer, explaining that they had been struck last visit by a crazy, ranting old man who ran the town stoplight and promised to repeat his actions if he ever saw them again. They had phoned Sheriff Sephus Adonis to seek charges against the perpetrator. Sheriff indicated it must have been an out-of-towner or "ferneer" in that no one matching their description had ever resided in Hardlyville to his knowledge. The delegation was taking no chances that time around.

The mayor nodded his condolences, hoping that the incident hadn't soured their enthusiasm for Hardlyville. The delegation leader assured the mayor that it hadn't, so the mayor shared his platitude for the day, "Ol' Dill is a Pill," to the confusion of the visitors and smirks from the locals.

Banker Jamin suggested, through Captain Happy, that the delegation divide into separate groups to meet with ad hoc citizen committees, all of which were aggressively involved in analyzing all implications of the deal. Jamin had only one question before the group divided: What if no one comes to visit the town?

The delegation leader seemed stunned with the simple gravity of Jamin's inquiry and promised to have an answer for him before they departed that day. She also noted that, if Hardlyville had a motel, all could stay as long as it took to answer any questions, an implication which was lost on no one.

She joined the soft issues committee, which met in Pierce Arrow's conference room at the *Daily Hellbender*. Pierce met her attempts at charm with an icy stare that only deepened as she slipped into a covertly sexy sideshow. She began by untying her Hermes scarf and flipping it casually on the conference table while releasing the top three buttons of her silk blouse, baring cavernous cleavage. Pastor Pat immediately went beet red while The Donald slipped into a bizarre Dinky Doodle bug-eyed gaze.

The delegation leader began by welcoming questions from the floor. Pastor Pat stammered something about "bountiful beauties" before concluding that what he meant were the generous profit-sharing proposals included in the deal.

Pierce Arrow's silent treatment quieted the others, who waited with trepidation for what he might be thinking.

"Come on," she encouraged, noting that she hadn't driven that far just for pleasure, though she was sure a quaint village like Hardlyville had plenty to offer.

This set off the editor of the *Daily Hellbender*. He had heard and seen all he could handle. His tirade was centered around the question of what right current residents of Hardlyville could possibly have to sell history and their souls to the highest bidder. This was a Faustian bargain of the seamiest sort.

What price for Octavia Rosebeam, her multigenerational contributions, including the Rosebeam Foundation, so ably administered by Ms. Bloom? How much is village founder Thomas Hardly's name and vision worth? Can they place a value on hero Lucas Jones' life sacrifice for the sake of the village children? How much for any life, name, or sacrifice?

And what about the true hero of Hardlyville's history, the village itself?

What about a community that always bounced back and a citizenry who forever carried the day after, no matter how difficult or challenging it loomed—a merry band of misfits who, throughout village history, had never thrown in the towel, never whined about murder or pig shit, or even asked for timeout? Every single Hardlyvillain was a link in an unbreakable chain from then to now. What price? What cost? What worth? What right?

The delegation leader listened quietly through his fifteen minute rant, which ended only when he finally ran out of breath and began hyperventilating. Ms. Bloom called Doc Karst on her cell and began mouth-to-mouth efforts to restore normal breathing. This got The Donald to briefly consider a similar attack in that the delegation leader was seated closest to him and might feel compelled to intervene in his best health interest, but Doc Karst's quick arrival ended that pipe dream. The last thing The Donald wanted was that old fart's goat breath singeing his tonsils.

With order restored, the delegation leader allowed that placing a price on history was difficult, but that her investors had given her some leeway to negotiate a sweeter deal if that was the issue. True value was always market driven, and the village was entitled to whatever the market would bear.

This set off Pierce Arrow on another run until Doc Karst could pop a valium down his throat to restore some semblance of a normal heartbeat. Doc was now getting worried about Pierce's ticker and led him quietly from the room for calming and observation.

He would be a difficult one, the delegation leader concluded, dropping one more button to free a touch more bounty. She soon had at least two of three remaining soft issues committee members inhaling her answers deeply. She would deal with the Arrow fellow in time.

The financial impact committee seemed content to rely on Jamin's original mind-boggling back-of-napkin calculations and spent their time merely tweaking assumptions and numbers.

As the day came to a close, the delegation leader returned to Jamin's office at Bank of Hardlyville to address his initial question. She slammed reams of marketing data on his desk, including demographic analyses, scientific surveys, societal trending studies, and public opinion surveys. Under no circumstance would no one come. She asked Jamin to review her package and suggested that she return to discuss it with him one day the following week. Jamin nodded without even noticing the buttons or what lurked behind them.

The delegation's Hummer escaped unscratched and unscathed, to Sheriff Sephus' great relief.

The delegation returned the following Monday to meet with Banker Jamin. As members gathered around his conference table to discuss his top of mind analysis, the delegation leader excused herself. She had an important personal call to make.

The Pitch

Pierce Arrow was beginning perhaps the most important editorial in his last decade in Hardlyville. He didn't know what it would say, but he knew it was momentous. He toyed with a title in bold black letters that read "**SOLD**" followed by "**FOR SALE???**" which carried less finality yet still spoke to the deep mistrust he had in those faces blurred with anonymity who wanted to buy his village. The "whys" of it all rang out to no answer, except money. Which simply raised another "why." Why Hardlyville?

He didn't hear the tap on the door below, the gentle tread on the stairs, or the creak as his office door swung open. Or the light footsteps that soon placed the delegation leader directly in front of his desk. It took a second sense, perhaps of danger, to snap his attention to full alert. He looked up into the seemingly innocent gaze of a beautiful, sexy lady intent on capturing a "yes" vote.

He motioned for her to sit as she expressed her regrets for the awkward beginning of their relationship. She continued that she was sure that, once he had a chance to observe and consider all the "facts," he too would come to the conclusion that the sale and rebranding of Hardlyville to caring and savvy investors was in the best interest of all.

This was the first time Pierce had heard the term "rebranding" and pounced on her to elaborate, wondering how one could rebrand something not yet labeled. She assured him it was simply a marketing term, carried no meaning beyond that, and then began to reveal her set of facts.

Fact #1: The delegation leader had enormous breasts.

Fact #2: The delegation leader was not wearing a bra.

Fact #3: The delegation leader would allow Pierce Arrow to observe and consider them.

Fact #4: The delegation leader had additional facts to reveal and consider as well.

The delegation leader began a sultry striptease, which ended only when she stood birth naked in front of Pierce Arrow, arms spread open in welcome.

Pierce stammered something about her needing to rerobe not rebrand and leave his office and village at once.

The delegation leader, of course, continued to strut toward a disbelieving Pierce Arrow, coming to rest on his desk mere inches from his nose. She was prepared to seal the deal, whatever that took.

Neither had heard the door open down below or the soft steps of Lettie Jones as she ascended to Pierce's office. Lettie stared for the briefest of moments before slamming the office door, stomping back down the stairs, and yelling at Pierce to enjoy himself.

The delegation leader smiled softly at Pierce, slid lithely into his lap, grabbed his cell phone from the desktop, and snapped a quick selfie of she and he, whispering that he seemed to have nothing to lose and might as well love the one he's with. Pierce could only slump in stunned disgust as she e-mailed the incriminating photo to a colleague.

PURGATORY

Banker Jamin called all committee chairs to join him and the investment banker delegation in his office immediately to review the additional marketing data and raise any further questions that had surfaced in their deliberations. All gathered, with the surprising exception of Pierce Arrow, who no one seemed able to raise. One banker thought that was perhaps who the delegation leader was meeting with, given some of the weighty concerns Pierce had raised during the last visit. Jamin shrugged and beckoned Billious Bloom to represent the soft issues committee at the important meeting.

Ms. Bloom entered the conference room at exactly the same moment as Chuck Hendricks, chair of the financial impact committee. They took obvious note of one another. Chuck was far removed from a troubled marriage, and Billious was finally of a mind to consider betrothal after her wild run of wanton catch-up. They grabbed facing chairs around the table and cast occasional glances that vibrated in the air. Jamin asked if either had questions for the visiting professionals before deducing that not only did they not have questions but they probably couldn't care less at the moment.

One investment banker glanced at his e-mail, opened a photo attached thereto, and smiled at members of his team with a nod of affirmation. "Done deal," he whispered to himself. This was clearly not the delegation leader's first multimillion dollar closing.

Banker Jamin asked for a couple of more days to restudy the marketing data, but he did confess to being impressed with the breadth and depth of the analysis. It had become obvious to him that "what if no one comes?" was a moot question.

The delegation leader stepped confidently into the conference room, oozing charm and expensive perfume, while winking slyly at Captain Happy. She silently hoped she wouldn't need to stoop that low but certainly was up to it if needed. She had slept with worse, if not as odiferous, on her way to the top.

Jamin welcomed her and hoped her conversation with Pierce Arrow had been productive. She nodded in the affirmative, adding that they had found common ground among several irrefutable facts. She was certain that Editor Arrow would announce his support of the project. Jamin promised to get back to her in a matter of days.

Meanwhile, Pierce Arrow headed straight to Lettie. He could only beg forgiveness for allowing himself to get in such a compromising circumstance. He then went on to set the record straight, trusting that she would believe him. He explained that what Lettie stumbled onto was no more than a blatant attempt to slander a major stumbling block to "the deal" and a significant closing fee the naked lady was pursuing without conscience or constraint.

Lettie didn't know much about the deal but nodded that the lady was definitely naked. She also knew that Pierce was amongst a minority that were digging in their heels, though she thought he looked pretty compliant at the moment of their encounter.

He assured Lettie that what she saw was as bad as it got. Well, almost.

The bitch had leaped into his lap as Lettie exited and snapped a selfie of naked self and victim Pierce. Then she began to nibble at his ears, which had snapped him from his shocked despondence.

Pierce had ordered her to get her fleshy ass off his innocent lap immediately or he would call the sheriff. That set her to laughing uncontrollably as she e-mailed the compromising photo to a colleague, wondering what Pierce Arrow was going to do now beyond voting "yes" on her business proposition.

Of course, if he chose not to, Pierce Arrow's colleagues in the press would soon be presented with a different side of him. She would claim that he forced her to disrobe at the point of a gun and sit naked on his lap, cold gun barrel jammed between the cheeks of her buttocks. He had demanded that she smile as well. She had followed the only course available to escape from a certifiable sexual pervert.

Pierce had then lifted her gently from his lap to the desk, the only touch he initiated during the entire ordeal, and left her to run to Lettie. Pierce would never vote "yes" to selling Hardlyville and would see that the delegation leader would be exposed to the village for what she was: an extorter, a slanderer, a cheap pimp of the deal.

Pierce again promised to a skeptical Lettie that he had not touched one breast, let alone both, that he had hoisted her by her hindquarters from his lap to his desk, that he had enjoyed neither the view nor the touch, and that, no matter what the photo that would certainly be circulated would show, he did not "enjoy himself" as Lettie had encouraged him to do.

Lettie could simply not not believe one so sincere. A quick peck on the cheek confirmed his credibility and innocence and sent Pierce Arrow striding purposefully toward the Bank of Hardlyville and Banker Jamin.

The delegation had already departed. On the way out, the delegation leader had felt secure enough to promise a visit from potential project managers within two days so the committee chairs could become more comfortable with the proposed day-to-day operations and the twin brothers who would lead them. Jamin thought this was probably a good idea before asking the community to endorse a final conclusion.

Ol' Dill, who had gotten wind from Sheriff Sephus that the secret big city delegation was trying to get him arrested for dinging their fancy car and that they had returned in a Hummer, was waiting at the town stoplight, pulled to the side of the road as if parked. The Hummer sat through two green lights just to make sure no cross traffic would materialize. At the third green, the Hummer driver pulled slowly and cautiously through. Ol' Dill popped up from his prone position in the driver's seat, jammed his old car into drive, and squealed through the red light, clipping the Hummer's rear bumper before carrying on downtown, horn blaring. The delegation was shaken but grateful to be leaving this crazy burgh.

Pierce Arrow barged into Banker Jamin's office, catching both he and Captain Happy napping. His agitated state caused both to sit up and stare. Pierce explained briefly what the delegation leader had attempted in his office while the others were meeting, namely the purchase a "yes" vote for the sale of Hardlyville. He added that an incriminating photo would likely surface if he refused to submit to bribery. He then shared the image with both from his phone. Banker Jamin blushed deeply and covered his eyes. Captain Happy asked Pierce to e-mail him a copy.

Pierce reported that he had told Lettie everything and that she was comfortable with bearing the embarrassment that would be forthcoming. He intended to go directly to the president of Lolly, Gag, and Maggot, LLC, PC with the whole sordid tale and demand that the delegation leader be removed from the Hardlyville negotiations.

Pierce Arrow could not support the transaction but sought no more influence than to simply share his reasoning. The final call, whatever that might be, belonged to the voters. But to witness citizen leaders dealing with a crook was more than he could bear. He intended to flush her supple ass down and out.

Captain Happy acknowledged that, while his vote might be for sale under such circumstances, he admired Pierce Arrow's morality. Banker Jamin could only shake his head in disbelief. All agreed they would keep this blatant attempt to extort Pierce Arrow to themselves until Pierce had a chance to pursue his strategy, as there was no need to unduly alarm the citizenry because of the actions of a bad character with evil intentions and a world-class body.

Doin and Goin

As promised, project site managers, Doin and Goin Voit, arrived in two days. Captain Happy called a quick introductory meeting in Banker Jamin's office for all committee chairs.

The identical twins were clad in matching overalls and straw hats. Doin would manage the motel. Goin would coordinate guest visitations to the village. Both were ready to start immediately if and when the deal closed. They were clearly putting forth their Hardlyvillain wannabe best.

Pierce Arrow couldn't stand either. First was the false air of authenticity worn like a fresh skunk bath. Second, he couldn't figure out how to pronounce their strange names.

Was Doin named after an act, like doing the wash? Same with Goin, as in going to town? Or were the trailing and identical letters like the twins themselves—odd, odder, and oddest? And did they rhyme with groin? When they nodded "yes" to everything, Pierce felt justified in his snap judgement. Yet another link in the rusty chain of unsavory characters and intentions emanating from the bowels of Lolly, Gag, and Maggot, LLC, PC.

He decided to call them Dong and Gong as a statement of disgust. They appeared to answer to that as well.

Pierce left shortly thereafter for the big city to meet with the big man, who had reluctantly agreed to his request for an urgent personal discussion. Big Man did not like members of the press, but this was an important enough deal for the firm that he felt he had better hear him out. Pierce actually had a strangely comfortable feeling for the guy as he grasped his firm handshake.

After pleasantries, Pierce described in great detail the efforts of the delegation leader to buy his vote. He closed by sharing the cell phone selfie and demanding that she be removed from Hardlyville negotiations immediately. Big Man muttered something about "not again" and nodded his concurrence. He started to explain to Pierce that the delegation leader was one of his most successful sales professionals but that, on occasion, she got carried away with the whiff of victory, the thrill of the deal, the climax of closing, so to speak. But then he recalled that Pierce was press and simply promised a new delegation leader immediately.

After Pierce expressed his appreciation, he noted that this successful sales professional was anything but, and he hoped she would not realize a single penny of commission if the transaction indeed closed. He also asked that Lolly, Gag, and Maggot, LLC, PC destroy any copies of the offending photograph and agree to disavow its accuracy if it should ever surface publicly. More concurrence and a quiet word of apology followed Pierce through the office door.

It hadn't taken Billious Bloom and Chuck Hendricks long to discover that they had several things in common.

First, they were physically attracted to one another. Second, they were both sex-starved—Chuck from months of divorce mandated abstinence in the interest of his child custody image,

Billious from years of virginity that she had just begun to catch up on. Finally, they both loved to travel—Billious to all corners of the earth in search of rare Latin manuscripts, Chuck to famous trout and salmon fisheries around the globe in search of fly-fishing nirvana.

In fact, in their first postcoital conversation beyond customary intimacies, Chuck had regaled Billious with his recent Mongolian adventure, which had taken him to the world-famous Eg River to seek giant taimen. One that he landed exceeded fifty-five inches in length. Billious teased that it was only slightly longer than that which had just pleasured her, sending Chuck into waves of deep-red blush and laughter. This is fun, he grinned.

Billious wondered aloud what might be Latin to pursue should Chuck invite her on a return visit to Mongolia, then remembered that Genghis Khan had ruled what is now Italy and surely had looted ancient treasures that made their way back to Mongolian museums. Chuck issued such an invite on the spot, and Billious made a note to commence research on Latin antiquities in Ulaanbaatar, Mongolia, as soon as she dealt with Chuck's resurgent needs.

Their shared commonalities had taken only two conversations to materialize. The first, over coffee immediately following their initial meeting in Banker Jamin's office with the creepy investment bankers, had resulted in an invitation to dine at Billious' residence the following evening.

Billious knew that she was feeling something special about Chuck after spending the whole afternoon preparing a homemade Bolognese sauce for her hand-cut tagliatelle noodles and putting together a tiramisu to die for.

When Chuck arrived with a bottle of Super Tuscan, Billious took it from his hand, placed it on the dining room table next to the steaming pasta, kissed him softly on the lips, and led him to her bed.

When they emerged two hours later, the cat had eaten most of the pasta, the simmering sauce had crusted around the edges, and the tiramisu was elevated to main course. They could not have cared less and were lost in the glow of mutual satisfaction.

They grew in lust and love on a daily basis thereafter, and the village smiled its blessing on their comingling. Their trajectories had taken different orbits to the point of concurrence, but neither could question the propitious timing of their intersection.

Pierce went straight to Banker Jamin's office after his successful confrontation with the Lolly, Gag, and Maggot, LLC, PC top brass. He caught Jamin and Captain Happy napping again and begin to wonder if this is how they passed most days.

Jamin nodded his approval to the outcome of the meeting and the promise of a new delegation leader. Captain Happy was less enthusiastic in that he still had a vote for sale but congratulated Pierce on his quick and decisive action in the name of honesty and fair play. He could always hope for another looker in the delegation leader succession. It was such a scumbag industry, this world of investment banking, that anything was possible.

Then Pierce Arrow laid it all out on the table as clearly as he could paint the picture of his own conflicted conclusions.

He promised that he only wanted what was best for Hardlyville, whatever that might be. Financial security for a village that had never had the comfort of such was a valid objective. He simply did not believe that selling out a name, a village, a history, and a heritage was right under any circumstance. Or for any amount of money.

He also believed in the rights of those who disagreed with him and with the due process that had been laid out to bring the final decision to a full vote of the citizenry. He wished Thomas Hardly, Octavia Rosebeam, Lucas Jones, and other dear deceased had votes as well, but he understood that this was not Chicago. A free vote after a thorough and unbiased analysis was the Hardlyvillain way, attempted sexual suasion and misconduct notwithstanding.

But this was where he was going to draw the line. Like any sincere Hardlyvillain, he too had a right to express his opinion on such a weighty decision. And he happened to own the *Daily Hellbender*. Its editorial voice was his voice, and he had been working on putting that voice to paper when the cheap bitch had come peddling her wares to steal his vote.

This editorial, he explained, would be the most provocative, controversial, and widely read since his piece on "passion" and the visit of French porn actress Florence Hormel several years back. While much attention had been focused on airbrushed photographs of the scantily, if not unclad, Ms. Hormel, some readers had actually read his insightful analysis of the inspiration she had brought to the village with her unadulterated sense of passion shared. His conclusion that she had left Hardlyville better than she found it was embraced by most. He hoped his current editorial position—that selling Hardlyville to the highest bidder was a really bad deal—would be greeted with equal enthusiasm. People were anxious to hear from his paper on this critical issue, and he would not disappoint them.

Jamin shook his head in concern. He knew most who had been involved in the analytical work of the three committees were in favor of the Lolly, Gag, and Maggot, LLC, PC proposal, perhaps with a few tweaks here and there, but rock solid in their determination to move the community forward. He also knew that Pierce's avowed opposition would resonate with many in the community. After all, they had all voted for him.

Jamin's real dilemma was trying to figure out what he himself thought. He had rolled the numbers through his subconscious time and time again, awake and asleep. They seemed to make sense, but he was a banker. Something could always go wrong, something he couldn't anticipate but had a vague sense of in the back of his mind. And he was really struggling with rationalizing the right to sell something no one really owned—Hardlyville's history.

At the bottom line on the far horizon, Jamin saw a community that had pulled together through unmitigated disasters—from the Big Pig Flood to floating naked dead men to terrorist attacks and an attempted lynching. Hardlyville was in a fragile state of togetherness. Should they risk ripping asunder the bonds that bind for a few dollars more?

Captain Happy suggested an emergency meeting of the committee chairs, their members, and the civic leaders to thrash it all out. Namely: Should the issue of selling Hardlyville be taken to the voters or pulled off the docket? Jamin and Pierce agreed that this was the appropriate course at this critical juncture in Hardlyville history.

As the meeting commenced, Captain Happy served as moderator and opened the floor for opinions. He made it clear that this was not an official committee report but an informal forum for expressions of support or concern. Everything was off the record and nonattributable.

Most present felt the sale of Hardlyville to a consortium of investors under the general terms of the deal crafted by Lolly, Gag, and Maggot, LLC, PC was in the best long-term interest of the community. Pierce Arrow was eloquent in his opposition. Several supporters of the deal flinched with guilt when he invoked the name of beloved souls long gone, who had invested their lives in Hardlyville. One rebutted that they had invested in fellow citizens, not a name. Jamin wore a particularly pained look.

Captain Happy suggested that each participant reflect on each other's thoughts overnight and that they gather for breakfast at Tiny Taylor's Greasy Spoon Grill and Bar at six a.m. the next day to see if a consensus on how to move forward could be reached. If not, committee work would proceed at an accelerated pace with the goal of scheduling a community vote within a week. Tiny didn't mind the early morning griddle work or the income, but she wanted assurance that her input would be heard between bacon and eggs. Most parted with a sense of looming conflict and division.

About midnight, a solitary match sparked a trail of gasoline that snaked toward the front door of the *Daily Hellbender*.

Fired

The big man at Lolly, Gag, and Maggot, LLC, PC summoned the delegation leader to his office immediately after Pierce Arrow exited. She greeted him with her customary passionate embrace. Their relationship was well known to all in the firm, as well as his spouse. All overlooked their thinly veiled indiscretions in the interest of income, spouse included.

He filled her in on Pierce Arrow's report and demands. Big Man guessed he would have to fire her again. He smiled wickedly. She shrugged and reached for the zipper of his suit pants.

Her cell phone rang, and the caller ID provoked an immediate response. Her frown caught his attention and tamed their ritual. After hanging up, she shared the news just provided by a committee member whose vote she had successfully acquired, and saving the deal moved front and center. The bastard Pierce Arrow was laying it all on the line to derail that very deal and would use his *Daily Hellbender* to sway the community.

As she laid out her plan, the big man marveled that the delegation leader had been able to secure the services of a severe scoundrel, whom she had learned about from Sheriff Sephus

Adonis himself in casual conversation. The most wanted man in Hardlyville history had been hard to track down in hiding, but once contacted, he had been more than willing to accept her retainer. He had also proven to be a surprisingly palatable lover for a badass ol' hillbilly in their one encounter to negotiate a deal. He hated Hardlyville as much as they hated him and was willing to do anything to expand on that premise.

She excused herself from the big man, promising to return soon so they could consummate her firing. He smiled broadly, repeating again how much he valued his most dedicated deal closer and assuring her that this termination would be no more problematic than previous ones, provided consummation lived up to expectations.

Her call to the scoundrel's cell was answered immediately, though reception was prickly due to his location deep in the Ozark hills. She emphasized the need to silence the *Daily Hellbender* within the next twenty-four hours. She didn't care how it was done, but it must be shut down before Arrow could stir up the community against the deal. She promised to deliver ten thousand dollars personally once proof was established of the paper's incapacitation and noted that she particularly looked forward to the "personally" part. She needed to know nothing more than "mission accomplished."

Aimless Bevel gathered two of his top aides and vetted options and opportunities. Within hours, a final solution for the *Daily Hellbender* was in play.

Being a Thursday, Tiny Taylor was in route home from her monthly visit to Ol' Dill. He had been unusually lethargic that particular evening, and even her most provocative striptease had failed to energize him enough to do more than just watch. They had lain together until he drifted into sleep, and she had gently lifted his arm to reclothe and head for her own bed.

It was a cool evening, threatening rain. Thunder rumbled just beyond Skunk Creek. She would have to hurry to avoid getting drenched, not a pleasant thought in her tiny faux-silk nightgown and nothing else. Maybe next month with Ol' Dill would be more rewarding for both.

She walked briskly through downtown before slowing to listen to a brief exchange of words, most unusual for that hour. Who could possibly be up, let alone conversing, on a stormy midnight like that one? She caught a brief whiff of smoke before the skies unloaded, followed closely by a boom of thunder.

As she ran toward home, she turned a corner into a fiery blast at the front door of the *Daily Hellbender* . . . and Aimless Bevel, who grabbed her about the waist and ran toward a waiting pickup and two more of his heathens. Amid her panicked screams, he tossed her into the lap of one in the backseat and crawled into the driver's seat, engine roaring.

Tiny Taylor was no stranger to violence. She had been sexually abused or raped by two of her many previous husbands, as well as several assholes she had dated. As the laughing backseat visage belched whiskey fumes and grabbed at her tiny breasts through the flimsy material, Tiny Taylor, all eighty-eight pounds of her, did what she had been taught in the self-defense class she had finally taken after the last sexual assault.

She karate chopped his windpipe, rendering him gasping for air, bit into his earlobe, bringing blood and screams of pain, reached across his lap to the car door handle with one hand and pounded his gonads with the other, before leaping through the door as it swung open. Her groper was left only with what remained of her nightie, the one so dear to Ol' Dill.

Tiny Taylor landed hard in the gravel—rain pouring, wheels spinning clouds of wet dirt into her nostrils before braking and reversing in pursuit. She realized that something was broken on her left side and that blood was spurting from an open wound on her arm, but she had to run clear of the truck or she would surely die an evil death.

Suddenly, shots rang out from the second floor of the *Daily Hellbender*. One shattered the pickup's windshield, spraying glass into Aimless Bevel's face. A second broke through the driver's side window, planting shotgun pellets in Aimless Bevel's neck and shoulder. He had enough presence of mind to shift back into drive before passing out across the front seat. The backseater leapt into the driver's seat, shoving Bevel to the floor, and roared away, leaving Tiny Taylor covering her nakedness with small bloody arms and Pierce Arrow, who had been sleeping at the *Hellbender* so as to get an early start on his lead editorial, trying to reload the shotgun he so despised so he could get just one more crack at the departing devils.

The pouring rain tamped down the flames closest to the front door of the *Hellbender*, but the gasoline trail that spread beneath the door exploded in a small firestorm that spread through the front of the first floor. Pierce Arrow raced down the stairs, grabbed a wall fire extinguisher, and sprayed the advancing flames, standing his ground on top of his antique printing press.

Sheriff Sephus was awakened by the ruckus and drove up with his siren blaring. Airreal, clad in a robe and gown, ran to Tiny Taylor, curled naked on the ground, and wrapped her in the robe. Both were sobbing now.

Sheriff screamed to Pierce to abandon ship and leave his burning building behind. Then, seeing Pierce atop his printing press, locked in hand-to-hand combat with the advancing fire line, Sheriff plowed through the burned-out front door, unloading one of two fire extinguishers along the way before emptying the second one into Pierce's front line of defense. The two stared at each other as their efforts finally reduced the roaring flames to a whimper.

Sheriff Sephus Adonis would always remember a defining image from the moment: Pierce Arrow, covered with soot and coughing up smoke, atop his press, protecting its and his freedom with his life.

Sheriff stomped at the remaining embers and was soon joined by Pierce in restoring singed order to prior chaos. They embraced amidst the smoke before stumbling back through the front door to find Airreal holding Tiny Taylor close in the now slacking rain that had saved the *Daily Hellbender*. Tiny had passed out from the pain of her fractured leg and the loss of blood from the gash up her arm. Doc Karst arrived in time to stem the bleeding with a tourniquet and carted her to his office to deal with the rest.

Many in town were now awake and wandering about in confusion. Lettie came running to the *Hellbender*, unable to find Pierce at home and sure he had retreated there for the night. She sobbed when she saw the burned-out building and again when she found Pierce and Sheriff huddled in the now misty night, trying to figure out what had happened.

They determined that several things were clear:

✓ Someone had set out to burn down the *Daily Hellbender* and had nearly succeeded.

✓ Tiny Taylor had been abducted by several men in a pickup and thrown naked from it.

✓ She may have saved Pierce's life with her screams.

✓ He may have saved hers with his shotgun.

No one could hazard a guess as to the who or the why. Maybe Tiny could fill in some blanks when she emerged from Doc Karst's sedative. Who in the world would do such a thing?

All were stunned the next morning when Tiny Taylor confirmed that Aimless Bevel and several of his boys were the arsonists. Tiny confessed with a blush that she stumbled on to it all as she was returning from her monthly date with Ol' Dill, which explained her state of undress. They had attempted to abduct her, and she had escaped the clutches of a nasty hillbilly in the backseat with her self-defense techniques. She confirmed that Bevel had been driving and thus was likely the "who" Pierce wounded, perhaps mortally. The "why" hung in the air like a soiled question mark.

Tiny would be fine, despite her broken leg and the arm gash that required sixteen stitches. What was certain was that she would not be serving breakfast to committee and civic leaders, whom Jamin herded back into his board room for a final sit-down.

Captain Happy asked Pierce Arrow to share what had happened during the night with those who had not heard. He added that Tiny Taylor regretted not being able to serve breakfast that morning but wanted it known to this gathering that she was opposed to proceeding with the sale of Hardlyville at that time. She had grave concerns as to whether it was right, or even legal, based on Pierce's comments, and she was particularly spooked by the events of the past six hours, which seemed intended to shut Pierce Arrow up. Her instincts screamed to her that there was more to that effort than Aimless Bevel.

At the exact time that the critical discussion was taking place, one committee chair was sitting in Sheriff Sephus Adonis' office, not Jamin's board room. Undertaker Bob was sobbing. Sheriff Sephus was confused but knew better than to undertake the aggressive questioning he was best known for.

When Undertaker Bob regained his composure, he asked Sheriff not to compromise his long marriage to wife Peaches with what he was about to share. Sheriff nodded, adding that only if it did not involve an illegal act on the undertaker's part. Sheriff had always been quite fond of the man, as was all of the community.

Undertaker Bob said he had sold his vote on the sale of Hardlyville transaction for oral sex. He resumed sobbing. Sheriff didn't know whether to join him or laugh.

Undertaker Bob recounted the visit he had received at the small morgue from the delegation leader on her last trip to town. It had begun with normal pleasantries, but when it became clear that Bob was a fence-sitter on the final decision, she upped the ante. She inquired what it would take to convince him that the deal was in the long-term best interest of Hardlyville. He shrugged, not knowing where she was headed. That changed in the time it took her to completely disrobe and place his hand on one of her gorgeous breasts. Having never seen or touched anything like it, he couldn't restrain himself from grabbing the other.

The delegation leader began to fondle Bob in such a way as had never happened in thirty-eight years of marriage. Or before. Bob moaned that he had never cheated on Peaches, and the delegation leader assured Undertaker Bob that what she was about to do would merely confirm that the sale of Hardlyville to benevolent investors was the proper course of action for a village at constant risk of insolvency, would not be considered cheating on his wife by even strict constructionists of fidelity, and would feel better than anything he had ever experienced. When she was finished, he had to agree with all of her conclusions.

She asked only in passing as she reclothed that Undertaker Bob contact her on the cell phone number she scribbled on her souvenir underwear, with a heart encasing her name, if anything appeared to put the deal at risk.

He had called her after it became clear that Pierce Arrow was preparing to unload on the deal in his upcoming lead editorial. He suspected that she had something to do with the attack on the *Daily Hellbender*. Sheriff Sephus Adonis agreed with his conclusion and promised to protect his confidentiality.

Sheriff strode immediately into Banker Jamin's office, announcing to all assembled that he had important information to add to the discussion. He shared that the lead delegate from Lolly, Gag, and Maggot, LLC, PC was a principal suspect in the arson attack on the *Daily Hellbender*. He confirmed that he had learned of her probable involvement from a confidential but reliable source. He was prepared to issue a warrant for her arrest immediately and have it served by local law enforcement at the investment banking firm's headquarters. He confirmed Aimless Bevel as the direct perpetrator of arson, but he hinted at a broader conspiracy keyed to coercion and bribery centered in Lolly, Gag, and Maggot, LLC, PC. He recommended to all assembled that they table any further discussion of the deal until his investigation was complete and justice was served.

Banker Jamin nodded in shock and agreement as those gathered whispered their concurrence.

Chuck raised his hand, which had been resting on Billious Bloom's thigh beneath the conference table, to ask a question about how long such an investigation and legal proceedings might take. Sheriff could only shrug and offer "maybe months or even years." Chuck replaced his hand to its happy resting place, where it was stroked softly by Billious. Both realized that their time together would be coming to an end and stared at each other with questioning eyes, Billious' leaking a tear. They had much to discuss.

The delegation leader and the big man had celebrated far into the night. As promised, he fired her, she applied for reinstatement, he agreed to consider a probationary arrangement, and they concluded the discussion with an extended frolic in his private sleeping quarters nested just behind the office confines. Two bottles of Dom Perignon helped seal this particular sub-deal.

Her cell phone rang early the next morning. Aimless Bevel was barely coherent, but he was able to confirm that the *Daily Hellbender* had been consumed by fire, presumably with asshole Arrow trapped within, but he, Aimless Bevel, had been seriously wounded during his escape. He also shared that a witness had stumbled onto the scene and would be able to ID him as the arsonist. He would survive but be incapacitated for several weeks, according to the country doctor he had kidnapped to provide urgent medical attention. He assumed that the firm would provide a stipend to cover the bills associated with his heroic service in addition to the flat fee and personal attention promised by the lead delegate. She agreed with a smile that the mission had indeed been accomplished, and Mr. Bevel's compensation would reflect the risk incurred in executing his brilliant scheme.

She returned to her pardoning benefactor, reaffirming that the deal would be consummated before resuming negotiations of another sub-deal. She was at her best with many balls in the air.

They were interrupted by a voice behind a knock on the office sleeping quarter's door that demanded immediate entry by virtue of police authority. She crawled under the rollout bed in all her naked glory while the big man threw on a bathrobe and unbolted the lock. He demanded to know the cause of the intrusion into his personal sleeping quarters. When advised that the presenting officer had a warrant for the arrest of a female employee of the firm, who was last seen in the big man's office, he stated that she had left the premises long ago and he had no idea where she was.

One officer wondered to whom the red thong in the corner might belong. The big man presumed it was his wife's, though he couldn't remember for sure. She had joined him during the night before leaving for an early appointment. The officers parted with the admonition that the big man contact them should he become aware of the whereabouts of the female employee in question. He nodded in affirmation, closed the door, and dialed first his wife, demanding that she confirm his story, and then his attorney.

The delegation leader crawled out from beneath the rollaway and sat a few moments in stunned and naked silence. She cursed the bastard undertaker with the silly name. She wondered what she could do next. She had often traded sex for profit and rarely left either side of the transaction lacking. Nothing illegal in that, as far as she could figure. But then along came that sanctimonious newspaper editor Arrow, who was too good for her finest offerings. That had never happened before. And the idiot undertaker, who had obviously squealed on her after sampling her business acumen. That was a new experience as well, as most begged for more.

What was with this crazy village of Hardlyville? She had originally sensed the moral compass of a town drunk, the greed of a bank robber, and the intelligence of rock, all buried deep beneath a simpleton facade. She had been wrong. The deal was brilliant, easy to understand, and beautiful. Everyone gets rich, just like that yahoo Captain-something had pointed out. Who couldn't see that? Evidently, a few hopeless hicks. There was more to that village, that space in the road, than misplaced history.

And now, talk about different. Arson? Attempted kidnapping? Maybe even murder? What if her man, Aimless Bevel, got caught? They surely knew it was him by now if there had been a witness, as he had suggested. If authorities could link the delegation leader to his acts of violence, she too would be would be indicted, perhaps as the premeditator. That spelled jail with a capital J. The corporate attorney had confirmed as much to the big man in their short conversation, warning that even he might be dragged into a web of deceit, bribery, and mayhem. He had warned Big Man to stand down from the delegation leader immediately and to whisk her to the outer ends of the earth until the air cleared. She asked what that meant, tears forming along her mascara-caked eyes. Big Man didn't know but ordered her to reclothe and exit his back office hideout immediately.

He then changed his mind, as Big Men are prone to do.

"What if?" he conjectured. "What if I whisk you off into the very Ozark woods where this guy Bevel and his boys are hiding out?" She could hang there for a month or two until the two-bit town completed its investigation and lost interest in justice. She would return to the firm on a probationary basis until another major deal that needed help closing presented, then earn her way back into corporate good graces by sealing it successfully. Delegation Leader Extraordinaire. Again.

She really didn't like the idea of spending weeks or months with a bunch of dirty, horny hillbillies, but alternatives were hard to come by. Besides, Bevel hadn't been that bad. He claimed that his hideout was comfortable and beyond detection. He had, in fact, invited her there for a long weekend once their business relationship was culminated. He promised that his running mates bordered on being gentlemen and that she would be treated as one of the gang. She wouldn't even have to sleep her way to the top as she was already starting there.

The delegation leader accepted the big man's offer of exile and transportation thereto. He dialed the firm's transportation pool and requested that a modest pickup truck be dispensed immediately to the back door of the back room of his office. He promised the delegation leader that this deal was the best he could offer under the threatening circumstances that hovered over him and the firm.

Big Man was certain Hardlyville would reject the deal, but he would beat them to the punch, personally calling on village leaders that very afternoon with a message of condolence for their travail. He would suggest that the deal be tabled because of extenuating circumstances, perhaps allowing for a revisit after the village had time to settle down and potential investors were given breathing room. It was all in the spin.

In addition, he would advance twenty-five thousand dollars in cash to the fired delegation leader to pay off Bevel and his medical bills, as well as provide her with living expenses, though he doubted there would be many. It was just another "win-win."

Her call to Bevel was accepted immediately. He was delighted that his long weekend offer was not only accepted but extended indefinitely because of her interest in getting to know him and his colleagues on a more personal basis. She was directed to the small town of their first encounter for rendezvous. He would personally pick her up there and escort her to their three-star hideout. He knew there was nothing to worry about, but she should be aware that her delivery vehicle would be trailed by several of his boys to assure that no one was following. Simple safety precautions for a daring and debonaire criminal and lover.

The big man wished the fired delegation leader safe travels and promised to call her when the furor died down, as it most certainly would. He would reserve a place on his rollaway for her return.

How do sleazebags part? With gropes, passing of funds, and mutually despicable lies.

It took several hours to reach the small-town destination where Aimless Bevel waited in his wounded pickup truck. He explained that the windshield had been shot out by Pierce Arrow from his burning office and that the driver's window was the one that had caused Aimless the most pain, pointing to his bandaged face and shoulder. He asked for the cash before releasing the delivering pickup from duty, then heartily waived it on after counting out fifteen thousand dollars.

His boys led the way on a dirt track about ten miles out of town off a gravel country road that had begun as pavement. Deeper into the woods they wound before crossing a small creek and ducking into a cave garage just beyond. They covered the vehicles with camo netting and led the fired delegation leader through a narrow passage to a large common room, well lit and adequately furnished, where other females in various states of dress waited with cold beer drawn from kegs situated in a large spring. A shared rough-hewn table was set with smoked meats and large bowls of sweet potatoes.

At the meal's end, Aimless Bevel took the fired delegation leader's hand and retreated to his own private rock crevice bedroom. Their reengagement disappointed neither. As they drifted off to sleep, she asked if he had ever thought about robbing banks.

Redeal

Banker Jamin gathered committee chairs and civic leaders for a formal debriefing.

All agreed the deck had been stacked. Even Steele, a strong supporter of selling Hardlyville in the interest of long-term financial security, acknowledged that someone had gotten into the wrong bed with somebody before Hardlyville was offered the transaction.

Were the numbers flawed? Probably not, confirmed Banker Jamin. Were there investors out there who would consider buying Hardlyville or someplace like it for a speculative ROI? Probably, confirmed Chuck.

But Lolly, Gag, and Maggot, LLC, PC were bad characters all the way around. That their big man CEO had showed up the very afternoon of the attacks on Pierce Arrow and the *Daily Hellbender* to offer condolences and request that the deal be tabled had only added to the stench.

All also agreed that further discussions with anyone about selling Hardlyville should be discontinued, at least for the present. The big man had intimated that he knew of other investors who would be interested in some iteration of the original deal, and he said he would endeavor to pull them together over time with an even more favorable proposal for the village's consideration. Jamin nodded no, and Captain Happy confirmed the same message verbally.

Steele, Mayor, and several others professed to retaining a sincere interest in considering a comparable or even more favorable proposal sometime in the future. The philosophical split among community leaders had not been bridged, though all agreed that only players of the highest repute and integrity be given consideration. Several wondered if such an animal existed in the world of big deals.

Pierce Arrow agreed not to further enflame passions. He would pull his lead editorial from the following morning's *Daily Hellbender*. That was a bit of an exaggeration. With his office in shambles, he had prepared a one pager on his Mac to read on the street corner to any and all who would listen. Now he would limit his remarks to observing that the village had been offered an interesting investment opportunity that all involved in the analysis thereof had concluded was not in their best interest.

Sheriff Sephus, who had been invited to the final wrap-up meeting, assured all that he would work tirelessly to track down Aimless Bevel and his brood. He wasn't certain about the lead delegate, as she had apparently disappeared from the face of the earth per her local law enforcement. Not much to pursue against Lolly, Gag, and Maggot, LLC, PC in that they would claim that all wrongdoing was the result of a rogue official acting totally on her own. Sheriff would focus all of his energy and efforts on Bevel.

Banker Jamin adjourned the final meeting of community leaders analyzing the sale of Hardlyville with a short admonition, issued through Captain Happy, that the village be grateful for its blessings not covetous of what it lacked. The small, somber group parted weary but without regret.

Except Chuck Hendricks and Billious Bloom. Their romance had blossomed during this time of crisis in Hardlyville. Chuck had been well paid by the Bank of Hardlyville for his consulting services, but with the final meeting, his hourly billings ceased. His big city firm would not understand if he lingered much beyond the term of his engagement. He had treasured the time with his mother, Flotilla, and his nephew, Otis, son of dear departed Sabrina. But more significantly, he had fallen in love.

Billious Bloom was everything his first wife wasn't. She was engaged, energetic, sexy, and at times wanton. Such a difference from bored, lazy, cold, and predictable. Well, maybe he had contributed to the latter's state of mind and body, but it had just never worked. And she got the kid.

Chuck took Billious to Tiny Taylor's Grill and Bar for lunch and to pop a serious question or two. Billious ordered her favorite off-menu item: Tiny's famous *vaccinium erythrocarpum* stew. Chuck followed suit before asking why, his mind and heart on graver matters, but the question soon followed. In answering, Billious proclaimed her love of the melodious Latin name, the savory aroma, and the unique texture. Chuck inquired as to the translation.

"Dingleberry stew," Billious replied with a wicked grin on her face that sent Chuck racing to Tiny's kitchen to change his order.

Tiny laughed heartily at Chuck's sense of urgency before observing that she handpicked her dingleberries to assure ripeness and proper aging. This sent Chuck running to Tiny's one holer out back of the grill, moaning that he had kissed lips through which dingleberry stew had passed.

He soon returned, pale and sweating, to Billious and Tiny, who were doubled over with laughter. Once she regained steady breathing, Tiny explained that her dingleberry stew featured southern mountain cranberries, real not slang dingleberries, that flourished on small bushes throughout the Southeast. Her tiny transplanted patch found Ozarkian soil to its liking and thrived.

Chuck reluctantly allowed his original order to stand until Billious added that Rocky Mountain oysters add substance and flavor to Tiny's stew. Chuck swore off *vaccinium erythrocarpum* stew on the spot and forever. He would stick with fried catfish for the remainder of his stay.

Menu issues resolved, Chuck proclaimed straight up to Billious his need to be with her. He asked her to move to be with him. She hesitated before declining because of her responsibilities and loyalty to the Rosebeam Endowment, all the while shedding heartfelt tears. Plus, she loved Hardlyville.

"Why don't you move back home?" she suggested.

It would place him closer to his dear mother and nephew and securely in the arms of one who loved him. He waffled around about what he might do for a living, as no one in the region could afford to pay him what he currently earned.

It was the same old round about and back and forth that professionals in love with another engage in and become entrenched in when big decisions are required. Chuck finally asked if it would make any difference if he asked her to marry in terms of moving. Billious again hesitated before confirming "no," and they remained stuck in a traffic jam of wishful thinking.

Chuck even tacked on two weeks of his vacation to postpone the inevitable parting. Still, no budge on either front. He did reconfirm his invitation to take Billious to Mongolia when he returned there fishing the following season, but that was the extent of their shared commitment. It seemed that each thought the other would give, but neither did.

Their lovemaking became even more passionate as much of Hardlyville lived vicariously through their antics. Ol' Dill even tried to sneak a peek through Billious' drawn curtains one moonlit night but couldn't even begin to describe what he had seen to Tiny Taylor. Something about costumes, foreign language recitations, and flying feet. Tiny could only shake her head at his intrusion into their privacy. She did wear an exotic dancer costume to their next Thursday playtime and uttered a few phrases in Spanish, bringing out the best in her old gentleman friend and lover.

And when it was time for Chuck and Billious to part, both swore that they would pay the other a visit soon but left it at that. Chuck's departure was a sad occasion for a village that liked happy ever after endings.

The Garden, Again

Sally Jones threw a plate at husband Jimmy. This had never happened in their short but blissful marriage. The plate missed Jimmy but shattered against the wall, sending him scrambling for cover.

Sally was pretty far along with their second baby to be, likely the result of their most recent visit to the garden. Three visits there together, two impregnations. The garden was clearly a very fertile place. Though neither would admit it, both sensed this one was a boy and that it would bear the name of Jimmy's deceased cousin-hero Lucas. Doc Karst didn't believe in the ultrasound stuff because he got so much pleasure announcing gender at the moment of truth. He would bellow out "penis" or "vagina" with such enthusiasm that it sometimes caused a baby to have second thoughts on what he or she was getting into.

Sally had a hormone rage every now or then. But this was not hormones. It was all about Cathy Cobb.

Cathy, or CiCi, as she was known, had always had a thing for Jimmy Jones, going back to Hardlyville High School days. Rumor had it she had acted on said thing several times before Jimmy and Sally became an item, but Jimmy had learned long ago to never confirm or deny. Nor had he ever catted around on Sally, before or after their betrothal. He was loyal to Sally, and little Girl Jones and her soon to be brother or sister sealed the deal.

Still, CiCi flirted with Jimmy Jones incessantly. She dated a fishing buddy or two of his so as to serve as shuttle driver for their float trips, and she dressed provocatively at every put-in or take-out as needed. Jimmy pretended not to notice, but he did. What's a young lad to do when every important part of a young woman got flashed at him when no one was looking? CiCi had no regard for marriage or spousal obligations. She simply fancied Jimmy Jones and would not abandon her quest for his infidelity until he broke.

The current crisis evolved from such an occurrence. Jimmy had chased topwater bite with his buddy Quarter Bogus one lovely warm day. Quarter was named in honor of the cost of admission to a neighboring town cinema, where he was likely conceived in the dark back row of a premier showing of *The Lion King*. He lived up to his moniker in every way possible.

Quarter's latest love interest was CiCi, though he hadn't a clue as to why such an attractive young lady would reach out to him. He was far too shy to have initiated any physical contact, let alone the deed itself. CiCi had simply made it impossible for him not to. That she was using him to get to his fishing partner Jimmy Jones had never crossed his mind, though he did take note of the flashes of brilliance CiCi shared with both at put-in or take-out time.

On this particular day, Sally had driven down to Skunk Creek Bridge take-out to provide her own personal greeting. She was feeling fat and full and was perspiring heavily under the ugly pink sweat suit she clothed her girth in. Still, she wanted to see her man, to let him know how much she loved him, and to share in his normal post-float-trip euphoria at its peak.

What she got instead was a peek at CiCi laying a liplock on Jimmy while pressing him against the pickup truck with her body to die for. Sally screamed an obscenity, turned heel, and strode back to her car, wondering why she had ever trusted the sorry son of a bitch to start with. She seethed for the hour it took Quarter to pull CiCi off Jimmy and join him in creating and personally delivering a credible alibi.

Quarter first had to immediately bring himself to break up with CiCi because of her attempted temptation of his best fishing buddy. This was not easily done because CiCi was the first and only filly in Quarter's stable, but Jimmy was worth it. CiCi huffed off, unfulfilled but carrying a half-smile knowing Jimmy's spouse had seen it all and might leave Jimmy for her, CiCi, to pick up the pieces, so to speak.

Jimmy was embarrassed, angry, scared, and innocent. The latter condition he doubted would sell under any current circumstance. He and Quarter tried a dozen scenarios—from CiCi trying to remove a fishhook embedded in Jimmy's lower lip, the result of an errant cast by Quarter, to Jimmy trying to save CiCi's life with mouth-to-mouth resuscitation after she had been bitten by a cottonmouth, to Jimmy trying to show Quarter what a worthless concubine CiCi was by flushing her out in the open, and on and on. Jimmy remembered that he had never really lied to Sally, and now was not the time to begin. He would lay it all on the line, and Quarter would back him to the last honest detail. Except Quarter didn't really know what that detail might be since he had been taking an extended pee break and had only seen what Sally saw—CiCi thrusting herself onto Jimmy, freed breasts accentuating a passionate kiss. For all Quarter knew, Jimmy was just messin' with his best friend's girlfriend, knowing Quarter would forgive him later.

So off they marched, soldiers of truth, to ease Sally's mind. She listened without expression while Jimmy explained how he had been bushwhacked, then wished he had used a different term. Quarter jumped in with his own version, which resembled what Sally had seen and only reinforced Sally's personal observations.

"So much for the truth," moaned Jimmy to no one in particular.

Sally shrugged, Quarter crawfished quickly out the front door, and Jimmy begged Sally to believe him. The plate that whizzed by his head said it all. Except Sally's final order for him to leave immediately, to get out while she figured out what she would do next.

Jimmy was heartbroken. He sobbed an "I love you, Sally" as he closed the door to his house and his life behind him. The only thing he knew to do was to go to Pastor Pat for counseling and advice, which he did. Surely the good preacher had helped other parishioners through situations where nothing appeared as it seemed or something like that. Whatever, Jimmy was short on options. Oh, how he wished Cousin Lucas was still there.

Pastor Pat welcomed Jimmy into his office, unsure what could be the purpose of the visit. When Jimmy explained, Pastor Pat simply nodded. They sat in silence for fifteen minutes or so—Jimmy waiting for Pastor Pat to share valuable advice and insight, Pastor Pat waiting for Jimmy to tell the truth.

When neither budged, Pastor Pat commanded Jimmy to "come clean" in a deep, otherworldly voice that reeked of religious authority. Okay, Jimmy confessed, he had noticed CiCi's flirtatious advances and even wondered if a brief indiscretion might not be worth it. That truth was tangential to the real truth. He had never initiated nor executed even his deepest lustful urges. He had not given in to CiCi and had remained true to Sally.

Pastor Pat thought he was getting somewhere and launched into his "peeling an onion" metaphor. It was keyed to the theory that removing each layer to the truth produced more tears but, in the end, the fragrant aroma of mercy. Jimmy was having trouble relating the core of an onion to fragrance and mercy. He sensed he was being prejudged but decided to play along.

Pastor Pat followed with one of his favorite questions for philanderers, something about why Jimmy reckoned God made sex feel so good. Whatever Jimmy answered, Pastor Pat could wind him back to mercy and forgiveness, the pedestal upon which all good marriages were built. Then he would help Sally understand the core of Jimmy's weakness and that it had nothing to do with her, except his need for her mercy and forgiveness, to which she must ultimately accede if she loved him. This line of twisted logic had worked impeccably in nearly every instance of marital infidelity that Pastor Pat had counseled.

Jimmy's response broke the mold and the model. Jimmy reckoned it was because we'd have babies and procreate ourselves, then God wouldn't have to mess with us no more. It wasn't exactly "God is dead," but not far from it. This threw the good reverend in reverse.

Pastor Pat asked Jimmy to repeat his version of the facts, including the corollary lusting in heart considerations. He did and, to Pastor Pat's amazement, his encore did not deviate from the original in any way beyond the corollary considerations. He must be telling the truth, Pastor Pat concluded.

Trying to dig his way out of a dead-end, Pastor Pat challenged Jimmy to reason beyond established parameters. If Sally wouldn't believe the truth, why not tell her a lie? What if Jimmy confessed to carrying on with CiCi far beyond the casual groping Sally had witnessed? What if sex with CiCi felt so good it became something he could simply not not pursue? That would get Jimmy back to the pastor's tried-and-true context for the whys of infidelity and the needs for mercy and forgiveness, all of which gave Sally the consummate power in their marriage. If she loved Jimmy, she would grab it and surely forgive him. If she didn't, she would likely cheat on him at some point in the future and Jimmy, in turn, would govern the balance of power for the duration of their days together.

Jimmy was long lost and asked Pastor Pat if he could diagram this trail of reasoning on a piece of paper. The pastor declined but suggested that Jimmy think it through, sleep on it in the sanctuary that night since he had nowhere else to go, and reconvene for morning prayers at five thirty a.m. Jimmy generally only rose at that hour to go fishing or respond to one of Sally's touches, but in that the latter was clearly at risk, he accepted the pastor's offer.

One of Pastor Pat's greatest gifts was to make nothing out of something in the name of his faith. Jimmy's case had been a tough one, but he went to bed patting himself on the back and praising the power of forgiveness.

Unfortunately, or otherwise, Jimmy awoke with no more inclination to tell Sally a lie than he had gone to bed with. He would trust the truth to carry them through and thanked Pastor Pat for his time and circuitous reasoning before heading back to Sally.

Then it hit him—an urge, a compulsion, a need to be in the garden again. He didn't know why, only that it was this, not CiCi, that he could not not do.

Two hours later, Jimmy rolled the big stone aside, tied his rope to the tree trunk, and slid slowly down into the garden. As always, there was a dim back light in the cavern and a temperate feel engulfing him. He had only been there a few times before, three with Sally and once in the wake of the Big Pig Flood, and had never left unfulfilled, be it conception or confirmation. He sensed that this time would be no different.

He sat in silence for an hour—meditating, praying, absorbing, hoping, begging that Sally might take him at his word, take him back, and put trust back in their relationship. Lust and love had always carried their day, but both knew trust was the solid foundation on which their marriage was built. He must find a way to patch the crack that threatened its collapse.

He snapped out of his trance and decided to explore a bit. All the creatures and critters seemed alive and well. He even saw two baby hellbenders squiggling in their mother's wake. The whole colony seemed to be flourishing.

He poked around a couple of corners in hesitant search of the source of the constant subterranean dimness. He had always been wary of finding or understanding it. Some things were better left to themselves, he had reasoned. But he was focused on truth and understanding in his real life just then, so why not stretch a bit.

He slid through a narrow crevice along a side spring branch. As his eyes adjusted, he sensed a shadow and crawled farther, bending slightly right. He gulped in disbelief. Seated ahead on a rock, facing away, backlit from the dim glow, was a human figure—flipping a coin in the air, catching it, examining it for heads or tails, then flipping it again. The ritual had a vaguely religious feel to it.

Jimmy knew without knowing that it was Cousin Lucas, squashing the doubt in his left brain and nourishing the possibility in his heart. He squatted in silent wonder, not knowing what to do next. That it was done for him provided comfort.

Lucas welcomed Jimmy to paradise. He quoted the one about "many mansions in my Father's house," which Jimmy thought he remembered from New Testament John. Lucas confirmed Jimmy's recollection and explained that this spot happened to be his with a slight nod. Their communication was implied, not heard. Lucas wanted Jimmy to know that he would always be there for him, unable to explain why or how, but firm with the always.

Lucas had dreamed Jimmy to the "X" on the map, the season and day of sign visibility, and the garden itself. That's how Jimmy had found the garden in the first place. Jimmy blushed at the thought of Lucas witnessing, up-close and personal, he and Sally's cavorting around in the raw and their love games. Lucas claimed to have nothing to do with conception, which was beyond his realm of contemplation, but he did not discount the magic of the place.

He had watched Jimmy from afar with pride as his young protégé had grown and matured and become a man of purpose and his word. He respected Jimmy's loyalty to family and village and occasionally trailed behind him when the topwater bite was on. Jimmy said he had sensed that Lucas was there sometimes.

Lucas dipped into the water and lifted a hellbender to briefly caress before passing it to Jimmy, still facing away. Jimmy accepted the priceless gift, acknowledging that he was fearful of touching them on his own, of somehow altering their pristine existence. Lucas nodded his approval of Jimmy's reticence, as well as his gentle stroking.

Lucas knew of the many tragedies to befall Hardlyville and Skunk Creek. It had hurt him to be powerless to help. But he could help Jimmy, and of this he was certain. And he would always be there in times of need. Lucas even knew of Jimmy's current crisis with Sally, which is why he had lured him there.

"Stick with the truth," he counseled. "Just tell the truth."

"Even the part about a tiny bit of lust for CiCi?" Jimmy blushed.

"Nah, too much information," laughed Lucas with that big, deep, joy of life guffaw that made Jimmy smile.

"And Jimmy," he warned, "you can never tell anyone about this, or I will lose my mansion. I am trusting you deeply, for this is indeed heaven for me."

"Not even Pastor Pat?"

"Especially not Pastor Pat." Lucas smiled.

Lucas also suggested that Jimmy seek Pierce Arrow's counsel in that he had just extricated himself from Lettie's doghouse for a similarly connived set up by a nasty investment banker. Jimmy wasn't sure what Lucas was sharing, but he would surely talk to Pierce.

Jimmy hesitated to ask but went ahead anyway. He wondered how Lucas took to having his friend Pierce so deeply involved and in love with his very own Lettie. Making a baby, no less.

Jimmy could feel the warmth of Lucas' smile, though he couldn't see it. Lucas was happy for his friend and widowed wife, that they had found a spark with each other. Sparks were the cat's meow, the rabbit's tail, the homemade cherry pie with ice cream, and Hardlyville was blessed with a fresh harvest of them from Lucas' vantage point. Ol' Dill and Tiny Taylor, Sheriff Sephus and Airreal, The Donald and the Sisters Sledge, Chuck and Billious, Booray and Lil' Shooter, and even Pastor Pat on his occasional forays afield were all on his radar. No, Lucas concluded, sparks were good for a village like Hardlyville and helped it cope with whatever came its way. And since they didn't do sex in God's mansions, at least as far as Lucas could tell, he would have no problem welcoming Pierce and Lettie into his paradise when their time was up. Lucas didn't understand it all, but he knew sparking was good.

Jimmy wanted to hug Cousin Lucas, but he figured that was probably a pretty bad idea. If this was only a dream, he would wake up. If it was real, it might mean he was dead too. Better leave Lucas and the dim light source alone and head straight back to Sally. Lucas nodded his approval, still facing away from Jimmy. Jimmy wondered if he could come back and commune with Lucas when he needed to. Lucas nodded again, rose slowly, and walked away from Jimmy into the shadows. He stopped and flipped a coin over his shoulder. It landed at Jimmy's feet. Jimmy lifted it and, even in the dimness, could see the same big breasted lady and scrawny bird on the front and back respectively. He rubbed it for luck and stuffed it into his jeans pocket.

Jimmy's drive back to Hardlyville offered time for reflection. Except there was nothing to reflect on. There was nothing tangible to bring to the table of common sense except a silver coin, dated 1803. The rest either happened or it didn't. He did feel secure in trying once more with Sally, and that somehow Lucas would have a hand in the outcome and others far beyond. He took comfort in that.

Jimmy found Sally crying in the corner of their living room. Girl was curled up beside her. It was late, and Sally was worried sick. She had seen or heard nothing of Jimmy for over forty-eight hours. Both Quarter Bogus and Pastor Pat had stopped by to beg her to believe Jimmy. She so wanted to, she confirmed, but what she had seen spoke against it.

She had finally called CiCi Cobb and asked her straight up if she and Jimmy were having a go of it. Cici had laughed out loud and affirmed their frequent trysts. When Sally didn't budge and asked for proof, CiCi Cobb began to stammer about one time here and one time there and how fortunate Sally was to have such a stud lover with hands of silk and the staying power of a stallion.

Now it was Sally's turn to laugh. Jimmy's hands were rough as a cob, blistered from woodwork at Rifleman's and scarred from tangles with hooks and fish. CiCi asked why Sally was laughing, and Sally confirmed that at least half of CiCi's equation didn't balance. She couldn't opine on the other but guessed he was more yearling than stallion. "Lucky bitch" were the words Sally heard just ahead of the phone slam and lost connection.

Sally had been wrong to judge Jimmy so harshly. Nothing he had done in their marriage deserved such shallow respect. He had told her the truth, as he always said he did, and now all she wanted was him back.

He knelt beside her as she sniffled, unaware of his return. He gently touched her cheek, arousing her to the reality of his presence and his love. His short-lived absence from her life was over, and her embrace branded him with trust, followed shortly by lust, once Girl was tucked into her crib.

Jimmy patted Sally's belly in the afterglow of their reunion. Her baby bump seemed but a logical extension of time and place.

Reprise

Yet another celebration in Hardlyville. Yet another visit from the president of the United States, his second in fewer than twelve months. The press wondered why he had singled out this tiny burg tucked deep in the Ozarks for so much attention and affection. He responded about "getting back to America's roots and whiffing the scent of what made our country so great."

In actual fact, it had been the provocative follow-up invitation from Miss Lettie that had jerked his chain and twirled his tiny swizzle stick.

On his previous visit to Hardlyville, he had experienced passion and lust on a scale only imagined in the nation's capital, where everything had a price. That tryst had been free. Sure, it represented repayment of a debt, consummation of a deal that had been bought and sold but never closed. Still, it was offered solely in a spirit of good will since his leverage with Miss Lettie, namely the Skunk Creek Watershed National Refuge, had been sacrificed on the altar of a nuclear war near miss. She simply was a lady of her word, and her word was the nectar of the gods.

The president had framed the past visit around a campaign stop for candidate Pierce Arrow and the announcement of the wildlife refuge, but it was the luscious and delectable Miss Lettie that lay at the heart of the matter. And she was everything the president dreamed her to be—a lady of mystery, an ardent lover of insatiable lust, finally accepting of the president's package, and an admirer of the president's stamina. He had returned to Washington energized and inspired to tackle the next global crisis. And though he had never known the concept of love, he wondered if the faint beating in his heart whenever he thought of Miss Lettie was an attendant condition.

The president hadn't a clue that he had been scammed and duped—that he had consumed what he wanted, just at a different and more welcoming trough. All he knew was that he was ready for more.

Lettie had all but promised more on top of more in her handwritten note of invitation to the dedication of the new National Hellbender Memorial. Plus, it would be wise to reprise his role in just elected Congressman Pierce Arrow's shocking upset of Washington insider Larry Larrsnist and leverage it for political influence in a decidedly red part of the country. "Win, win, sin" the president disclosed to his principal aide with a wicked grin. It was up to her to craft a plausible method for the president's apparent madness.

Lettie and Pierce could only smile when the president called personally to accept. Billious Bloom was beside herself that she would get to screw the president of the United States again, even if only under the cover of Lettie. Ms. Bloom had been only too willing to serve as surrogate lover, in the interest of history. Perhaps Hardlyville would never know of or share her sense of triumph, but she was damn sure that she was the only in Hardlyville's storied history to have lain with a sitting president. And to do so in the noble interest of protecting her friend Lettie from the indignity of cheating on her beloved Pierce Arrow to "Save the Skunk" doubled the fun, doubled the pleasure. Billious

Bloom had simply come to love sex for sex's sake, to love Lettie and Pierce for the fierce lovers of each other and the creek that they were, to love her unique role in history, and to love being the facilitator of all of the above.

At least before Chuck. Much had changed since. She knew she was in love with the man and felt he reciprocated her passion. She hadn't slept with another since their first time together. Her fleet of past lovers was adrift and baffled, but they still served her well professionally.

Chuck claimed the same. But still he wouldn't budge on moving back to Hardlyville, nor she on her insistence that she stay put. Her work at the Rosebeam Foundation was simply too important to abandon. Sure, she could relocate it anywhere, but Hardlyville was where it was meant to be. At least she was free to have another go-around with the president and create more Hardlyville history. She wouldn't be entirely guilt free, but not wallowing in it either.

If Chuck wanted her, he would move to Hardlyville, and she would be true in every way. He had visited just the prior weekend and, as always, lust ruled the home roost. But he chose to return and leave Billious alone. At least the president of the United States would pay more attention to her, though he didn't know it was her, Billious Bloom, serving her nation and her Commander in Chief.

The president arrived with his entourage the morning of the dedication. He would lunch with Hardlyville civic leadership, break for a short "nap" in an undisclosed napping place, and break a bottle of cold duck on the nose of the unsuspecting bronze hellbender to seal the deal. That was all Tiny Taylor could find in the wine cellar of her Grill and Bar that had bubbles.

Lunch went well, and the civic leaders applauded his role in helping restore the community. The president basked in their praise and photo ops abounded.

Post lunch, Lettie led him, again on tour, to her secret nesting place. It was darker than a snail's butt, and she suggested that he strip naked and get comfortable on the blanket he could feel below. She promised to return in something more intimate. Just like last time.

And as before, it was the voluptuous Billious Bloom who serviced the president's every napping need. He wondered again to himself why her breasts seemed so much more ample than Lettie presented in public, but he chalked it up to Victoria's Secret and Lettie's natural sense of modesty. After multiple consummations, the president moaned that duty called and promised to return to Hardlyville again and again to pleasure poor Lettie, who was obviously underserved by her live-in partner Congressman Arrow, nothing personal, of course.

He also hoped they could get together with more frequency after she was settled in Washington and while her husband was busy legislating. Billious wasn't quite certain how to answer that one, so she simply squeezed his now deflated member, after searching high and low to find the pitiful little thing. Though she had not seen it in person, she knew it well, and though not large, it was—more importantly—truly presidential. The president pinched her butt with love and affection and wished her good day, promising to see her on the dedication podium as soon as they reclothed. He spoke again of his admiration for a lady of her word. The president even felt his heart flutter and ordered it to be still.

This monument dedication was more somber than the refuge announcement of months past and drew environmentalists from around the country. They gathered to honor the hellbender and its memory as a Skunk Creek resident. Scientists doubted that the species had survived the infamous Pig Flood in any form or fashion. All present wanted to pay tribute to its long run in the Skunk Creek watershed. That the statue would stand on the site of Hardlyville founder Thomas Hardly's original house added historical context and meaning for Hardlyvillains. It could not replace the ancient structure, which had drifted downstream amidst the hog carcasses to a Skunk Creek burial, but it could commemorate it.

As they approached the podium, the president looked in wonder at how poised and professional Miss Lettie looked in a formal business-like suit with nary a hair out of place. He felt a little mussed and frumpy himself and could not believe how quickly she had reassembled herself. They traded winks as Bilious Bloom glowed in the crowd.

The president's remarks were brief and to the point. Greedy corporate interests had dealt a blow to the groin of loyal American Hardlyville, and he, the president of the United States, had stepped in immediately to ease the pain and right the wrong. All of Hardlyville erupted in praise.

In the front row, where they had been given honorary seats, Ol' Dill asked The Donald who had gotten kicked in the nuts and why. The Donald could only smile, confirm it had been the president of the United States, and challenge Ol' Dill to right the wrong.

"Sing what song?" asked Ol' Dill.

"Your call," confirmed The Donald.

Ol' Dill limped to the podium as the president concluded his remarks, grabbed the mike, patted the president's privates, apologizing on behalf of Hardlyville for whoever did the dirty deed, and burst into an old white boy rendition of Marvin Gaye's

"Sexual Healing" before Secret Service agents could wrestle him to the ground.

The president looked desperately at Lettie, fearing they had been caught. Lettie could only laugh as Sheriff Sephus Adonis and The Donald joined the fray to rescue their good buddy Ol' Dill. Even Tiny Taylor leapt on top to protect her rumored part-time lover.

Pierce Arrow tried to restore order by yelling "fire," which prompted Rifleman to empty multiple rounds into the air, dropping a stray mallard on the platform scrum. Combatants looked at one another in fear, wondering if more animal corpses were on their way down Skunk Creek.

Pierce finally asked little Lettie to cut loose with one of her bloodcurdling whistles. That stopped all in their tracks. Pierce promised that all was well in Hardlyville and called for one more round of applause "for our beloved president."

As Sheriff Sephus escorted Ol' Dill back to his honorary seat, Pierce Arrow handed Lettie the bottle of cold duck, who in turn passed it to the president with a warm smile of her own. He pinched her behind as he accepted it, drawing a slap to his hand from Pierce and a hearty laugh from the crowd.

Pierce raised the cloth cover from the statue of the bronzed hellbender and urged the president to smack it with the cold duck, which he did.

"You would think they would have already killed the critter before mounting it on a granite base," observed Ol' Dill to no one in particular.

The president waved goodbye to the Hardlyville he so loved and blew a kiss to Lettie, which she returned with a wink. Billious Bloom swooned in the swaying audience as the motorcade pulled away. The whole party returned in five minutes for directions in that they had gotten lost on the way out of town and landed on a dirt road. They pulled away again to an encore.

As the president sat basking in the glory of a truly exceptional day, his principal aide shoved her camera in his face, suggesting he would enjoy the candid photos she had taken during his "nap" time. He smiled as he riffled through the digital images until he realized that there was Miss Lettie at the beginning, there was Miss Lettie several times in the middle, actually waving to the camera with a big grin and wink, and, of course, there was Miss Lettie at the end. His smile turned to a frown as he asked his principal aide if the images were in chronological order. She confirmed that they were. How could that be, he wondered aloud, since he had been with Miss Lettie throughout "nap" time?

"Obviously not," beamed his principal aide, who had become a bit jealous of the president's Lettie fetish.

"I knew those breasts I was caressing were bigger than what I had seen on Lettie," he moaned. "Who knew whom the president was screwing and where?" shouted the befuddled chief executive.

His principal aide could only shrug and smile. *Can't wait to pass that one along to Woodward and Bernstein for a sequel to "All the President's Men,"* she quipped to herself.

In Memoriam

Pierce Arrow, Lettie Jones, and Sheriff Sephus lingered at the hellbender statue after others had left. Pierce was deep in thought as Lettie and Sheriff Sephus were doubled over in laughter at the naughty trick played on the president. Both were delighted they had pulled the charade off again but knew the jig was up after Lettie had mugged in the principal aide's photo shoot. The principal aide had actually seemed to enjoy that part. Lettie shared that Billious Bloom had claimed to as well. One last presidential go for the home team.

Sure, Billious was in love with Chuck, but he would still be there long beyond the memory of an inconsequential presidential tryst. At least she hoped so. She might even tell Chuck about it one day if they ever got hitched. She guessed he would find the whole thing amusing and might even take pride in counting himself in pretty hifalutin' company. The first time had been historical and pre-Chuck. This one was hysterical, and she was sure Chuck would find it so. She was simply honored to have been a major player in the whole deception.

Sheriff Sephus' walkie-talkie cackled, and he stepped aside to hear better. Seemed that there had just been a violent bank robbery in a small town some thirty miles to the southwest. Two employees had been killed and a customer critically wounded. The suspects included a woman and a man wearing toothless hillbilly masks. They had fled in an old pickup truck. Sheriff excused himself to offer his assistance at the crime site. A bank robbery with multiple casualties? Where did that come from?

Pierce Arrow resumed staring at the two-foot long, green-and-brown statue of the noble hellbender, wondering when the entire species would be lost to humankind. *And at what cost to the civilized corners of our minds and hearts?* The setting sun glinted on the flat head, lighting the beady little eyes. It almost looked alive. Pierce wished it were.

What gives us the right to wreck the habitat for one so durable and strong? How can we accept extinction of a species which has evolved to survive for over ten million years only to finally fall prey to the moneychangers and unholy alliances of the corporate-political complex of today? These were the questions rattling around in his head, and he was now part of that desolate landscape. Could he make a difference? Certainly not much as a one-term congressman from Podunk Hardlyville, which was his stated intention. Lettie called him one and done, with a clear understanding of the concept.

Pierce had run against a ten thousand count industrial piggery in the Skunk Creek watershed. That was gone, now and forever, he hoped, but at great cost to the creek itself. The victory was hollow and scarred. Skunk Creek Ranch and Swine Branch just should never have been.

Of course, the same could be said of the coven of evil, the demon lady with the glaring yellow eyes, the murders of Lucas Jones, Thomas Hardly, innocent floaters, and three naked dead men without gonads, the rape of Octavia Rosebeam, or any of the tragedies in Hardlyville's colorful history.

Still, for every loss there had been a gain of sorts—he and Lettie Jones' affair of the heart, their beautiful little adopted baby daughter with the big yellow eyes, little Mona of their own accord, Ms. Rosebeam's bank theft and subsequent funding of the Rosebeam Endowment, and even the passionate pixie dust sprinkled by the ebullient Mademoiselle Florence Hormel on all of Hardlyville one beautiful spring break, which lingered in the community emotional coffers still. "No pain, no gain," as they always said.

Big Pork can bear the blame for eliminating the Skunk Creek Branch of the hellbender family, but in the end, we are all guilty, Pierce confessed to himself. Perhaps that tiny creature of the deep creek was the most significant unransomed loss of the Hardlyville centuries.

Pierce studied the inscription on the granite base beneath the day's honoree. It would serve nicely in broad, bold print as a front page for the next day's *Daily Hellbender* and set in history that particular moment of celebration and mourning.

IN MEMORIAM OF THE SKUNK CREEK HELLBENDER
Rest in peace, tiny Skunk Creek hero,
lost to greed and avarice forever
from these precious Ozarks waters.

—THE END—

BUT WAIT! THERE'S MORE ...

Don't miss books One and Three in the Ozarkian Trilogy!

Available in print and ebooks.

SKUNK CREEK

~ BOOK I IN THE OZARKIAN FOLK TALES TRILOGY ~

Who knows what lurks in the deep, dark corners of the Ozarks?

A gruesome murder on the banks of Skunk Creek leads to a mystery and a rollicking adventure story. Populated by the crusading editor of a small town newspaper, an oversized Sheriff, a lovable band of merry misfits, and an evil cult, an Ozarks village is steeped in beauty, tragedy, love, and lust.

Hardlyville and her colorful, unforgettable Hardlyvillains bring laughter, tears, and celebration of life at every turn as they seek to prevail over natural and unnatural threats to their way of life.

Warning: Do not read if you blush or tire easily. Skunk Creek grabs readers from page one and rushes on through each disaster and fiasco. In the end, love of place and people carry the day to an unlikely conclusion.

Skunk Creek is rowdy, ribald, insightful, and grounded in Ozarks waters and history. It confronts and entertains amidst the vexing questions of our times.

READ A FREE CHAPTER NOW AT
WWW.PEN-L.COM/SKUNKCREEK.HTML

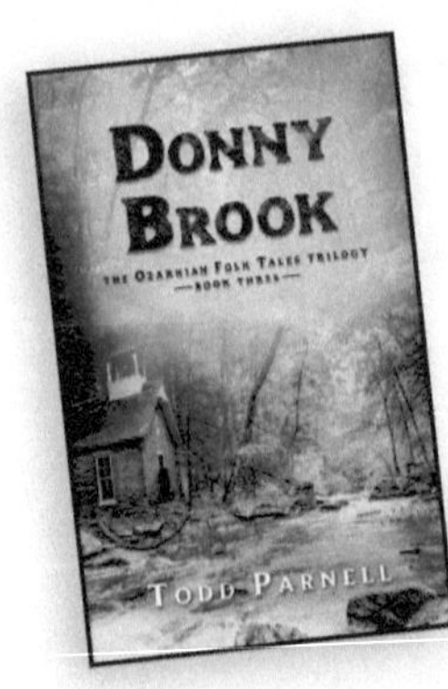

Donny Brook

~ Book III in the Ozarkian Folk Tales Trilogy ~

Who knows what lurks in the deep, dark corners of the Ozarks?

The colorful characters of tiny Hardlyville are thrown into a panic when brutal murders, environmental disasters, corruption, and threats to their beloved and pristine Skunk Creek arise and upend their bucolic lives. Larger-than-life Sheriff Sephus Adonis, devoted newspaper editor Pierce Arrow, libidinous librarian Billious Bloom, and Hardlyville's most influential citizens are forced to contend with a community divided by greed and self-interest to solve the riddle of a mother's love vs. inherent evil.

Will the Hardlyvillains stop the murders and save their indispensable water?

Get yours now at
www.Pen-L.com/DonnyBrook.html

About Todd Parnell

Todd Parnell began writing nonfiction during his years as a banker and educator, including published books *The Buffalo, Ben, and Me*, *Mom at War*, and *Postcards from Branson*. He is an award-winning author inducted into the Missouri Writers Hall of Fame in 2012. He tried his hand at fiction upon retiring as president of Drury University and hasn't stopped writing since, completing the Ozarkian Folk Tales Trilogy, published by Pen-L Publishing, and is hard at work on a second trilogy, Children of the Creek.

In his own words, "I've had great fun writing about the Ozarks and tackling important contemporary issues in that rich and captivating context!"

Parnell is a civic leader, environmental advocate, co-founder of the Upper White River Basin Foundation, and retired CEO of THE BANK in Springfield. He recently completed his term as Chairman of the Missouri Clean Water Commission. He holds Masters degrees in Business from Dartmouth University and History from Missouri State University, and is a graduate of Drury University.

Born in Branson, Missouri, Todd is a sixth-generation Ozarker. He resides with Betty, his wife of forty years, in Springfield and is blessed with four children and five grandchildren, so far.

Connect with Todd at:
www.ToddParnell.com
Facebook: Todd.Parnell.7

Dear Readers,

If you enjoyed this book enough to review it for Goodreads, B&N, or Amazon.com, I'd appreciate it!

Thanks, Todd

Find more great reads at
Pen-L.com

www.ingramcontent.com/pod-product-compliance
Lightning Source LLC
LaVergne TN
LVHW091042080826
845145LV00002B/593

* 9 7 8 1 6 8 3 1 3 0 4 5 1 *